Pra

Eleanora and Joseph is an imaginative novel of the intersecting narratives of two intriguing historical figures whose lives span the Old World and the New, and the Age of Enlightenment as it explodes into the Age of Revolution. Novelist and scholar Julieta Almeida Rodrigues draws on her own wide-ranging background in Europe and America to draw a sympathetic portrait of two brilliant Portuguese characters. Eleonora is a poet and revolutionary, Joseph a conflicted man navigating a career in the church, botany and diplomacy. The personal and intellectual drama of Eleonora Fonseca Pimentel and Joseph Correia da Serra plays out amidst the revolutions sweeping Europe at the end of the eighteenth century and the intellectual oasis of Jefferson's Monticello whose master's own internal contradictions presage the war that would later engulf America as well. An absorbing tale of passion, clashing ideals, guilt and devotion.

—*Ambassador Laura Kennedy*

This historical novel uses three keys to open one door, a door that offers readers access to a world of cultural treasures and political contradictions at the turn of the eightieth century in both Europe and America. Julieta Almeida Rodrigues juxtaposes opposites in this story of passion and revolution: beauty and ugliness, wealth and poverty, refinement and ignorance, liberalism and despotism. Eleonora Fonseca Pimentel, a gifted aristocrat, becomes a leading revolutionary in Naples, an unusual role for a woman in her day. Joseph Correia da Serra, a diplomat and internationally recognized naturalist, struggles with ambition and what is right. Rodrigues's erudition steers the reader through the conflicts of the past that currently inform our present. The ill-fated love between Eleonora and Joseph reflects the many moral issues of our contemporary world. Thomas Jefferson, a former president of the United States, owner of plantations and slaves, plays a prominent role in this story as a liberal intellectual whose domestic life we come to understand.

There is a jewel in this novel, delicate and stoic at the same time. It is the *Madre Superiore*, the Reverend Mother, in charge of the female section of the Vicaria prison where Eleonora becomes imprisoned for her political activity. A feminist *avant la lettre*, she professes a gender ideology before her times. Compassionate, she touches the reader in tantalizing ways.

Rodrigues's novel is a page turner—I was glued to the pages from beginning to end.

—*Amadeu Lopes Sabino, Portuguese writer*

Eleonora and Joseph. An enticing take on the Enlightenment set in eighteenth century Naples and the newly minted United States, as seen through the lens of two powerful historical figures: doomed revolutionary poet, Eleonora Fonseca Pimentel and Abbe Joseph Correia da Serra, artfully re-imagined as star-crossed lovers. Thomas Jefferson, debating ideas with Correia in Monticello, is a wonderful part of this story.

—*Novelist Hope C. Tarr w/a Hope Carey*

In *Eleonora and Joseph*, Julieta Almeida Rodrigues shows vividly how politics and culture join hands to illustrate the eighteenth century's illustrious lives that she both captures and celebrates. Eleonora Fonseca Pimentel was in no way inferior to the two eminent male characters in this story: Joseph Correia da Serra and Thomas Jefferson. With a masterful literary approach, Rodrigues addresses the bonds of long-lasting love that tied two adolescents—Eleonora and Joseph—who lived in Bourbon Naples. With an exceptional literary imagination, Rodrigues opens our horizons to the contrasting and diverging feminine and masculine worlds of the era. By sharing on a first-person basis the vicissitudes and dilemmas of the protagonists, readers experience their story as if present on the scene and readily take sides on the exchanges skillfully depicted. Parallel to Eleanora and Joseph's story is a passionate portrait of Thomas Jefferson's way of life. Here, the author details not only Jefferson's family's domestic life on the Monticello plantation, but also his illicit relationship with a younger black slave with whom he fathered a number of children.

Eleonora and Joseph is a compelling read for both European and American audiences, the story's action taking place on both continents. The narrative offers a heightened sensibility that subtly reflects on history, femininity, and the love of nature. The distant eighteenth century comes up close for our enjoyment and serves as an omen of the gender issues and achievements of the future.

—*Zília Osório de Castro, Professor (ret), Faculty of Social Sciences and Humanities, The New University of Lisbon, member of the Portuguese Academy of History, and Founder and Director of the literary magazine, Faces of Eva*

Novelist Julieta Almeida Rodrigues has lived a life of broad and varied adventures that positions her well to write this story. Following the strong tradition of Portuguese female writers, she brings to her novel *Eleonora and Joseph* her experience of both the 1974 revolution in Portugal and her life in diplomatic circles around the world. The life of Joseph Correia da Serra has been the subject of biographies in Portuguese, while his contacts with Thomas Jefferson deserve to be explored in English. In addition, Eleonora Fonseca Pimentel's narration from prison is a striking frame from which to foreground issues of passion, patriarchy, inequality, slavery, and struggles for female independence.

A must read of imaginary lives in European and American intellectual circles at the turn of the 18th century!

— *Kenneth David Jackson, Professor of Portuguese, Yale University*

As the Cultural Counselor at the Embassy of Portugal in Washington, DC, I became aware of Joseph Correia da Serra's towering figure in Portuguese-American relations soon after my arrival. As an ambassador, Correia da Serra embodied the vast and influential Luzo-Brazilian Empire from 1816 to 1820 in the United States. For us, he had always been part of a domestic and engaging cult.

That Correia da Serra finds in Thomas Jefferson's library Eleonora Fonseca Pimentel's memoir written from prison before she dies in 1799, stands as a credible and ingenious literary device. Reading her manuscript, not only does he find the reasons that turned her into a revolutionary, but he also discovers her revelations of their adolescent love in Naples. Concomitantly, Julieta Almeida Rodrigues brings to light the astonishing friendship between Correia da Serra and Thomas Jefferson with Monticello as background. What initially binds these *philosophes* is botany as an emerging science at the time. What follows are shared secrets, discussions of love affairs in libertarian Paris, and a vivacious display of mutual weaknesses.

Like Plutarch, Julieta Almeida Rodrigues gives us a book tuned into two voices. She aptly brings to light the much-neglected Southern European Enlightenment, adding the irresistible Thomas Jefferson to plot and discussions. The social and moral issues that fall under scrutiny in this historical novel are well worth contemplating, and debating, in the twenty-first century.

—*José Sasportes, Portuguese Writer and Former Minister of Culture of Portugal*

Eleonora and Joseph. Two distinct lives with parallel destinies, portrayed with literary and sociological imagination by Julieta Almeida Rodrigues. Lives that plunge us into *Les Lumières*, the French Revolution, and the apocalyptic events that followed. Unknown to us if Eleonora and Joseph ever met, let alone fell in love, it is plausible that their lives crossed paths during the 1770s, when both lived with their families in urbane Naples. This novel's evocation of a past world is exceptionally well-plotted, and leaves the reader wishing the two talented and youthful idealists had indeed crossed paths and fell for each other. Eleonora, the Jacobin Marquise, fought noble causes despite an array of adverse circumstances that led, inevitably, to a tragic fate. Joseph, scientist and citizen of the world, cultivated knowledge and scholarship in Lisbon, London, and Paris, ending up his academic life between Philadelphia and Monticello—fortunate to enjoy the advantages of a close friendship with Thomas Jefferson. Jefferson gives this well-conceived story its beginning and its end. It is also Jefferson who introduces us to the lure of a century that glorified freedom without abolishing slavery, that proclaimed equality without eliminating privilege. Remarkably, it is also a story about human nature and the unchanging ways of the world that Julieta Almeida Rodrigues examines between the lines of two destinies that so provocatively cross each other.

—*José Luís Cardoso. Research Professor, Institute of Social Sciences, The University of Lisbon and Fellow, Lisbon Academy of Sciences.*

Eleonora and Joseph

Eleonora and Joseph

Passion, Tragedy, and Revolution
in the Age of Enlightenment

A Novel

Julieta Almeida Rodrigues

THESPRING

Washington, DC

Library of Congress Control Number: 2020907642
ISBN 978-1-7348659-1-2 paperback (alk. paper)

THESPRING | THESPRING is an imprint of New Academia Publishing

New Academia Publishing
4401-A Connecticut Ave. NW #236, Washington DC 20008
info@newacademia.com - www.newacademia.com

Author's contact:
jar@julietaalmeidarodrigues.com
www.julietaalmeidarodriguesauthor.com

To Anne Clark Christman, Washingtonian and Friend,
and
to my son, Julian, as always

Contents

PROLOGUE

Standing Before the High Court

Kingdom of Naples, Naples, August 17, 1799

This might well be the last entry of my memoir. I, Eleonora Fonseca Pimentel, am standing before the Giunta di Stato—the High Court of State—of King Ferdinando and Queen Carolina, the Kingdom of Naples's Bourbon sovereigns. The session is taking place at the Convento di Santa Maria di Monte Oliveto. It is hot, and the sky is overcast. I have three judges in front of me; there is no scribe in the room to take notes of the proceedings. It will be easy, one day, to erase the historical record of my trial. My hands are tied up in the back. Eyes wide open, I see only three colors: black, white, and gray. I am wearing a black, dirty dress with holes at the seams. The walls are white. The judges wear black robes decorated with white jabots. Their powdered wigs are white. Their expressions are gray—like the iron crucifix behind them. They sit at a long, wooden table. Royalist soldiers fill the room, guard the entrance door, and surround my fellow *literati* waiting outside to be sentenced.

We're the defeated revolutionaries of the Neapolitan Republic of 1799.

"Answer me!" the judge sitting next to the window yells. "Why do you want a republic in Naples fashioned after France?"

"The Republic comes from Plato, not France." I lower my gaze as I reply.

"You think so? We confiscated books of French authors in your home."

Defiant, I choose not to reply.

"Do you believe in the French Republic?"

"A republic brings liberty to all because its laws protect the citizens."

"You disregard our established order. You don't believe in God the Almighty."

"I respect the will of the people," I say, my gaze still low. "My only enemy is tyranny."

"You're still a Freemason," the judge concludes as he assembles scattered papers into one single pile.

The judge opposite the window speaks now. "From Sant'Elmo's fort, you helped the French Army enter Naples last December. You befriended the republican government. You edited the republican newspaper *Il Monitore Napoletano*. Why?"

"The citizens of a nation, if educated, have a duty to help those less fortunate rise above their lot."

"You disagree with King Ferdinando, who says the three Fs should rule Naples: *forca, festa, e farina*—gallows, festivities, and grain."

"I believe our sovereign can do better," I answer in a neutral tone. My composure adds to my bravery.

"You're a damn liar. The people just acclaimed the king upon his return from exile. You're only a woman, and a reckless one at that."

"Women should be given the chance to express themselves."

"Express themselves like you?" The judge laughs while looking at his colleagues. *"La repubblica è sporca!* Any republic is dirty."

The judge next to the window leans forward as he resumes his interrogation. "I want to know why you betrayed Queen Carolina."

"I did not betray the queen." I stop. The less I say, the better.

"Yes, you did!"

"No. I read books and my ideas changed."

"What's your view of the friendship between Queen Carolina and Lady Emma Hamilton, the wife of the British ambassador?"

"The matter doesn't concern me." My voice quivers as I say this.

"It doesn't? Your indictment says you stated their friendship imperils the Kingdom of Naples."

"I never said that." But the reference is clear, Carolina demands my doom. All along, I dreaded her power over my trial. My hands are in back of me, I cannot see them. Neither can the judges. But my fingers quiver as much as my voice.

"You were once the queen's librarian. You paid back the privilege by slapping her majesty's face with treachery." I suddenly see red spots in the judge's face. They show on the visible part of his neck, too.

"I never intended deceit, I trust reason over perfidy." I think to myself, let these high bureaucrats figure out why I am a daughter of the Enlightenment.

"Don't pretend to be who you are not. We know you incited the people to rebellion."

I do not reply, afraid my words might bring my doom.

It is the middle judge's turn to question me. He seems to be the one presiding over my trial. "Do you regret the decapitation of Marie Antoinette, our queen's beloved sister?"

I look at him as an equal, my gaze is locked with his. A hyena stands before me, ready to devour its prey. I remain silent.

"I accuse you of treason. Women's heads are rolling. Yours might be next." As he speaks, the judge adjusts his voluminous wig with both hands, as if caressing it.

"If I am to perish, I request to be beheaded." I speak slowly, my breathing is uneven, and my mouth dry. I feel on fire now.

"This court decides, not you. You're Portuguese. Naples received you as a daughter, but you weren't born here."

"In 1778, King Ferdinando granted to my father, a titled aristocrat in Portugal, the same prerogatives given to the Neapolitan nobility."

"Those prerogatives no longer apply to you."

"My request isn't unusual. I respectfully ask that you honor it. It's customary for aristocrats to be beheaded, not hanged." The judges know this, but I state it anyway.

"We only grant our own nobles the dignity of being beheaded."

"I have the right to die under the blade."

"The monarchy has been reinstated, we have jurisdiction over you!" The judge appears in a hurry now. "We might hang you in the scaffold as an example. So that you'll die like a plebeian, like the criminal you are. The people of Naples, those you claim to love so much, might enjoy the spectacle."

I kneel; my heart is broken. I'm not wearing undergarments, they are long gone. If I'm hanged, my body will rise in the gallows and everybody will see my private parts. Nothing matters from now on. So I scream loud and clear, "If I die, I'll die a citizen. Whereas you, the three of you, will die vassals, servants of a tyrant."

The judge jots down a few notes. Then, not losing a second, he stands and tells the soldier by the door to escort me out. And bring in the next *"reo di stato,"* the next state prisoner, without delay. "

My trial is short. It couldn't have taken more than fifteen minutes. The loneliness I feel is astounding.

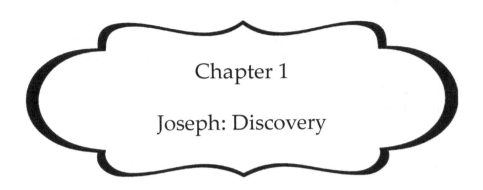

Chapter 1

Joseph: Discovery

I shall be very happy to receive you at Monticello, to express to you in person my great respect, and to receive from yourself directly the letters of my friends beyond the water introducing me to the pleasure of your acquaintance.
—Thomas Jefferson's letter to Joseph Correia da Serra,
 April 17, 1812

//"Come and live here. I'll give you the chair of botany at the University of Virginia. You're the most learned man I've ever met." Thomas Jefferson's boisterous voice echoed through the dining room and filled my heart with joy.

"What an invitation. Thank you, my dear Sir," I replied.

"How wonderful you've finally made it to Monticello. I never imagined I'd have to wait for more than a year to meet you." Jefferson touched my arm.

"Your reception is captivating." My eyes shone as I said this.

I arrived in Monticello, Jefferson's mountaintop plantation near Charlottesville, well past six o'clock. Jefferson had kindly waited for me to have dinner. This gave us the chance to dine alone. A rare opportunity, since I had heard his daughter Patsy and her family always kept him company during mealtimes.

Monticello's dining room was an intimate space painted in a stylish, bright color—so-called chrome yellow. It was June, and the first thing I noticed was that the floor-to-ceiling paneled windows allowed the summer light in, despite the time of day. As I looked up, I saw a skylight. A lot of the furniture was European, undoubtedly pieces Jefferson brought to America after his ambassadorship to France. The golden clock at the center of the fireplace was the epitome of refinement. The atmosphere was stylish and, at the same time, relaxed.

I had dressed for the occasion. I wore my best jacket, my Florentine breeches, a clean white shirt, and my only pair of black silk socks. My shoes had buckles, and I made sure my garters would be in place the whole evening. Jefferson, on the other hand, was dressed in a modest blue coat and black breeches; his soft leather shoes looked like slippers. His republican simplicity was patently displayed.

There were no servants around. Jefferson addressed the matter saying he enjoyed talking to his guests uninterrupted. There was a dumbwaiter on the side of the room and serving plates, filled with food, lay on various shelves in a revolving door. Jefferson said the fireplace had a side mechanism to transport bottles of wine up from the basement—he would show it to me later.

"I plan to attract to Virginia the best European minds." Jefferson had a suave manner. "You already live in this country, which is an advantage. André Thouin's letter of introduction for you is outstanding."

"You flatter me." I trembled with excitement while looking through the windows at the west lawn's vibrant grass.

Upon arriving in the New World, I swiftly wrote to Jefferson from Philadelphia asking to meet him. I had carefully chosen the friends who could give me the best references. I knew beforehand that my success in America depended on the good fortune of making prominent acquaintances. A botanist, I was already a member of the American Philosophical Society, and Jefferson continued to be its president. As I intended to pursue my long-life interest in the natural sciences, Jefferson was at the top of my list of people to meet.

André Thouin was the chief conservator of the Jardin des Plantes, the main botanical garden of France. He was a towering figure of the French establishment, a man of influence, and a good friend of Jefferson. Of all the recommendations I had brought with me to America—and I had several from renowned European lumi-naries—I particularly appreciated Thouin's. He told Jefferson that I was a naturalist of the first order. He said my scientific creden-tials were the best among the best, and that he could rely on my botanical expertise. I was a *philosophe* with a practical mind, who enjoyed field trips into the countryside, and therefore believed in the usefulness of science. Moreover, he said, Jefferson would enjoy my conversation and company.

Jefferson replied to my initial contact with an invitation to vis-it Monticello. An exchange of correspondence ensued. Needing to establish myself first in Philadelphia, and hesitant about a journey through uncharted territory, I kept postponing the trip.

Now I had the privilege to be his guest at the dinner table.

"Friends tell me you might be waiting for a diplomatic assign-ment from the Kingdom of Portugal. But knowing your passion for botany, I'm confident I'll steal you away." Jefferson rested his glass of Bordeaux back on the table.

"I see you're well-informed. But correspondence across the At-lantic is slow and unreliable, therefore my assignment might never come through. One thing I know for sure, I plan to stay here, I love your country."

"I'd like to work out the statutes of the University of Virginia with your counsel. They've been worrying me and, after all, you set up the Royal Academy of Sciences of Lisbon. May I count on you? Your reputation is widely acknowledged."

"I would be honored to be at your service." I hoped my smile indicated to my host how happy I felt with his request.

"I want to create a state institution paid for through public funding. But my university must be free from religious affiliation, unlike those in the North."

I nodded. "I congratulate your originality of thought." Jefferson filled my glass a second time.

The food we were enjoying was first-class. We had *Beef à la Mode*, eye round cutlets, accompanied by white onions, carrots and mushrooms. The brandy gave the meat a most delicate taste. Jef-ferson explained his cook used the art of French cuisine, following his taste. The china, the glasses, and the silverware were all French.

As the dinner proceeded, I was delighted to confirm that the sage of Monticello and I had a lot in common. The University of Virginia was a monumental initiative, something the two of us had already touched upon in our letters. These exchanges, even if brief, convinced me that we shared the same encompassing love of the natural world. I was confirming my impressions.

As we moved from topic to topic, my host said that he very much enjoyed the company of regular visitors since retiring in 1809. I could see he was a gregarious human being: he gesticulated, looked me in the eyes, and touched my arm cordially once in a while. His guests, he said, were American and foreign alike, people he knew enlivened his inner world. He abhorred cities now, and preferred the ease of plantation life. Surrounded by his family, he had found the peace and quiet he needed for his projects to mature. Establishing the University of Virginia was a major one.

Jefferson reminded me of a well-bred Frenchman. I knew them well, I had lived in Paris the previous decade. Although born and raised in the privileged landowning class of Virginia, Jefferson was wholly down-to-earth, which struck me as surprising. As we talked, he seemed to embody the soul of the new America.

From the outside, we were an odd pair. Jefferson was tall and lean, I was—and still am—short and stout. His face was angular, mine was round. His eyes were a deep blue, mine were brown. His hair, now white, still had reddish overtones, mine was still black. His complexion was fair, mine was olive. My face was pale. His was pale, too, but had freckles. Our age disparity—I was in my early sixties and Jefferson in his late sixties—didn't make any difference.

The French loved Jefferson and stories about his demeanor still abounded when I arrived in Paris, many years after his sojourn there. The inconsistencies of his life were a perpetual topic of conversation. He had written the American Declaration of Independence, declaring we were all created equal. But he had two mulatto servants with him, and Parisians knew they were his slaves. These enslaved individuals were members of the Hemings family; their offspring, if they had any, would also be Jefferson's property. Furthermore, it was well-known that Jefferson had helped the Marquis de Lafayette draft the French Declaration of the Rights of Man and of the Citizen, also ensuring equality to all in France. The document had an enormous influence at the start of the French Revolution, and the two men had remained life-long friends.

These ironies excited the French elite. Jefferson never mentioned his mulatto slaves in the salons he regularly frequented, but people said he treated them as well as his paid French domestics. He never mentioned, either, his help to Lafayette. As an ambassador, he was forbidden to meddle in French affairs. So, he had advised his friend in private. As I heard these stories many times over, I had an insurmountable curiosity to meet the man in person. The descriptions indicated a unique individual with exceptional qualities of heart and mind.

When we finished the meal, Jefferson got up from the table. "I'd like to show you the drawings for the university. Let's go to my private quarters." It was now getting darker outside. He took a large candlestick from the table to light the way across the entrance hall.

So here I was, astonished, as I followed Jefferson. A priest from Portugal, in the company of one of the most—if not the most—famous man in America. Moreover, he wanted me not only to help him establish his university, but also be a professor there. Soon, I suspected, I would be agonizing over my decision. I knew I wanted to remain in America. But what would I prefer? A diplomatic assignment, undoubtedly prestigious? Or devote my time to scholarship in rural Virginia? In due time, it appeared, I would have to make a choice. Even if it didn't seem an easy one, how much more blessed could I be?

Jefferson's private quarters comprised a suite that started with his library, which he called his book room. The area was lit with well-placed candleholders. When I mentioned how bright the ambiance was, Jefferson said he used spermaceti wax candles made from whale oil. According to him, they gave the best light.

Similar to the dining room, the library's décor also favored intimate exchanges. The doors were made of exquisite dark wood. The space was filled from floor to ceiling with books, maps, pictures, and paraphernalia. An engraving in a corner showed Benjamin Franklin with his peculiar beaver cap.

"I now have time to devote myself to the things I value," Jefferson said. "Come here to see my sketches. I very much enjoyed designing these plans for the university."

I sat down at a table near the window—it had a rare hexagonal shape—and Jefferson brought the drawings from the desk nearby.

"Look at this," he said. "I like to call the university my 'academical' village. At the north end, there's a Rotunda where the library will be located. The Rotunda will be modeled after the Pantheon in Rome. I want a dome with a glass oculus in the middle, but I can't leave it open. It'll be a space that's used daily, rain can't come down through a hole in the ceiling."

We chuckled. "True," I said.

"There'll be a central, rectangular lawn with two rows of pavilions on each side. The first row will have a succession of gardens in the back."

"I didn't know you enjoyed architecture so much," I said while admiring the drawings.

"It's one of my pleasures. I love the Italian architect Palladio, so I want the grounds to be enjoyable to the eye."

"How do you plan to use the buildings?" I pointed to them in the drawings.

"On each side of the lawn there'll be apartments for students and faculty. The gardens behind the first row of buildings will have vegetables, flowers, and trees—and, possibly, livestock. The green areas will be enclosed in serpentine brick walls. The houses further away from the lawn will be meeting areas: classrooms, dining halls, living rooms, and whatnot."

I examined the sketches in detail. "You draw like a savant," I said.

"There's something I want to show you about the pavilions in the first row, facing the lawn. The light of Virginia will be mirrored in the building's white facades. I call this the '*Lumière Mystérieuse*,' the mysterious light. I like to think this beauty will inspire the students—not to mention the professors—to feel not only a sense of joy but the urge to practice virtue." As Jefferson said this, his eyebrows seemed to flare.

"It might!" I wasn't sure how serious Jefferson really was, so I decided to play it safe. "As a Portuguese, I know the importance of sunlight in determining a sensible mood. And that feeling might inspire good character and bring hard studying. When will the university open?"

"It all depends on funding, but I've started to talk to the Virginia legislature."

"These drawings are classical, but planned for a tranquil and pastoral environment. There's a sense of community here. You're a visionary! Who else would think of constructing such fine buildings in the middle of nowhere?"

The project was fascinating, and we discussed a few more architectural details. Then, as Jefferson put the drawings away, he said he would show me the location he envisioned for the buildings on the morrow.

I rose up from my seat at the table and perused the nearest shelf of books. Jefferson's library was huge and diversified. Some books were simply bound in leather; others had elaborate designs or lettering in gold leaf. I noticed a shelf with books on *Révolution*, the titles on the spines all written in French.

"I'm glad I don't have to translate the French titles for you. I started collecting those when I lived in Paris," Jefferson said. "I visited booksellers every afternoon."

"How lucky for the French to have, first, Mr. Franklin and then you as ambassadors."

"Mr. Franklin had all the social skills I lacked: he loved Parisian salons and their women, young and old. He also loved defying French protocol by dressing as a simple Quaker."

"When I prepared my eulogy on Mr. Franklin at the Lisbon academy, I read all about him," I said.

"You gave a talk on my friend?"

"I described Mr. Franklin as the ultimate representative of *Les Lumières*, the Enlightenment. I spoke about his revolutionary ideals, his internationalism, and his experiments in electricity."

"Did your colleagues enjoy the talk?" Jefferson crossed his arms, as was his habit. Was it a defensive stance? I couldn't say, but I hoped he wasn't jealous of my praise of the old American icon.

"They did. Mr. Franklin was an *'indagador da natureza,'* an inquirer into nature—something I've always tried to apply to my own work."

"I loved the French calling him 'the electrical ambassador,'" Jefferson said. "The French knew of Franklin's experiments in electricity. And his nickname had a hidden meaning: liberty had become inevitable."

"Our own Franklin is a Brazilian scholar called Andrada e Silva, someone the Lisbon academy sent on a tour of Europe when he was a student, all expenses paid. Afterward, he was for many years a professor at the University of Coimbra."

"Why do you find these two people similar?" Jefferson asked.

"They combine scientific fervor with revolutionary zeal."

"What's Andrada e Silva doing these days?"

"He's positioning himself to be one of the fathers of Brazilian independence, if that possibility ever arises. I hope not, I prefer the Portuguese empire to remain intact."

"You see what happens when you give people wings to fly? They desert you," Jefferson said with a sprightly laugh. I smiled back at him, he was absolutely right. I enjoyed my host's frankness. It was inspiring and, moreover, put me at ease.

Jefferson now approached a small table and poured Madeira into two glasses. I joined him.

"To the University of Virginia," he said, raising his glass.

"I'll drink to that," I replied.

"Interesting that you spotted my books on revolution, I haven't looked at them in a while," Jefferson said. "With the French Revolution underway while I was in Paris, I laid my hands on topics dear to my heart, the sacred fire of liberty above all."

"Themes dear to you, to me, and to our Republic of Letters," I replied.

"Indeed," my host said.

"I have something on that shelf written in Portuguese that's rather intriguing. It must have been sent to me after I returned to Monticello. As I don't read the language, I wouldn't have bought it myself."

Jefferson took out a black leather case tied with a red ribbon and brought it to me. "This is a manuscript and it seems one of a kind. I've always been curious about it." My host looked at me with inquisitive eyes.

"Let me see," I said, taking the case from him and opening it.

"As you see, it's handmade and has a small pocket at the back. Inside, there's a folded letter written in a different hand."

As I examined the booklet, I felt faint. I'm sure I turned pale for Jefferson asked whether I was alright.

"You're not going to believe this," I said. "This is a memoir writ-

ten by a Portuguese woman I was very close to in Naples. My Eleonora! Our families knew each other; we all moved from Rome at
the same time. She was later famous as one of the revolutionaries of
the Neapolitan Republic. The king and the queen of Naples—Ferdinando and Carolina—had her executed in 1799."

"What was her surname?"

"Fonseca Pimentel. She was the daughter of the Marquis and
Marquise Pimentel, members of the Portuguese nobility."

"Her calligraphy is rare. It's so well designed that I imagined it
belonged to a proud woman," Jefferson said.

"How did you get this?" I asked.

"A French bookseller must have sent it. I still receive packages
with books from France."

"Neapolitan revolutionaries escaped to France after the Republic failed. They sailed to Toulon, with many settling in Paris later.
Someone must have brought Eleonora's manuscript and sold it to
feed the family. Once they were in exile, the French government
was far from welcoming."

Jefferson remained silent.

"My dear Sir, you and I have had a long day. I see it's close to
nine-thirty." I felt now an indescribable need to be on my own. I
wanted to read Eleonora's words, feel her near me. "Do you think I
may retire and bring the manuscript with me? I promise to tell you
all about it when I finish."

"*Certainement!*" Jefferson's gaze was gallant as he replied in the
French affirmative. "I'll show you to your room, and I hope you
have a good night's sleep."

"You're a generous host," I answered. "We had a delightful
philosophical evening."

"The chair of botany at the University of Virginia would give
you great happiness," Jefferson said. "Besides, you would get a
comfortable and lucrative retirement."

"Thank you, Sir, I'll consider your offer. But I must wait for
news about my assignment. As you know, the Portuguese royal
family is established in Rio de Janeiro now. Brazil is so far away! I
wish I received news more often." I didn't want to appear ungrate-
ful, so I added while caressing my chin, "I've heard these woods
offer a sound occupation and countless opportunities to a botanist
like me."

As we crossed the entrance hall once again, with Jefferson holding yet another candlestick in his hand, I was reminded my host didn't live alone. A few of his grandchildren—he had eleven—encircled us momentarily to greet their grandfather. They were a lively set. Two or three put their arms around him and said they had missed him at dinner. My host kindly introduced me as a friend of Thouin, saying I would be staying for a few days.

"Can you repeat his name, 'Correia'? It's Portuguese," Jefferson said to the children. A girl he introduced as Ellen took to the task with a strong English accent. All the other children laughed, for she wasn't even close.

"One day, I'm sure, you'll get it right." Jefferson laughed, too. "You just need practice."

"Grandpapa, can we look at Thouin's calendar now?" a younger girl asked. "I want to see those pictures again."

"It's too late now, but maybe tomorrow—that is, if you all behave and go to bed on time."

The group left moaning with disappointment. How much fun for the children to learn from their grandfather, I thought to myself.

My host showed me to my bedroom as we entered the north corridor. Finally, I was by myself, alone with my thoughts. I closed the door and leaned against it. It was a balmy summer night, comforting. I noticed the bedspread of my alcove bed had been tastefully turned down, making it easy for me to slide into bed. A blue and white chamber pot had been removed from under the bed and placed at its foot. Several candles illuminated the space, giving it a cozy feeling.

Sagging against the door, I pressed Eleonora's leather-bound manuscript to my chest with both hands. Life was, sometimes, extraordinary. Then, I turned the pages feverishly, reading a line here, another there. Was I really seeing, really holding, what I thought I was? Was this indeed a memoir in Eleonora's own hand—Eleonora the love of my youth in Naples? Indeed, it was! Not only did I recognize a few descriptions of the city where I had grown up. The author's signature, Eleonora Fonseca Pimentel, was something I recognized distinctly. How could I ever forget it? This was the woman I had wanted to elope with; someone who had stayed in my memory throughout my life. Someone I hadn't been able to purge from my memory.

My legs felt wobbly, my knees quivered.

I now searched the booklet's back pocket while pacing the room. It smelled of mildew, it hadn't been touched in years. As I took out the letter folded inside, a sprig of rosemary fell to the floor. Oh my God! Eleonora's habit of pressing herbs to dry them inside a book stayed with her to the end. The letter's title at the top was *An Execution in Naples*, and a sister, Suor Amadea Della Valle, had written it. She said she was the Madre Superiore, the Reverend Mother, of the female section of the Vicaria prison where Eleonora had been incarcerated.

I started reading. To my horror, the letter described Eleonora's death. I lived in London at the time of her execution and knew from the English newspapers that she had been sent to the scaffold. But I didn't know the details.

When I finished Suor Amadea's letter, I hid my face in my hands. The scent of blood filled my nostrils. Eleonora had paid for her ideas with her life. A feeling of shame came over me; I had abandoned the love of my youth to her fate.

And now I was reading the gruesome details of her execution, things I preferred to leave behind. Eleonora had combined a powerful intellect with a disposition for writing lyrical poetry. She believed the poor deserved to be educated in order to have a better future. I turned to the memoir's initial pages and recognized the discussion that had gone on in France after the revolution. Dr. Guillotin, a French physician after whom the guillotine was named, proposed a reform for capital punishment. His "machine" was merciful because of its surgical speed. And it should be applied to all slayings—not just those of the aristocracy—as an egalitarian measure. Hanging, on the other hand, was long, inhumane, and brutal.

Eleonora's character, as I turned page after page, outshone many of the people we knew in common. It not only set her apart from all the other women I had met in Naples, but also those I met later in life.

Her boldness, in particular, set her apart from me. I could be a world-renowned botanist praised by Jefferson. But I had failed Eleonora. She was unswerving in her convictions. Was she—after all those years—still the better part of me? If I dared to answer my question with feeling, the answer was an undeniable yes.

For a split second, I wondered if Suor Amadea was the person she said she was at the end of the letter. The narrative was respectful, and the nun had written as one of Eleonora's admirers. It was the work of a compassionate woman describing another's ultimate plight. This writer was educated, knew how to express herself. Could the name be a pseudonym? That didn't matter, I concluded.

Inspired, I brought the sprig of rosemary to my nose. No scent remained, too many years had passed. But it reminded me of the day I had delivered my goodbyes to Eleonora.

I pressed it firmly between my fingers.

This was the moment I decided to take notes of my stay, or stays, in Monticello. The future would tell me what to do with them. I wanted to preserve a fragrance, a redolence, from my past. Something that would carry me into the future.

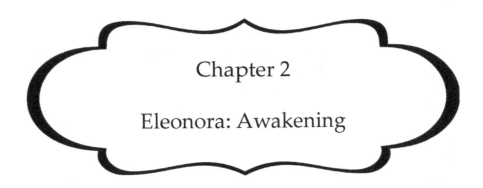

Chapter 2

Eleonora: Awakening

At the Vicaria Prison, Castel Capuano, outskirts of Naples,
June 29, 1799

As I stare at the blank page of parchment paper that Suor Amadea handed me, I might as well start to write. I don't know how much longer I have to live. But I'm here, now. It's the middle of the night and I have all the time in the world. I pick up my quill pen.

It all started with Joseph, our passion, and our parting.

To this day, I remember the moment we fell in love. How could I forget? His mother died in 1765, at the age of thirty-one. At her funeral, his father, feverish with grief and anger, appeared shattered. Joseph's family filled a dark, wooden bench at church; the father stood at one end, and Joseph, the oldest son, stood at the other. In between them sat his two brothers; and his grandmother, who held his two young sisters on each side of her lap. The Neapolitan church where mass was celebrated was uncomfortably warm, since it was June, and the light coming through the stained-glass windows was colorful but opaque. I noticed Joseph's stare wandering aimlessly. First, he looked up at the frescoes of the saints displayed. The holy images illustrated the survival of those devout souls: theirs were lives of adversity and sacrifice. Some were hunchbacks; others used canes to walk barefoot through narrow trails paved with stones, and, still others pierced their bellies with spikes. Lowering

his gaze, Joseph rested his view on my family to his right. Mesmer-
ized among the mourners, I felt unable to keep my feelings at bay.
Tears rolled down my face, I couldn't control my sorrow. It was my
first funeral, I was almost fourteen years old. How was it possible
that a mother of five, so beautiful, had died so young?

Joseph's gaze fell on me, on and off, for the rest of the ceremony. It was as if my tears expressed the emotions he was unable to
show himself. The mass was long, it lasted well over an hour. And,
throughout, Joseph's stare wandered the church, it seemed, just to
come back and rest on me. A few pews away, my crying seemed
to comfort him, to create a soothing bond. Joseph was a year older
than I—and we barely knew each other—though we had met on
several occasions. I thought our silent communication was a way to
uplift our spirits above and beyond ourselves.

Our two families had known each other for many years; we had
left Rome for Naples at the same time. Our move had been forced.
The prime minister of Portugal, the famed Marquis de Pombal, had
expelled the Jesuits from Portuguese territories, and the Papal State
had retaliated by ordering its Portuguese colony to leave. We all felt
insecure, fearful of the uncertain future. The order to depart came
in 1760, and set off three months of chaotic transitions.

I was of noble descent, my parents being the Marquis and Marquise Pimentel, but this didn't prevent Joseph and me from moving
in the same social circles. Joseph's father was a well-known gentleman: a small landowner, a merchant, and a medical doctor who
had graduated from the University of Coimbra. His mother had
been a lady of good birth, with a warm smile. She had admirably
fulfilled her roles of wife and mother.

I adored Naples, where Vesuvius's mysterious presence reflected on the Mediterranean Sea. There was something unique,
and exciting, about living in a city whose volcano seemed ready to
erupt at any moment. Neapolitans called their city *città-spettacolo*,
spectacular city, and I agreed. Its coastal geography was wholly
seductive. It was a place full of sunshine, with perpetual blue skies
and a blessed climate. The port was captivating with royal sailboats
running leisurely with the breeze, small fishing boats dealing with
their daily catch, and cargo ships unloading goods from all over the

world. The city itself exported fine wines, liqueurs, cotton, dried and fresh fruits, fish, and timber.

I lived with my parents, brothers, and Uncle António Lopes, my mother's brother, in the Quartieri Spagnoli, the Spanish Quarter. My mother's domain was our home and, as my father was always busy with my brothers, I shared a special bond with Uncle António. He was a respected Catholic man of the cloth. In Naples, this designation applied to abbés, priests, and presbyters. Since my uncle enjoyed my company, I often accompanied him on errands throughout the city. Our excursions filled me with joy.

We loved to stop and admire the Palazzo Reale, the Royal Palace, situated close to the bay. The building was reddish, of monumental proportions, with a private quay. Here lived King Ferdinando IV, a member of the royal Bourbon family, and Queen Carolina, who were recently wed. The queen was the daughter of Empress Maria Theresa of Austria and sister to Marie Antoinette of France.

Ferdinando was called the king *lazzaroni*, king of the dispossessed, a term of endearment. He was uneducated, weak, and lazy, but devoted to his subjects. Carolina became the more powerful ruler of the two as the years passed. While the king believed he ruled by divine right, the queen was strategic and shrewd. As her mother had stipulated in the marriage contract, she made sure she was granted a seat in the Council of State as soon as she delivered a male heir.

Uncle António shared details of the monarchs' flamboyant lifestyle that delighted me. I dreamed about court life, for Carolina and I were the same age. The royal couple entertained luxuriously and supported a wide range of *literati*.

Joseph and I moved in the aristocratic, educated circles of the Naples *nobilissima*. I still remember how timid I felt when first introduced to the literary salons. Months after the funeral, Joseph and I met by coincidence at the home of the Duchess of Popoli. The atmosphere emanated refinement and elegance, her library was one of the best in our city. My uncle António had been invited, and I was allowed to go with him. As Naples encouraged female inclusion, I had the same access as Joseph to literature, the sciences, philosophy, and the arts. I was a quick learner under my uncle's tutelage and, soon, everybody knew I wrote poetry. Much in vogue, I cultivated the French fashion of letter writing; this became, for me, as necessary as breathing.

The Popoli had several parlors where guests congregated, and Joseph and I happened to be in the same one that day. We were dressed in our best attire: I wore a light, dark red, taffeta and silk dress, and Joseph wore an impeccably ironed white shirt under his nicely cut jacket. The light from the candelabras was low to give the room an enigmatic glow, as if we inhabited a world of fantasy.

For everyone's delight, when the Duke of Belforte finished reciting a poem that linked Mount Vesuvius's unpredictability to the character of our local people, he turned to me and said, "Eleonora, dear child, your turn now."

I blushed, all eyes were on me. Joseph's too.

"I didn't prepare," I stuttered. "I would prefer to be excused."

"It doesn't matter if you are prepared or not," the duke said with glee. "Recite for us the latest poem you wrote!"

My uncle, always protective, whispered quietly in my ear, "It will be good for you to practice recitation among friends."

I felt I couldn't refuse. I looked at Joseph standing nearby, and it was as if I saw his heart pounding inside his white shirt. I got up from my chair and brought myself to center stage. I enjoyed sonnets, so I started one I had recently composed in the Neapolitan dialect. It was about the goddess Aphrodite, born from the ocean's foam, and the passion of love.

I spoke quickly, I wanted everybody's attention to shift away from me as fast as possible. When I finished, I bowed to the applauding audience and returned to my uncle's shielding figure. While everybody shouted "Brava! Brava!" I sat down and pressed my head against my uncle's shoulder, seeking comfort.

Joseph was looking intently at me. His body seemed to have frozen, as if he needed to escape the weight of his own feelings. Soon afterward, he left the room. He probably wanted to turn to discussions on agriculture, commerce, and economy. I had heard my uncle say that Joseph was studying with the great Antonio Genovese and relished those subjects best of all.

The Naples Joseph and I enjoyed was very different from the rest of the city. My poetry might have been lofty, but I didn't shy away from what I saw outside my world. The city was populated by so-called *lazzaroni*, people who lived in the poorest, dirtiest conditions. Under different names, they existed in many other European nations: they were the *arraia-miúda* in Portuguese and the *canaille* in French. I looked at them with pity and indignation. They were idle and illiterate, superstitious and religious, brutish and savage all at once. But they needed compassion, help, and education not pity, hate, or contempt. They were human beings who struggled constantly to find meager food for themselves and their children.

Naples still had no sewers and the population performed their physical functions wherever. Children ran the streets at all hours of day or night collecting excrement in wooden carts. Dogs followed them, they wanted a meal. Deadly infectious diseases like cholera, smallpox, syphilis, typhoid, and pneumonia spread easily, killing rich and poor alike.

Soon after my poetry recital, Joseph and I began seeing each other on a regular basis. We attended the Latin lessons of Professore Grassi, a *literati* friend of our families. My education in the ancient language turned into an opportunity for the two of us to get to know each other. We were five pupils in the class, and I was the only girl. Unlike some of the young men, I never missed a lesson.

Like me, Joseph was always in attendance. Our group sat at Professore Grassi's small, round living-room table. We read, learned grammar, and recited the language's declensions for a couple of hours. Our purpose was not only to *introdurre le luci*, enlighten the mind, but also to expand our knowledge by becoming familiar with ancient texts. Since my family and Joseph's spoke Portuguese at home, and Neapolitan outside, these lessons gave us a third language. Joseph and I always sat next to each other, as if our seating arrangements took place by accident. From the beginning, he would sit in such a way that our legs touched under the table. When we got up to leave the room, however, it was as if nothing had happened. In my bed at night, I would recall Josephs pleasurable touching.

Joseph's company filled my life with zest. We loved learning together. Moreover, when our eyes met, there was a sweetness I hadn't ever experienced. He made me feel alive, filled with femininity. When his leg moved closer under the table, I welcomed it brazenly. These emotions were new and thrilling, and I knew they were mutual, even if left unacknowledged.

Over time, we became comfortable in each other's company. Certainly one of the reasons I liked Latin so much! Our notebooks were neat and clean, just as Professore Grassi demanded, but we used them to communicate further. Our touching under the table wasn't enough. Joseph drew plants and seeds in the last pages of his notebook, and he enjoyed sharing them with me. Little red hearts were mixed in; I found them lovely. His drawings had, of course, Latin names, and I could see how much he enjoyed the natural world. I, on the other hand, had the habit of drying herbs between my notebook's pages—they spread a nice scent.

I kept my feelings for Joseph locked deep in my soul, they weren't something I wanted to reveal. Besides, there was no one with whom I could share them. My family had decided long before that I would marry my first cousin Michele. Marriage between first cousins was common in Portuguese families because it kept money within the family. It wasn't that I was against the life that had been determined for me; it was that Michele and I were very different. We had played together all our lives, but I had never felt the attraction I felt for Joseph.

When Uncle António fetched me from Latin one glorious spring day—hot and humid as only Naples can be—he suggested we go for a lemonade at a fashionable pastry shop in the Strada di Toledo. This was the main street of Naples, recently paved with dark lava flagstones. We walked alongside carriages pulled by horses and carts dragged by oxen while my uncle entertained me with explaining the various uses of lava. As we were about to enter the pastry shop, I saw Joseph close by and wondered if he had followed us. I waved discreetly, indicating that he should keep a distance. He licked his fingers, as if to say the pastries were tasty, and I couldn't help but feel his sensuality.

Uncle António and I sat at one of the shop's tables by the window, and I felt relieved that he hadn't noticed Joseph. Joseph was a *converso*. He belonged to a New Christian family—Jews who had converted to Catholicism and I was sure my uncle wouldn't approve of our relationship. It was one thing for the two of us to acquire a good education together, but a different matter for us to be friends. My uncle ordered an assortment of pastries: *susamielle, struffoli, roccocò, sapienza,* and *divino amore*. Such exotic names for the renowned Neapolitan pastries! Some were sprinkled with cinnamon, clove, and nutmeg, and the powerful aromas still linger in my memory today.

At this time, I was feeling confused about my future. Marriage was, for me, the natural course for a young, aristocratic woman. I wanted to be a wife and mother. My brothers would probably follow military careers and be stationed out of Naples. My betrothed Michele wanted to be a barrister, he had no inclination for the career of arms. Thus, my parents considered him a good fit for me. When they died, he would assume responsibility for our finances, while I would continue to pursue my life of the mind. However, after experiencing Joseph's closeness, and his sensuality, I was having serious doubts I could be satisfied in a marriage with Michele.

One day during our lessons, Joseph passed me a message saying he wished to meet alone. He knew my uncle had been invited to the Serra di Cassano and that I would be going as well. He, too, would be there. He must have felt it was time to make a move. He suggested a time we could meet on their terrace. I read the note and indicated with a slight nod that I would be there. The prospect of meeting Joseph alone thrilled me, and I couldn't think of anything else the rest of the lesson. It must have been the same for him, for his leg pressed ever more tightly against mine under the small table.

It was on the terrace of the Serra di Cassano that Joseph and I were alone for the first time. I was about to turn seventeen and wore a blue pretty dress. He said he was crazed with love; he wanted to marry me. He said he had heard rumors that Michele was a strong candidate for my hand, and he wanted to know how I felt about it.

"Eleonora of my heart, I can't sleep at night thinking of you," he said, pressing his chest against my breasts as we hid behind one of the terrace's marble columns. "You are the lady of my dreams!"

I smiled at his adoring gaze and said, "I feel the same for you."

"We need to find a way to make our courting official. I want to propose to you. I'll talk it over with my father and then we'll talk to yours. You know how sick my father's been is the last few years—he never recovered from my mother's death. But I'm confident that when I talk to him about our love, he'll understand."

As I listened, all I could see was Joseph's coarse beard; I was ready to faint with passion. My voice wavered. "My family wants me to marry Michele."

"But Michele can't make you happy!" Joseph now kissed my eyes, nuzzled my lips, and lowered his mouth to my breasts. The pleasure I had felt when our legs touched under the table accelerated to a pitch of excitement.

"You're daring!" I uttered with delight.

"We must find a way," Joseph said. "Either your father agrees to our marriage or we'll elope."

"I want to follow you wherever you go," I replied.

Dark blue light emanating from the sky bathed us like a blessing. The marble balcony seemed a divine enclave where our bodies nestled. I raised his head between my hands feeling his beard, and kissed his lips. Afterward, we both looked up at the moon—and she was smiling back at us.

Was this the call of love? My feelings had possessed me, as if I had experienced Joseph's hands on my body all along. Michele had never, ever, touched or looked at me this way.

When I heard Uncle António's voice calling my name, I hurried inside. I didn't want us to be seen together, let alone by my uncle. I told him I had been observing the moon, its soft and radiant glow spreading over the Bay of Naples.

That evening changed my life, Joseph and I now shared a secret. The question was whether we could bring our passion to fruition. His daring ways continued as we sat beside each other during lessons. Occasionally he would furtively lay his hand on my legs, his fingers swift and adroit. I didn't push him away, I welcomed the feeling of fullness that penetrated my whole being. If I turned red, no one noticed anything.

My involvement with Joseph affected my poetry. I felt unleashed, more capable of expressing the essence of my soul. Meeting fellow poets and reciting became easier. It was as if my sexual awareness had given me freedom to express myself. Queen Carolina enjoyed my poetry and its celebratory vein. I had written a poem she particularly enjoyed, *Il Tempio della Gloria, The Temple of Glory*, celebrating the joining of the Houses of Hapsburg and Bourbon by her marriage. I felt accomplished, and I enjoyed the royal praise. There was talk the queen might appoint me her personal librarian one day. If that ever happened, Naples would see me in a new light.

Joseph mentioned he was waiting for the right moment to speak to his father about us. Since the old gentleman was in a bad spell, he hadn't had a chance yet. I felt sure of Joseph's love, so, even though disappointed, I was willing to be patient. The months proceeded for me in this idyllic state. Both Michele and Joseph were in my mind, but I didn't have to make a public choice. It was late spring; my life was sweet and full of expectation.

As summer approached, Joseph passed me another note in class saying the opportunity to speak to his father had arrived. They would be traveling to Rome, where his father was to meet an old colleague from Coimbra, João Carlos of Bragança, the second Duke of Lafões. I knew the duke was a close relative of Queen Maria of Portugal. Joseph said the duke had lived abroad for many years, but he now wanted to return to Lisbon to establish an academy of sciences. Since his father's business wasn't doing well, the duke's patronage, if he was willing, might help the family finances. Joseph's note finished by reassuring me he would be back in no time, and that we were made for each other.

But I didn't hear from Joseph when he returned to the city. It was summer now and our lessons were over. I felt anguished. My parents were talking insistently about Michele. They saw my resistance and wanted to set an engagement day. I kept saying I wasn't ready; I even pretended to be sick to gain time. I missed Joseph terribly, and I missed his touch most of all. Since I couldn't understand what was happening, I turned to my poetry for refuge.

One day our maid Clotilde said she had a message for me. A young man had approached her in the street and had asked for her confidence. She had raised me and although surprised by the request, passed on the note without comment. The missive was from Joseph and asked to meet at the small garden near our apartment in Via Platea della Salata. He suggested the following afternoon, and that I tell my mother I needed to go out with Clotilde to buy new notebooks.

And so, the next afternoon, shopping with Clotilde, I made it seem like the two of us had bumped into each other by accident. I told Clotilde to wait for me a few yards away. As I moved away to join Joseph, I breathed in the garden's rosemary — it was intoxicating.

The marvelous sensation vanished as soon as I reached Joseph and saw the gravity in his eyes.

He first said he was in a hurry. Then he handed me a letter he said I should read at home. I felt shocked that he had no more to say. His former personality had vanished, replaced by something I didn't recognize. With a dark expression, he cautioned me.

"Eleonora, your head is full of naive fantasies and this is good for the art of poetry. But I would like to think of you as being grounded, as I plan to be," he said, looking me straight in the eyes. "Concentrate on being a virtuous wife and mother. I fear for you; your imagination is fertile, but it can turn against you."

When he finished, he leaned over and picked a sprig of rosemary from the nearest bush. He smelled it with closed eyes and then offered it to me.

Without another word, he left. I waited for what it seemed an eternity to see if he would look back before exiting the garden's iron gate. He did, just as I put the rosemary into the bosom of my dress.

Distressed, I called Clotilde and we went home. Alone in my room, I read Joseph's letter:

My Dearest Eleonora,

Our love is impossible and we must renounce it for our own good. My father opened his heart to me on our way to Rome and I must free him from feeding one more mouth. I'm his oldest son, I have responsibilities I can't discard. The Duke of Lafões advised that I follow a religious career in Rome. If I do, he will promote my future in Portugal and, therefore, assist our family. I will help him with his scientific pursuits and, in turn, he will provide for me through various tenças—subsidies or financial ecclesiastic benefits that he can dispose of as he pleases.

Miraculously—and impressed with my intellectual abilities—the duke decided my future for me. I've found his offer irresistible, a way out of my family's predicament. You are lucky that, due to your family's social standing, you are already on the way to be well-established in Naples. But my father is nearly penniless. Thus, there is no way I can ask your parents for your hand.

We must quiet our feelings, promise never to see each other again. Our determination should be, moving forward, our only ally.

I am going to Rome to start my religious studies soon. Later, I'll take my Catholic vows. An ecclesiastical life will provide me with erudition, something I very much want. I sincerely hope your marriage to Michele fulfills you. You must make the most of it. I will do the same with my own life. I wish you the happiness a life in Naples promises and can deliver.

Yours truly,

Joseph

I finished the letter and let it drop from my fingers. I felt abject, miserable. How was it possible that Joseph had turned his back on me? I had been abandoned, nothing else made sense anymore. Joseph's resolute voice told me that he wouldn't be changing his mind. This was the saddest day of my life. I was becoming a recognized poet in Naples, slated to become the queen's librarian. But it all seemed without grace now.

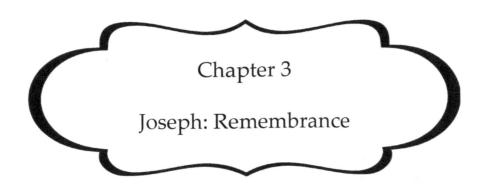

Chapter 3

Joseph: Remembrance

You know our course of life. To place our friends at their ease we show them that we are so ourselves, by pursuing the necessary vocations of the day and enjoying their company at the usual hours of society.
—Thomas Jefferson's letter to Joseph Correia da Serra,
    April 19, 1814

"Mr. Jefferson, I felt indisposed last night. It's already past noon, and I'm sorry it's only now I'm able to join you," I said, as soon as I saw my host enter Monticello's main hall, where I happened to be sitting.

"Are you felling well?" Jefferson asked.

"I wish I were." To find comfort I looked at the picture of *Saint Jerome in Meditation* that hung on the opposite wall.

"Let's sit in the tearoom and talk." Jefferson patted my arm. "My favorite variety of green tea, Young Hyson, along with our corn muffins, will make you feel better."

We crossed the hall and entered a formal parlor. Jefferson opened the French doors and, to my surprise, as one side slid open, so did the other. Jefferson said he had invented a device that made the entrance into his mansion's finest room a novel experience. As he went to a corner to ring a bell, I saw how dull and worn out I looked in the large mirror to my right.

"A servant will bring our fare shortly," he said with a smile. He then moved us through the parlor and the dining room into the tearoom. A colored man appeared, dressed like a European butler, and Jefferson gave him his instructions as we sat down. Soon afterward, the man returned with a tray that contained a teapot, two cups, and an assortment of muffins with butter.

"Thank you, Burwell," Jefferson said.

My host had called this man a servant, and indeed he was a servant. But I knew he was also a slave. Intrigued, I wasn't about to discuss this subject with Jefferson during our first encounter.

I had Eleonora's manuscript in my pocket and took it out. "I mentioned to you I knew the author of this memoir," I said.

"You did. "

"Well, I spent the whole night reading it."

"You must have felt the writing was important." Jefferson's head tilted to one side conveyed surprise.

"Eleonora Fonseca Pimentel was my first love," I said. "It was a shock, really, to find her memoir here. I was flooded with recollections. First her descriptions of our mutual attraction; then how I abandoned her to her fate."

Jefferson listened, his eyebrows lifted. He gave a slight nod for me to continue.

"Once I started reading, I couldn't stop."

"Tell me more—what does she say?" Jefferson fidgeted with his fingers.

"My Eleonora describes our families, the aristocratic salons we frequented, and the royal court's ambiance." I sighed. "Her descriptions are so real, I was brought back to the Naples I once knew."

"*Livres de Raison*, the description of one's life, if well written, touches the senses deeply." Jefferson offered me a corn muffin and then helped himself. I accepted but couldn't eat, I sipped my tea instead.

"The letter in the back pocket is a description of Eleonora's execution by a nun. I've imagined her death many times, but I didn't know the details. The whole thing has shattered me."

"I can imagine," Jefferson said taking a sip of tea. "Why did they kill her?"

"She was editor of the progressive republican newspaper, *Il Monitore Napoletano*."

"She strikes me as a daughter of liberty!" Jefferson said.

"She was."

"That's commendable. She believed in the holy cause of freedom."

"Eleonora was born in one world and wanted to invent another," I said.

"It takes courage to do that."

"But she paid for that daring with her life. She envisioned a republic of intellectuals for Naples. Change meant a radical break with the past. She wanted the Bourbon monarchy to go. Neapolitans called her the Jacobin Marquise."

"I like your Eleonora, she was a *literata* turned revolutionary. She preferred the boisterous sea of liberty to the idle calm of despotism." Jefferson's eyes burned with his own revolutionary passion.

"Indeed. But I feel blood on my hands. My abandonment of her—the love of my youth—was heartless. Maybe even cruel."

"What happened?" Jefferson asked.

"She was barely seventeen, just gaining fame as a poet as we parted. She enjoyed living in a world of make-believe. I didn't protect her as I should. She needed someone like me at her side—someone she loved and admired—to curb her emotions."

"But fantasies are good, they nourish the soul," Jefferson said. "For me, the world needs more idealism, not less." Jefferson now turned his gaze to the window as if contemplating the distant horizon.

"Her head was filled with lofty fantasies. If she recited a poem about the goddess Aphrodite, she became Aphrodite herself. I warned her of the dangers she faced the day we parted."

"Eyes in the sky and feet on the ground are not easily reconciled in the female character." Jefferson had a gleam in his eyes.

"Indeed, she had fire inside," I answered.

"That's attractive!" Jefferson said. "I hope you don't mind my candor."

"Not at all," My friend's remark lightened my mood, I now drank some tea and nibbled a muffin.

We were both silent for a moment.

"When was Eleonora executed?" Jefferson asked.

"In 1799, when the Neapolitan Republic—supported by the *Directoire*, the French Directory—failed."

Another silence ensued." I still don't understand why you didn't marry her," Jefferson asked.

"I didn't have the means. My family's Jewish and my father, like so many other Jews, was a doctor. As he didn't have a chance to practice medicine in Naples, he became a merchant," I said. "But after my mother died, he lost his will to live and never earned a living again."

"I imagine Eleonora's family was part of the elite in order for her to be recognized as a poet at such a young age." Jefferson pointed to a bust of Voltaire in the parlor. "As you know, our *philosophe* friend said that the ideal union was that of an aristocrat to one of the merchant class."

"Not in our case. I was the firstborn, I had the duty to help my father."

Jefferson looked at me and waited for me to continue.

"It was when I planned to discuss my marriage hopes with my father that I learned of his near bankruptcy. I then left Naples to enter the priesthood in Rome. The option soon gave me financial security and I could help my family."

Jefferson eye's opened widely as he said, "What a blow!"

"Had I been more savvy, I would have realized that Eleonora's dowry would've been enough for us. This, assuming, of course, that her parents blessed our union."

"Do you think they would have accepted you?"

"To this day, I don't know. My Jewish heritage might have affected them. We were New Christians, Jews who converted to Catholicism. Since I enjoyed the life of the spirit, the option of priesthood to help my family seemed a good choice. I put love aside."

"I married my late wife Martha for love." Jefferson crossed his arms on his chest, the same way he had done the night before. "Her family also had property, but that was not a consideration."

"You're fortunate. For me, my father's situation had a dire impact. A friend of his, the Duke of Lafões, offered to help us. If I entered the church, he would provide for me; in turn I could provide for my family. The duke was in charge of distributing a number of church monies. This is how I became the Secretary of the Royal Academy of Sciences. He founded it."

"At least your intellect found fulfillment. I'm sorry about Eleonora. Losing her then, and reading about her execution now, must be equally devastating. When Martha died, I experienced intense grief, I didn't know if I could survive without her." As ever the gentleman, Jefferson added, "Tell me if there is anything I can do for you."

"Your company has been my best solace, thank you." I finished my tea. "I already feel better."

"Then let's go out." With a cheerful smile, Jefferson got up from the sofa. "I'm going to show you one of the possible sites for the university. I want to see it from Monticello."

A few minutes later, we set off for the short walk from the house to a northwest pavilion that Jefferson said his son-in-law used as a work space. It was already the afternoon, but for the first time that day I was able to enjoy the weather—a light breeze touched my face, refreshing me. Jefferson pointed out the striking Blue Ridge Mountains. From there, his finger moved to the site he was planning for his campus. It was close to the town of Charlottesville, about seven or eight miles away. I commented on the Virginian landscape, how tranquil, soothing, and inspiring it was. Jefferson appreciated my enthusiasm, and for the moment I was able to put Eleonora from my mind.

My host had definite plans for his establishment. The Rotunda—the university's major building that would have a copper roof—was intended to be seen from various distant viewpoints. He hoped European professors would bring their knowledge and students to the place. He wanted the student body to be international to add cultural diversity to the classrooms. All the governing bodies would be secular, the grounds would have no church. He envisioned a bell tower whose inviting ring, heard everywhere, would call students to class.

Jefferson envisioned a curriculum based on reason and experimentation. The natural sciences would be strongly represented. There would be classes in botany, zoology, chemistry, mathematics, and astronomy; as well as anatomy, medicine, and surgery. The library would include books in all these growing areas of knowledge.

To create what he called a "society to our taste," Jefferson said he needed connoisseurs like me to lead the university's various departments. He called himself a farmer but said the life of the mind was paramount. He mentioned the names of his two most famous neighbors, James Madison and James Monroe. He also wanted them involved in his project.

"I hope you'll consider my offer for a professorship." Jefferson had an eager tone of voice.

I assured Jefferson I would. I clarified, however, that my future was not entirely in my hands; it had to do with the diplomatic assignment I might receive. Living in Brazil, the prince regent of Portugal had assumed governance of the Portuguese empire following Queen Maria's insanity. Medical reports confirmed his mother's recovery from the lethal condition was impossible. I added that as the university was still being developed, we had time for final decisions. My work with naturalists at the American Philosophical Society, people Jefferson knew well, gave me great satisfaction as well as scientific contacts. In due time, my work might well provide a worthy foundation for the position he was proposing.

As I described my work in Philadelphia, I was actually having reservations about his offer. The position was obviously a high honor that would culminate my life-long passion for botany. But my initial feeling was that an ambassadorship was a superior option. Becoming a representative of Portugal and Brazil brought with it the social standing I had always craved. Was I ready to sacrifice my life-long passion for botany to be in the public limelight? My financial security was also something to consider. These thoughts tormented me, and I calmed myself thinking that time would show me the way.

On our way back to the house, Jefferson said his grandchildren's music teacher would be arriving soon and warned me not to be surprised if I heard them playing. He also wanted to introduce me to his daughter Patsy, and her husband.

"The children will rehearse outside to enjoy the fresh air. Later in the day, their teacher, Mr. Valentin, will entertain us with a performance," he added.

"Music in Monticello, how delightful," I said.

"If you don't mind me asking," Jefferson's blue eyes pierced me. "Was Eleonora pretty?"

"She had the most beautiful, dark, expressive eyes," my voice whispered as if sharing the most intimate revelation.

"Our discovery in my library last night means so much to you. As a token of our friendship, may I offer you the manuscript?" Jefferson asked.

I shook Jefferson's hand. "I accept with gratitude."

Yet, I realized instantly, accepting Eleonora's memoir would keep open a wound I had wanted closed forever. I hid this feeling from Jefferson with a thankful smile.

Ever since the day I left Eleonora, I had developed a peculiar nervous restlessness. I was feeling it now. I had joined a satisfying life of tranquil scholarship and the pursuits worth of an international naturalist. The pleasure of collecting botanical specimens in field trips wherever I was had become a cherished habit. But I had split myself in two: I had crushed the emotional side of me, the part that had loved a young Portuguese woman with dark, contemplative eyes. The root of my spiritual alienation, if I could call it that, lay in this division. Sometimes I saw it as a form of lunacy; I even wrote to friends about it. I carried a heavy load on my shoulders, but I didn't dare to address its root. Thus, my wound hounded me wherever I went. It also constantly forced the question, who was I, really?

I returned alone to the tearoom, as Jefferson went for a ride on his favorite horse, Eagle. I sat once again on the sofa and this time closed my eyes. Sunshine poured through the large French windows, warming me. And it happened that, feeling such comfortable ease, I was momentarily transported back to the Naples of my youth. My father had once enjoyed a lucrative trade between the city and the Iberian capitals, Lisbon and Madrid. He had exported medicinal plants and herbs. And, with my mother's aesthetic, he had diversified the business to include textiles. One of our rooms at home was like a warehouse for all his goods. The diverse flora exuded exquisite aromas; those smells had predisposed me, I was certain, to my love for botany. I had early on recorded the name of those specimens in my Latin notebook, something I had often shared with Eleonora.

The evening I gave my goodbye letter to Eleonora had been dramatic. Almost eighteen, I didn't know how to quiet the burning of my soul. So, after I was sure the household was asleep, I tiptoed to my father's storage room. My siblings and I were hardly allowed into that space. I looked at the piles of silk, examined their colors and textures, and found a soft yellow moiré. I grabbed it, hid my whole face in it, and let my tears fall. I hadn't cried like that ever before, not even at my mother's funeral. At church that day, Eleonora's tears had seemed enough for the two of us. The fabric dampened little by little until it was completely wet. When I stopped, the delicate material was spoiled beyond repair. I hid it in the back of the room, in the middle of a stack of damaged goods. What a scolding I would get if my father ever found what I had done.

During the weeks that followed my separation from Eleonora, I wandered the streets of Naples, visiting every single fountain I knew. Most were made of stone, and the water gushing through the spouts soothed me. I made a point of observing the *palazzi* of the aristocracy, to admire the churches with marble and alabaster chapels, and to scrutinize the city's collection of obelisks. I felt I had to memorize the city by heart, for I might never return.

Naples was a place I had enjoyed since my arrival. Ties with Iberia were strong partly because King Ferdinando's father ruled Spain at the time. The city had a substantial community of Spaniards and Portuguese; its residents had lively faces and expressive gestures. Street life was theatrical and vivacious. Nomadic troupes of actors enlivened its piazzas with performances that could last for hours. Sometimes I strolled at night trying to relieve my churning mind. As only a handful of torches brightened the streets, the city was immersed in darkness once the sun set. Oil lamps, placed in dark alleys to illuminate shrines with images of the Virgin Mary, didn't guarantee public safety. But I never minded the danger.

The example of several priests I knew in the city made my transition easier. Innumerable abbés, including Eleonora's uncle, had independent careers of erudition, in some cases even enjoyed fame. Their lives were filled with intellectual freedom and scholarly leisure. I now wanted to share those same privileges.

I kept to myself how the Abbé Ferdinando Galiani and his adventures in Paris had showed me how to pursue my goals. He turned out to be, somehow, a more vibrant example for my future career than Genovese, despite the latter's great teachings. Galiani's life abroad was stimulating and exciting; he had made friends in the French capital with illustrious *philosophes* — people like Diderot.

Later, back in Naples, we all knew how he eagerly awaited letters from the celebrated Mme d'Épinay. He didn't need to marry to be intimate with a woman. I envisioned myself becoming, like him, a citizen of the world. The vow of chastity I took was a respectable cover for the life I intended to lead.

In fact, romantic liaisons were on my mind as I contemplated the celibate life. Dante Alighieri saw his secret beloved Beatrice only a few times. He probably never spoke to or touched her. She married a banker, a man of high standing. Yet, she remained his personification of spiritual and physical beauty, a holy figure, the love of his life. I thought Eleonora's memory might have the same effect on me.

Soon enough, my ecclesiastical career began in Rome. Not even the words of a close family friend, someone who considered all clergy "*manhosos, inúteis, imbecis*," sly, useless, and idiotic, could alter my decision. I didn't have to join any particular religious order—as an example, after the Jesuits were expelled, the Dominican friars were popular in Portugal—which I liked because it afforded me freedom from an institution's rules. After I celebrated my first Mass, my ordination to the priesthood was confirmed. Later, I graduated with a degree in ecclesiastical law. The three vows I professed—chastity, obedience, and poverty—allowed me to take advantage of and hide within the social structure I had entered. I was now part of a respected organization.

My reverie about my Neapolitan life faded when singing reached my ears. I got up and made my way toward the agreeable sounds. The scene I found on the mansion's north terrace was uplifting. Valentin, the music teacher, stood before a group of children gathered in a semi-circle. I recognized some of them from the previous night. A few were of mixed ancestry. Their skin tones ranged in color, some lighter than others. As they sang what I took to be Virginian ballads, a mulatto boy played the violin with feeling. Another played a fiddle. Valentin directed his youthful choir the same way a maestro would conduct a prominent orchestra. I felt blessed to be at Jefferson's hilltop mansion—it presided over a plantation with eccentricities I could never have imagined. I was experiencing an agrarian society filled with sophistication and culture, something I couldn't possibly have imagined from Europe.

A few minutes later, Jefferson called me to join him. He told me Valentin lived in nearby Charlottesville and was a great conversationalist. He was the son of one of the Italian musicians he had formerly hired to celebrate his first inauguration as president in 1801. Italians were great artists, he added, and Americans profited from experiencing their musicality. He then proceeded with the introductions in the main parlor, which doubled as the music room.

"Mr. Valentin, allow me to introduce to you my eminent friend, the Abbé Correia. He became a member of the American Philosophical Society as soon as he set foot in America," Jefferson said.

We shook each other's hands while I said, "Glad to meet you. Mr. Jefferson and I share a firm belief in the usefulness of science."

"True." Our host said. "We must understand the laws that govern nature. Only that will foster an enlightened viewpoint."

The three of us sat down to talk.

"Mr. Correia was the secretary of the Academy of Sciences of Lisbon for many years," Jefferson said to Valentin. "From there he moved to London and, later, to Paris. We're fortunate to have him with us in America now."

"I lived in Lisbon from 1777 to 1795, but was forced into exile," I said.

"What happened?" Valentin asked.

"Our academy met with opposition from conservative groups, including the crown. Most members of the academy were in the more liberal camp. Some of us were Freemasons, and we met regularly. The Inquisition didn't like us, its judges acted like an arm of the monarchy."

"It was expected that European kingdoms would fear social upheaval in the aftermath of the French Revolution," said Jefferson.

"I was considered a Jacobin, a supporter of the French. But I'm a reformer at heart. I've always been a believer in gradual change brought through small, steady steps. The social system is like the natural world: a tree, a flower, develops slowly, little by little. But that wasn't enough for the royal police."

"Our American envoy, my friend Mr. David Humphreys, wasn't able to help. Members of the academy weren't the only ones under close scrutiny. New ideas were in the air and threatened the authorities," Jefferson continued.

"I venerated our Queen Maria, who founded our academy. But when I figured out her chief of police—the dreadful Pina Manique—was about to arrest me, I fled wearing only the clothing I had on that day. I left everything else behind at the Grilo Palace, Lafões' residence, where I lived."

"How upsetting," Valentin said.

"My life was in danger, I had to act. I had nightmares as soon as I blew out my candles and lay in bed. Once, I even recalled the Chevalier d'Oliveira. The gentleman was an *estrangeirado* like me, a designation we use to describe Portuguese Europeanized intellectuals who live abroad. The Inquisition considered him a heretic but was unable to arrest him and bring him back to trial. So, in 1761—it doesn't seem so long ago—they burned him in effigy. They led an *auto-de-fé*, a ceremonial public procession of condemnation that displayed a long-size paper image of him being led to the stake. The image wore the dreadful penance tunic and the *sanbenito,* the tall dreadful hat. It lasted for several hours."

"I can't imagine how terrifying your nightmares have been!" Jefferson said.

Valentin spoke up. "As I told Mr. Jefferson once, we're also Sephardic Jews, originally from the Iberian Peninsula. What those nations did to us is vile!"

I nodded at my companions, somehow bewildered by my confessions. "I must admit I even contemplated suicide at the time."

"I'm happy you were able to regain your footing. Botany would have lost a lot without you, " Jefferson said.

"My friends at the academy and I were all fearful. It was impossible to challenge the Inquisition," I added.

We lapsed into silence for a moment. Then Valentin asked, "Did you admit your Jewish blood when you joined the Church?" Valentin asked.

"Never. How could I? They would never have taken me in."

"You did the right thing. Best to keep some things to yourself." Jefferson stretched his back and appeared even taller than he was.

I was struck by Jefferson's comment. As if he knew—as much as I did—that intimate details of our lives were better kept for oneself. Like me, Jefferson understood that reality had many layers. Some were visible, others we concealed. I felt Jefferson's remark as the solidification of an emerging, beautiful friendship.

Besides, all my European contacts had told me that Jefferson—like our friend the American envoy David Humphreys—was a Freemason. Another thing we had in common.

Even so, I wasn't about to reveal how the Inquisition had mistreated me when I was in Portugal. This incident had taken a toll, but it was easier to speak about others' tragedies than about my own. Once, the Inquisition had summoned me, forcing me to confess matters of a private nature. I will not go into this at the moment, but maybe I'll have the fortitude to address the issue later on. Suffice is to say now that, indeed, I had committed what the church called *delitos*, evil acts. Someone had denounced me, I didn't know who. At the time, I had seen my admissions as a way to be, finally, free from the fear of their questioning.

"Patsy and Maria, my two daughters, studied in a Catholic school in Paris, the Panthémont Convent, when I was ambassador there," Jefferson said after a short silence. "The convent was an elite school that catered to the children of well-to-do families. They never asked us about our religion."

"Catholicism acts differently in different countries. The Inquisition was at its worst in Iberia, Portugal and Spain," I said.

"What made you choose a Catholic education for your daughters?" Valentin asked.

"The curriculum was excellent," Jefferson said. "I was busy with work and the heavy demands of a social life. And, after my late wife's death, I thought my daughters might be better off in the company of women like them."

"Did you see them often?" Valentin continued.

"I saw them all the time, they spent week-ends at home."

Our host now turned to his daughter, Patsy, who had just entered the room. I had heard in Philadelphia that when she had voiced a desire to become a nun, Jefferson pulled his daughters out of the school. This coincided, luckily, with the family's return to America. Jefferson had witnessed French citizens storming the Bastille on July 14th, 1789, setting off the French Revolution. However, he had previously asked the American government to return home to his beloved Monticello. After several years abroad, he was homesick.

"Papa, dear guest, Mr. Valentin," Patsy said, entering the room with her husband and children. She wore a simple, cream dress that covered her ankles and an embroidered white cap on her head. "We're ready for your performance," she said to Valentin.

A few minutes of pleasantries followed before we sat down around the harpsichord. After a few chords to warm up his fingers, Valentin played several sonatas by Domenico Scarlatti, a composer born in Naples. To please me, I guess, he then sang a Neapolitan aria.

Jefferson's family life filled me with contentment, I was enjoying their warmth and connectedness. Jefferson sat amid his grandchildren, a smiling patriarch. The mulatto children I had seen outside earlier in the day had now vanished. Jefferson had not changed his attire for the evening. He could have put on a shirt with lace, had he wanted to impress me. But that wasn't his character. On the table next to him lay a bouquet of jasmine, spreading its scent. I was sure it had been picked not long before, for it still looked fresh and moist. The performance ended with both adults and children clapping enthusiastically to Valentin's delight.

The homey scene made me wonder if the position at the university wouldn't benefit me. I would be doing what I enjoyed most, studying botany. I had always been short of money, but my salary would be ample to cover my living expenses.

I left Monticello at the end of the week. Before my departure, I asked Jefferson if he would kindly show me the writing box—or a lap desk—where, at the age of thirty-three, he had written the American Declaration of Independence. Benevolent as usual, he led me to the mahogany piece. The portable desk was Jefferson's own design, smaller than I had imagined. I contemplated it silently, in awe.

As I thanked Jefferson for his lavish hospitality, I told him that not only had he and his family captivated me, but I also felt very much at home in Virginia. We promised to continue our correspondence. Affably, Jefferson said we were kindred spirits and that I should return to Monticello as soon as possible. I attributed his remark to his starving for intellectual companionship during his retirement, something his daily correspondence and study didn't entirely fulfill.

As soon as I settled in the coach back to Philadelphia, I took

Eleonora's rosemary sprig from the booklet's back pocket and held it in my hand. I was sure it was the same branch I had given her the day we parted. On my way out of the garden, I had turned for a last look and seen her tuck it into her bosom. After the excitement of my stay in Monticello, my trip promised to be long and contemplative.

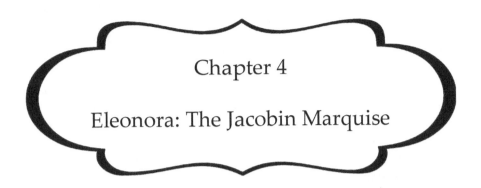

Chapter 4

Eleonora: The Jacobin Marquise

At the Vicaria Prison, Castel Capuano, outskirts of Naples, July 6, 1799

The roots of my revolutionary thinking started early, paradoxically, when I was the librarian to Carolina, the Queen of Naples. As Naples grew to admire my poetry, the queen appointed me to the position. This took place in 1775, after I wrote *La Nascita di Orfeo, The Birth of Orpheus,* celebrating the birth of the queen's first son. When I look back, my early years in the queen's service were the happiest of my life. Carolina and I were the same age, and both foreigners in Naples. As such, we wanted to fit in and embrace the city we called home.

I found the queen rather captivating the first time we met. The encounter had occurred at a poetry competition at the Royal Palace, many years earlier. Young, timid, and introverted, I'm sure I blushed when the queen awarded me first prize. I was competing against several priests, and she said she was thrilled a woman had won the competition. Her liking of me and my poetry was enthralling.

Carolina's conviviality was contagious and contributed to a lively and cosmopolitan atmosphere for all of us, the *literati*. She contrasted markedly with the ladies I usually met in Naples, even among the aristocracy. As the king's consort, she wanted to create a world of her own. And to find a role for herself as the queen of a Southern European kingdom, potentially hostile to her own views. Educated in Vienna, a city that dazzled with culture, she showed the court early on that she was going to influence her new surroundings. That her husband lacked the skills to be a worthy monarch—that he lacked a basic education—had been clear to her from the beginning of the marriage. The daughter of Empress Maria Theresa, Carolina combined birth and privilege with high intelligence and lofty ideas. She had been brought up in a Masonic environment: her father, her brother Joseph II, and two of her sisters were Freemasons. She respected self-discipline, manners, and decorum. But, above all, she arrived in Naples with a modern way of thinking: she valued equality, majority rule, and universal education.

Early on, Carolina realized she needed to win the confidence of the cultured Neapolitan elite if she was going to fulfill her agenda. An easy way to do this was to support free-thinking societies—a task she undertook by spreading the Freemason philosophy on her rounds of the city. I saw how, under her protection, lodges began to flourish both in Naples and its provinces.

Following French thinkers like Voltaire and the Encyclopedists, lodge members were soon discussing the reforms now occurring in France. These included citizenry and human rights; governance by the people and free speech; religious tolerance and separation of church and state; and the right to private judgment, the ability to express personal views.

Viewing the queen as a role model, a friend and an ally, I soon joined the Masonic Lodge for noblewomen presided over by the Venerable Princess Ottaiano, the Marquise Caterina di San Marco. Now, with the queen's blessing, female lodges—not only male ones—were spreading.

Like others, I befriended members of the Patriotic Society, this was the main Jacobin club of Naples. It was here I learned the origin of the term Jacobin: it came from Saint Jacques, the church in Paris where the French revolutionaries had originally met. Following the French example, the Neapolitan *literati* saw themselves as intellectuals ready to become revolutionaries—the so-called Jacobins.

Many of us met at the San Carlo Royal Theater, a general meeting place. I attended the performance when the prima donna Antonia Bernasconi interrupted her performance to make a Masonic sign. She circled her open hand three times from the end of the torso to her throat—a gesture greeted by the audience's applause. I was lucky that night to be escorted by Abbé Ferdinando Galiani, the distinguished diplomat. He had heard something significant was going to happen that evening, and I felt fortunate to be present at the event.

As the queen's librarian, I often had the honor to enter her private quarters at the palace. The atmosphere was informal with courtiers, visitors, and servants coming in and out of her boudoir at all times. The entourage was joyous, endearing, and I so enjoyed those visits with Carolina. There, I very much admired the *objets de vertu* she collected: clocks, statuettes, brooches, and miniatures. I particularly liked the potpourri, the large vases she had filled with aromatic herbs to freshen up the air. The queen was usually surrounded by her progeny. She had the good fortune I had wished for early on, but still lacked: a husband and children. It gave me satisfaction to witness how she wouldn't sacrifice her beliefs to please her husband.

At this time, people in Naples already called me the "Portoghesina," Little Portuguese. This was a term of endearment that included, from the start, a touch of rebellion. How I cherished the designation! Everybody knew I supported and encouraged the queen in her quest for reform. Portuguese by birth, I had always spoken my native language at home. All of us in the Portuguese community felt attached to our former homeland, a place located at the far end of the Iberian Peninsula. There was a small Portuguese legation in Naples, and my family fraternized regularly with its members. I looked at Portugal's history and culture as an illustration of what Naples could be one day. I had never visited the nation where my parents had been born but, in my view, it had modernized more rapidly than Naples.

The court's lively environment helped me put aside my doomed passion for Joseph. I was now ready to accept my parents' choice of Michele for a husband. Marrying a cousin was common practice for young, aristocratic women. My parents' arguments, increasingly forceful, convinced me.

I now lived among many distractions that kept me busy and engaged. The most notorious intellectuals of the day visited the palace to borrow books the queen had asked me to order from abroad.

Many offered fresh news on the latest political developments of turbulent France. Well versed in Latin due to Professor Grassi, and also knowing Greek, I spent hours translating ancient texts. These studies fed my passion for knowledge and change. Once in a while, I took time off to work on my own texts. I closed the heavy library doors and sat at my desk for the solitude I needed. Time flew by and how I cherished these precious moments alone with my inner world!

On one occasion—I was twenty-three and still single—I wrote *Il Trionfo della Virtù, Virtue Triumphant*. It was a cantata in the neo-classical style: poetry to be recited, accompanied by music. The text was as daring then as it remains now, so many years later. It demonstrated not only my political savoir-faire but, above all, my future revolutionary role. It was a step forward in my literary career because it made my political direction clearer. I'm not certain Carolina ever saw this work of mine, she was always exceedingly busy with her own court activities.

I know how proud my mother would have been had she seen my treatment of reform in Portugal. Unfortunately, she died before I had finished the work. She would have seen how I emerged there as the scholar she always believed I was born to become. Moreover, Carolina's cosmopolitanism had facilitated my task; we *literati* weren't restricted to discussions about the southern Italian peninsula. I sent my cantata to Vienna, to the greatest European master of the genre at the time, the famous poet Pietro Metastasio. He wrote back saying that he admired "the noble, poetic, and sonorous verses and the ingenious, robust, and proud thoughts."

Il Trionfo della Virtù reached Portugal in 1777, a few weeks after Maria, King José's daughter—young and sane at the time—was acclaimed first queen of Portugal. In the letter that accompanied the cantata, I dedicated my work to the Marquis de Pombal, the prime minister she had just deposed. He was an enlightened despot—our Cardinal Richelieu—and one of the most enlightened European reformers of the time. He embodied, in my view, the notion of public virtue. In my dedication, I call him "intrepid philosopher, defenseless minister and sensitive citizen."

These were political statements that took, at my age, a great deal of courage. My critics were confused with the letter's arrival date in Portugal, thinking that I might not be aware that Maria's father, King José, had died. But I was fully aware of his death and Maria's succession. If I hadn't been, why would I address Pombal as "defenseless minister?"

Maria—pious, Catholic and conservative—had dismissed Pombal as soon as she was made queen. I wanted her to be aware of my words of wisdom and, hopefully, consider my advice. As the librarian to the Queen of Naples, a *literata*, I imagined myself now capable of influencing the new queen of Portugal. Like all enlightened men and women seeking recognition for their work, I fancied I could shape the times in which I lived.

My dedication had the political purpose I will now explain below, so many years later.

Pombal's supremacy had depended on the king allowing him to carry out sweeping reforms. Maria loved and respected her father, but she hated his prime minister's enlightened policies. As soon as Maria became queen, Pombal was arrested, put on trial, and placed under house arrest. Further, a restraining order prevented him from approaching her. Rumors circulated in European capitals, Naples included, that Pombal might be sentenced to death, be assassinated, or simply vanish without a trace.

I felt alarm that Pombal's dismissal marked the end of the struggle between reformers and conservatives in the country. The conservatives had won, they now had power. But I was dismayed with the turn of events, and thus wrote in my dedication to Pombal:

> *Nothing is more difficult to find, nor more pleasing to the eyes of heaven and earth, than the sight of a righteous king served by a wise minister, the two equally able, where the former surrenders to the advice of the latter, and the latter sacrifices himself at the service of the former... Hence, this dual, delicate balance becomes the firm foundation equally of the dignity of royal power and the firmness of public happiness.*

With these words that I recall by heart, I asserted that King's José's policies were tempered by a wise and fair prime minister; someone willing to serve a just and provident king. My letter had a clear intention. If Maria jeopardized the memory of Pombal, she also jeopardized the memory of her father; she would appear to suspect him of wrongdoing. I hoped to prevent that from happening. My goal was to mobilize the liberal circles of Europe to Pombal's cause.

Why did I take pains to write *Il Trionfo della Virtù*? Quite simply, as a Freemason, I easily identified other members in our fraternity. And the Marquis de Pombal was one. Pombal and I were *compagnons de route*, regardless of our geographical distance. My letter was far-reaching. It aimed to protect a brother in trouble at the end of his life. Thus, the letter's date of arrival in Portugal needed to be crystal clear. When Pombal's reforms came under attack, I stood loyally behind him.

I'm still proud that I included the issue of public happiness in my letter. The theme had been consecrated in the famous Declaration of Independence written by Thomas Jefferson in America. I took his words to heart.

I deliberately evaded Pombal's most controversial deed in power: the barbaric execution of many members of Portugal's high nobility in 1759. I knew the brutal episode was Queen Maria's reason for so fiercely opposing Pombal; I knew these victims were like my family. But, in my view, some notables had to be eliminated for change to take place. There was no other way.

I never imagined the same tragedy might befall me one day. Imprisonment is often followed by death. I was either too young, or too innocent, or even too hardhearted, to fully consider the impact of my silence. Do I now regret this writing of mine? No, the answer is a definite no.

Buried here in this filthy dungeon, I must consider now what might happen to me one day. I've been disciplined; I've been writing a lot of the time. But will I be able to continue—given the disgusting food, the straw mattress filled with lice, and the putrid smell?

Only time will tell.

While at the Royal Palace, my work touched a variety of lives, not only those of the powerful. I talked to everyone: prominent and common, noble and plebian, rich and poor alike. One late afternoon, just as I prepared to go home, Queen Carolina came rushing into the library. I was surprised, she usually asked a courtier to fetch me to her private quarters.

As soon as I saw the queen, I rose to greet her. Carolina looked stunning that evening. She wore a tall wig in the French style, something she knew enhanced her appearance. Her dress was formal for the dinner she was hosting that evening. It had delicate white and pink frills that adorned her bosom and stiff skirt like tiny butterflies. She was in a good mood and said that the previous day the head of the Accademia dell'Arcadia, the most prestigious of our poetic academies, had praised my poetry. "Eleonora, my dear, I came here to charge you with a mission I wish to sponsor."

"What can I do for you, Your Highness?"

"The Madre Superiore, the Reverend Mother in charge of the feminine section of the Vicaria Prison, Suor Amadea Della Valle, wrote to me. She would like to start literacy classes for the prisoners. It pains her to see such idleness in the prison."

"To give inmates the rudiments of reading and writing is a worthy cause," I replied.

"Most of these women don't even know the alphabet. They sign their name with a cross. Suor Amadea is asking for basic texts. I thought we could donate a few of our catechisms."

"Of course—that's a great idea."

"Suor Amadea is also concerned about these women's situations, their background. Some are imprisoned for petty offenses and might leave soon. But others have committed serious crimes and might remain prisoners for the rest of their lives. The catechisms depicting the life of Jesus Christ might help them," the queen said.

"Many of them have the alphabet listed in the back pages," I added.

"Suor Amadea will be coming tomorrow to talk to you. The two of you can decide what to do. You'll enjoy meeting her—her family is originally from Portugal. But she was born in Naples and is a few years older."

"I'll be delighted to meet her," I replied, my heart pounding. I could be of service, and I was going to meet someone who shared my ancestry.

With a fond farewell, the queen left as quickly as she had arrived.

I lost no time familiarizing myself with conditions at the Vicaria Prison. I wanted to be prepared for meeting Suor Amadea the following afternoon, and I found out the women lived in deplorable conditions. They were fed a small piece of bread each day and a *caldo* that couldn't even be called a soup. They quenched their thirst with murky water. Bathing was unheard of and often the overworked prison guards didn't empty the latrines as regularly as they should have. The odor was horrific, and the lack of sanitation responsible for epidemics and death.

The next day, when Suor Amadea arrived, I felt immediately drawn to her.

"You look so Portuguese!" I extended my hand in greeting. She was short and muscular, with a plump face framed by the starched white wimple. Her habit covered her body, except for her hands.

"The pleasure is mine," she replied warmly.

"Before we discuss the women and their needs, could I ask if you've been to Portugal?"

"Unfortunately not," she said. "But I read and speak Portuguese."

"So do I, it's the language we speak at home."

"We do the same," Suor Amadea said with a smile.

"I'm so glad we can work together. I sympathize wholeheartedly with your mission to help the prisoners with literacy."

"This has been a wish of mine for a long time. I'd asked the royal administration for help earlier, but nothing ever came of it. I feel so happy I contacted the queen."

I showed Suor Amadea a few of the catechisms I had laid out and she chose the ones with the alphabet written on the back.

We talked for a while about her plans to use the booklets, and our connection was affectionate and genuine. Before she left, she told me she had taken her vows at a young age, envisioning a life of devotion to others. "You and I share the good fortune of an education, something that made us who we are."

I agreed.

"And if I only succeed in teaching these women to sign their names, I'll consider the effort worthy in the name of God."

As our meeting ended, I said, "Queen Carolina instructed me to give you all the support you need. The catechisms are cumbersome, so one of our coachmen will deliver them to you."

"Would you like to visit the prison? You'll likely be appalled by the conditions, but they might also be a mind-opener. An aristocrat like you hasn't been exposed to such harsh realities."

"We are all members of the human race. Your just cause has touched me, and it'll be an honor to accept your invitation. But my trip depends on whether Queen Carolina needs me the day the booklets are delivered. If I'm free, I'd be delighted to visit."

And it so happened that the queen did not need me the day one of her coachmen was available for the delivery. I sat in the royal carriage's back seat of dark-green velvet and set off with the coachman to the Vicaria Prison.

I never forgot the day I was first exposed to the desolation of poverty. I had seen it before in the streets of Naples, but this was different, it was close-up. The Marquis de Sade had described the jail at its arid location on the city's outskirts. It bore the name Vicaria because the Vicar of Naples presided over the judiciary, located in the same building. From my vantage point, the sight was sinister at first glance. In front of the main gate stood the horrendous stone pillory. This was a high stone pole where criminals, robbers, and debtors were commonly humiliated by having their private parts exposed to the public. It was cold that day, but I wondered how anybody survived the punishment under our scorching southern sun.

I felt fear and horror entering surroundings I could hardly have imagined existed, and wondered if Suor Amadea could detect this in my eyes. Little did I know! One day I would be the one locked up in this dreadful place. Not once, but twice. And how could I ever have predicted that I would need this same woman's protection and kindness?

Suor Amadea was eager to show me her office and also the small library room. Dust filled the latter, no one seemed to have entered it in a long time. There was plenty of space for our booklets, the wooden shelves were empty. A small mouse scuttled across the floor, but Suor Amadea didn't comment on it. The repulsive rodents must be everywhere, I thought, spreading disease. Sure enough, on our next stop at the infirmary, one room was full of prisoners with infectious diseases, kept in isolation from others. Suor Amadea didn't touch anyone but paused at each bed to ask how the patient was doing. Most were too sick to reply.

The apothecary needed constant supervision, Suor Amadea

told me, otherwise medication was stolen by guards who later sold it for high prices outside. We proceeded on, entering the dormitories. Here, hordes of women dressed in rags stood around idly or sat on their beds. They looked unhealthy, many had no teeth, and their matted hair looked as if it hadn't been washed in months. A few women were picking lice from each other's heads. The filthy odor is what struck me most. Our visit ended at the Vicaria's chapel in the main building. It was here that justices heard Mass before making judicial decisions. A picture of Christ's resurrection caught my attention, it was so vivid.

My visit to the prison had a powerful effect on me, and the next morning, first thing, I wrote Suor Amadea that it would be an honor to assist her further, if needed. I reminded her of our common heritage and said I was moved to see a woman dedicated to bringing the light of instruction to other females. I added I had been most impressed with her compassion and good will.

I kept in touch with Suor Amadea on and off in the ensuing years. We exchanged notes and greetings frequently, particularly until the time I worked in the palace. But not as much as I had wished. Intellectual work was my first priority and kept me busier than I sometimes wanted.

At the queen's library, I was acquiring firsthand knowledge of the reforms the Neapolitan *literati* craved. At the same time, I had the opportunity to witness the sad conditions in which the *lazzaroni*, the dispossessed, lived. How difficult to reconcile the contradictions flowing under my eyes!

I worked at the Royal Palace several days a month, mainly when the queen needed me. My schedule was flexible and, like everything else in Naples, varied with the seasons. My proximity to Carolina afforded me an extra chance: to know up close who was in her favor.

Even in retrospect, it's difficult to imagine how things could have soured so badly between the queen and me; we had started off on such good terms. How sad that she became conservative and vicious as the years went by.

In 1786, a new arrival at the palace immediately caught my attention. She was Emma Hart, and I saw how quickly Carolina took to her. She was the mistress of the British Ambassador Lord Hamilton, and breaking diplomatic protocol, he brought her along to the palace any time he was invited there.

Emma had an aura hard to escape. She was beautiful with alabaster skin, elegant manners, and dressed stylishly. She was a lively conversationalist up to date on the latest news from abroad, something the queen enjoyed. Rumor had it that Emma had been a former high-class prostitute. Now she was the concubine of the most important member of the diplomatic corps in Naples, treated like an international luminary. She entered the queen's quarters at ease from the beginning of her arrival, either to spread gossip or just discuss the latest fashion of the day. How she must have enjoyed the blinded-folded games, the masked balls, and even the duet singing with King Ferdinando!

Once, I had the chance to see the future Lady Hamilton perform one of her *"Tableau Vivants,"* theatrical pieces. She portrayed the mythological figure Circe as Ulysses sailed away. She wore a simple white tunic, seductively transparent, and her long auburn hair flowed freely over her shoulders. She used a black shawl as a prop. These so-called "Attitudes," or mimicking, were like a game of hide-and-seek because the audience was left to guess who Emma was impersonating. They would shout out a name when they found the celebrity—or thought they had. As she went about waving her shawl, and sometimes hiding her face behind it, she would acknowledge her viewers with her tantalizing eyes.

I was seated in the middle of her audience, my gaze rising just above the women's wigs and the men's long hair tied up in the back with colorful bows. Looking sideways, I could see how the men were unable to take their eyes off the enchantress. They were enthralled and ecstatic, including her future husband. I was shocked. I found the performance vulgar, with erotic overtones. That Emma could have no conscience about exposing her legs, bosom, and body to a public audience, appalled me. But the guests enjoyed her manner and seemingly innocent expression. Famous artists had already painted her portrait in London, and later I heard that Richard Cosway—married to Maria Cosway, the socialite that the American Thomas Jefferson was apparently in love with in Paris—was seeking the chance as well. Painting Emma Hart, it seemed, added to an artist's reputation. No one in my own circle would ever perform such an act as I was witnessing. But the court needed entertainment and Emma was willing to provide it. Rumor had it that Lord Hamilton had paid several actors to train her.

The future Lady Hamilton and Carolina spent countless hours together, alone. And, one day, an unfortunate incident occurred with frightful consequences for me. The palace's cheerful atmosphere included a lot of gossip; it was like a wasp's nest, the chatter never stopped. Gossip, among us, was rarely kind. Voices filled with intrigue and malice whispered that Emma and Carolina had become lovers. Stories circulated about how they enjoyed taking afternoon siestas in the same bed, the window curtains drawn. Or how they bathed together in the queen's bathtub to cool off during the afternoon heat, the water perfumed with rose petals.

I must have been distracted on the day of the incident for, what I'm about to say, should never have happened. But my personal life had changed, and I was less attentive than I should have been. A courtier came into the library and told me the queen wanted to see me in her private chamber. I sighed softly. I was in the middle of cataloging a series of Vesuvius paintings a Neapolitan aristocrat, recently deceased, had left to the crown in his will. I hated the interruption, I loved my desk by a window carved with a limestone trim. The work was pressing because we were exhibiting the art to the public the following week.

As I entered the queen's boudoir, I noticed her bedroom door was ajar. I was surprised to see no courtier or maid nearby. But, since I had been summoned, I walked into her room as I usually did. Immediately, I saw Emma and Carolina. Not only was their long hair loose—they were not wearing wigs—but they also wore chamber robes. I remember Carolina's robe distinctly, it was adorned with golden fleur-de-lis, the Bourbon symbol. They were undressing each other, while kissing. When the queen heard my steps, she turned and with the slant of her eyes, told me to leave. I disappeared as fast as I had come in.

After this episode, Carolina took over several weeks to call me again. The exhibition of Vesuvius artwork never took place. From then on, she only came to my desk to briefly discuss a few matters or give me orders. We no longer chatted as before. We still needed each other, on the surface our relationship remained the same. The queen must have her *literati* close to bring her projects to life; I required her power to develop my literary ambitions. Of course, we never spoke a word about the scene I had interrupted, but our relationship changed on that day. The queen put a wall between us, she became cold towards me. I had discovered one of her secrets. And since everyone now joked that the king of Naples was, in fact, the queen, I could be dismissed from a position I loved in an instant.

It goes without saying, I never told anyone what I had seen.

I married during my years of service to the queen. But not to Michele, in anger and disgust I made sure he broke our engagement. Michele's manner had been disengaged and distant all along. The memory of Joseph, and our seductive courtships, had been embedded in my soul forever. I knew the meaning of love, the excitement of touching, and the desires of the flesh. Instead of Michele, I married Don Pasquale Tria de Solis, someone my father took quite a bit of time to find. It might have been better if, instead of walking to the church altar at the age of twenty-six, I had broken both legs that day.

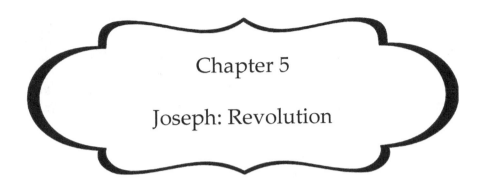

Chapter 5

Joseph: Revolution

I shall hope for your passing at Monticello as much of the summer
as you can.
—Thomas Jefferson's letter to Joseph Correia da Serra,
    March 6, 1815

❝If Eleonora could ever imagine me at a Virginia plantation that
    bears an Italian name, Monticello!" I said to Jefferson one late
afternoon during my second visit.

"I've had plenty of time to think about your Eleonora and her
manuscript. In fact, I'd like to talk more about her," Jefferson replied.

"Gladly!"

"Shall we talk as we walk? I'd like to plant magnolia seeds in an
area that I call the grove. This is an experiment of mine, one of my
pet projects," Jefferson said. "On such a beautiful spring day, we
can really enjoy nature. You know, the soil here is as fertile as parts
of the Italian peninsula."

We had been sitting in Jefferson's library and headed now to
the mansion's south terrace. "I'm so happy to be back," I said. "It's
indescribable! I feel like a pilgrim visiting a sacred shrine. Nature is
blossoming in May, and so am I. "

Jefferson handed me a pair of boots that were laid aside on the
terrace. Then he took his walking stick and offered me a spare. "I'm
so glad to see you again. As you know, spring is cooler here, and
healthier, than in Philadelphia."

For the past year or so, Jefferson and I had exchanged frequent letters. He had solicited my counsel on several occasions, and I had gladly given him my opinion. It was a pleasure to discuss the statutes of the University of Virginia, its natural sciences curricula, and the specifics of the courses in botany. I had also suggested plants for the arboretum Jefferson was designing for the grounds. An invitation for my next visit had concluded many of his letters. I was eager to be back, we both loved the culture of the earth.

As we walked toward the grove, I felt a profound sense of spiritual renewal. We passed a winding walk lined with fragrant flowers. The beds were oval-shaped, producing a riot of tulips, hyacinth, larkspur and other perennials. Everything surrounding us was fresh and dewy—the colorful flowers, the chirping birds, and the rustling bushes. My joy of combining traveling with pleasure was intense. I wondered if I would be able to open my heart to Jefferson; I had never been able to share my vulnerabilities with anyone. Time would tell if the moment was right.

I looked at my friend—I knew I could call him that now. He was holding the box of magnolia seeds and I saw a curious item coming out of his waistcoat pocket. It was a small ivory notebook, ready for use. It had several layers of thin ivory that were attached to each other by a metal piece. When I mentioned it, he described it as his portable companion. The ivory layers were like pages of a notebook. When they got filled up, he transcribed his notes to a larger pad, and then erased the ivory layers with cloth. The ivory pad was ready for use again.

As if on the same wavelength, Jefferson's hazel eyes looked into mine with brotherly warmth. He stopped and looked at me. "As I said earlier, Eleonora's been on my mind. I have so many questions—her marriage, for instance."

Stopping too, I answered with a burst of emotion. "If only I could describe her disastrous marriage to a despicable Southern European man, followed by the death of her only child, then perhaps you might feel her pain the way I have."

"How she must have suffered! Where were you when she perished?"

"I was living in London. I was there from 1795 to 1802," I replied. "Sir Joseph Banks kindly admitted me to the British Royal Society, where he was president."

"His favorable opinion of you is legendary. You know he calls you the most extraordinary animal in nature, don't you?"

I laughed because I had heard the description before. "I take it as a complement." And I continued. "During one of our botanical excursions, we discussed the revolutionaries' role in the Neapolitan Republic. But I never told him I knew Eleonora."

"I hope you don't mind my asking, but did you ever attempt to intercede on her behalf?"

"No, and I regret that I didn't. Banks and the British ambassador Lord Hamilton were both naturalists and good friends. They were forever exchanging letters on Mount Vesuvius. Had I asked, they might have intervened. But I was only thinking of myself. I was seeking a position at the Portuguese embassy in London and didn't want to jeopardize my chances."

"Silences are, sometimes, golden. In this case, you wanted to protect yourself," Jefferson said.

I was struck hard by his words. They showed understanding, compassion, and friendship. My heart stirred with gratitude and reverence. As during my previous visit, I had the feeling that Jefferson agreed with my silences because they mirrored his own.

"It was a hard choice." I said. "I feared repercussions if I interfered with Portuguese affairs. As a royal subject in London, I would gain nothing by trying to rescue an insurgent. I might even be considered one, too."

"I see."

"My reward came in 1802, when I was appointed Agente de Negócios, Commercial Counselor, at the embassy. But the job didn't last long—and that's another story."

"Why? Were you…?"

I interrupted Jefferson. "The Inquisition came after me again, even in London. Our ambassador's cousin was the Grand Inquisitor of Portugal. When I submitted my resignation—feeling unable to work for such a man—he wouldn't accept it. I was afraid he might arrest me; after all, we were in Portuguese territory at the embassy. So, I fled to Paris."

"What a life you've had!" Jefferson paused for a moment and then said, "But returning to Eleonora. I imagine you felt guilty about her death."

"I did, I still do. But I don't think that bloody revolutions pay off. Change should be lawful, without violence," I said.

"I have to disagree, my dear friend. Eleonora did as all revolutionaries do, she fought for her beliefs. As far as I know, a republic could have succeeded in Naples had the *Armée d'Italie*—the French Army—remained in the city to protect the newly established Republic."

"But the majority of the population, the *lazzaroni*, loved their king and queen too much for a bunch of *literati* to succeed, even with French support. As poor and destitute as they were, the masses adored their sovereigns," I answered.

Silently, we crossed a zigzagging path. It had narrowed, and I let Jefferson go ahead of me, I needed space for reflection. Here and there we swept our sticks from side to side to remove branches from the way. I was going to keep a secret from Jefferson, something I could barely even admit to myself. The author of the American Declaration of Independence had been at the helm of huge historical changes. He had leapt into the unknown; if the British had accused him of treason, it could have cost him his life. Thus, understandably, I thought, Jefferson might not agree with my conduct. He might interpret it as a flaw in my character, a dark side. And I didn't want his disapproval.

The truth is that Eleonora—determined as ever—had managed to contact me when she was a prisoner on the ship *San Sebastian*, while waiting in the bay of Naples to depart for France. I was horrified when I read her letter—dated June 23, 1799—only a few weeks before her execution. I've never forgotten its words:

> *Dear Joseph,*
>
> *I must be brief. You undoubtedly know I'm imprisoned on the San Sebastian in the Bay of Naples. Some of my republican friends are here with me. The terms of the signed armistice allow us to go into exile. There is no point in contacting the Portuguese Embassy for assistance, I know they will not come to my rescue. I fear for my life. You must talk to Sir Joseph Banks, he is a friend of Lord Hamilton. Lord Hamilton is a powerful man in Naples. A word from him will set me free. Joseph, we loved each other once. I beg you to take action on my behalf.*
>
> *Affectionately, Eleonora*

I read her letter one time and burnt it immediately. Even if, impulsively, I didn't want to read it a second time, its words had engraved in my mind. When I asked who had sent it, the messenger said he didn't know but that the gentleman lived close to the Portuguese embassy. I gave him a few pennies and hurried him out of the door afraid he might recognize me some day.

Reading the letter had physically shaken me. I felt horror, less for Eleonora's dire situation than for my own safety. Such a message could bring disastrous results. Walls have ears, we might have been overheard. Or, the messenger might have had contacts at the embassy, someone who might speak out one day. My valet wasn't at home when the fellow knocked at my door—a blessed coincidence. My fear that Eleonora's plea might jeopardize my chances of a position at the embassy determined all my actions. No one must know about it.

As described earlier, I have asked myself many times over the years who I really am. Those actions of mine lacked fortitude; I admit I am flawed. But I hope God will forgive me one day. It is not that I'm callous or heartless, it's that my need for self-preservation has been a constant throughout my life. I have always struggled for survival. The Inquisition lived in me and followed me wherever I went. Then, there was my need not only to support myself but my family as well. Mentally, intellectually, I couldn't have endured life without my travels; but they were costly. The many scholars I have met all enjoyed a better birth and family stations than I did. I've been in debt to friends for long periods of my life. If this counts for redemption of my soul, my two sisters never married, and I've supported them since the day my father died.

Up ahead, Jefferson waited for me, ending my musings. He smiled, eager to impart a thought. "Eleonora reminds me of the women I met in the Parisian salons at the start of the French Revolution. They were in favor of the new ideas of liberty, equality, and fraternity."

"Yes. And Eleonora could espouse her views as editor of *Il Monitore Napoletano*. Her calls for freedom were constant in the thirty-five issues of the newspaper," I said.

"I see her as a Martyr of Liberty, she carried its sacred fire. What do you think?"

"Heaven only knows how much I loved and admired Eleonora! But, regrettably, when she stepped out of her traditional role, she knowingly risked her life if the Republic failed. She wasn't prudent."

"My compatriots and I took risks when we declared independence from Britain. Had we been 'prudent'—had we avoided danger—we'd still be exploited by the British monarchy today," Jefferson said.

"Of course, you're right. But Eleonora was a woman, and needed to be especially careful. She had too much at stake. I warned her to be careful—curb what I called her fantasies—when we parted," I replied.

"Eleonora's only mistake was that she wanted change too fast. I looked favorably on the French Revolution, at least in the beginning. It was the continuation of the American project, the triumph of republicanism on European soil." Jefferson's eyes filled with passion. "Popular violence in France, even if tragic, showed republican vigor in the quest for a new society. Jacobins were virtuous, they had the best interests of the people in mind."

"I see why some Americans call you a Jacobin!" I chuckled.

Instead of commenting on my assertion, Jefferson shrugged his shoulders and changed the subject, "It seems doubtful Eleonora's life could have been saved either by you or anyone else."

Jefferson's talent for keeping his thoughts to himself was clear once again. I admired that quality. He didn't want to discuss with me why certain sectors of American society found him too liberal in his political thinking. It was also possible that he didn't see himself as a Jacobin.

"The king and queen of Naples wanted blood when the Neapolitan Republic was defeated. And they got it," I said slowly. "I'm so sorry for what happened to Eleonora! But if she hadn't become a Jacobin, she wouldn't have been executed. I firmly oppose disrupting the social order."

We reached the grove and the conversation shifted. Jefferson pointed to the area saying, "We've arrived. I would like to see this area filled with ornamental trees one day. I want it to be like a house—a house of nature. Monticello needs an Elysium," Jefferson said.

One of the gardeners, Goliah, had left us two shovels in the ground for us to dig holes and plant the magnolia seeds. We set to work, and I was glad the sun was getting lower; Jefferson had chosen the right time of day for our job. When we finished with the seeds, we covered the holes with soil, gently spreading it to a smooth surface. We marked each spot with a stake. Afterward, Jefferson took out his ivory notebook and jotted down some thoughts.

Then, he looked up at me and described gardening as a fine art. "I've been carrying out seed experiments in different locations around here. I look forward to seeing whether these trees will grown up; but I'm not sure they'll adapt." He added that botany was one of the most important of the natural sciences. While in Paris, he had imported innumerous American plant species to offer his French friends. Over the years, those same friends had kindly shipped him hundreds of seeds and bulbs. "A great way to cultivate friendships." He added, "I hope we can return here, one day, to see the results of our work. Plants, like people, have a sensibility."

We drank a few sips of water from a canteen Jefferson had brought along—his pockets possessed endless items. He didn't want to go back home immediately, so he showed me the way for us to proceed.

We stopped at his vegetable garden next, with its impressive view of the southeastern slope. The garden's built-in terrace faced south and had probably 1,000-feet of space still bathed in sunshine, despite the approaching evening. It contained more than two hundred and fifty vegetable varieties. Jefferson called this plot an experimental station, another one of his scientific ventures. Some vegetables were native to America, but many others had been imported. The assortment of broccoli, eggplant, cauliflower, cucumbers, and radishes was astonishing. I saw tomatoes, beets, okra, celery, lettuce, cabbage, and beans. The slope had more than twenty-three varieties of peas. This was a major horticultural achievement; it combined foreign and American samples to a degree I had never seen before. André Thouin from the Jardin des Plantes had been a major contributor to it.

We then walked down to the South Orchard, which sprawled below us. Its display of one thousand trees amazed me; I had never seen such a developed orchard. It combined Old World horticultural tradition with local Virginian varieties. I spotted French apricots, figs from Marseilles, and Spanish almonds; apples, peaches, berries, and cherries. And plums, pomegranates, pears, grapes, and currants. I couldn't help but feel that the orchard's abundance mirrored its distinguished owner's genius.

A large number of slaves—mulatto and negro—were working among the trees. I saw men, women, and children bending to tend the soil.

"The people we see working here are your slaves, correct?" I asked Jefferson.

"Yes, they are."

"How many hours a day do they work?"

"From dawn to dusk."

"Six days a week?"

"Yes."

This kind of servitude was new and troubling to me. I knew Jefferson's slaves lived in legal bondage, without pay or education. They couldn't leave Monticello, even if they wanted. Their lives depended entirely on their master. Jefferson and his family lived among people of a different race. They were white, and were surrounded by many more of darker skin. It was perplexing that a man like Jefferson didn't see the contradictions of his own life. Or, if he saw them, how could he so utterly ignore them?

We took a break in the pavilion in the middle of the garden terrace and admired Virginia's rolling hills. The gazebo was beautiful with its double sash windows, and Jefferson said he came here often to read and meditate. The sun was now setting, the sky a mixture of pink and blue. We took seats on the wooden bench and Jefferson offered me some more water. He then said, "I'm not yet finished with your Eleonora. How did the London press report the events in Naples in 1799?" he asked.

"Very thoroughly. The Republic only lasted a few months—from January to June. Admiral Horacio Nelson, of the British fleet, commandeered nineteen war ships to help the kingdom restore the monarchy," I said. "He himself was on the *Foudroyant*, and brought with him Lord and Lady Hamilton from Palermo to Naples when the Republic fell. They had fled Naples with Ferdinando, Carolina, and the royal entourage."

"The famous Tria Juncta in Uno!" Jefferson recalled. "Those three were, apparently, inseparable; one heart in three bodies."

"Yes, Nelson and Lady Hamilton were madly in love at the time." I said. "Nelson behaved despicably in Naples. He deliberately maneuvered the British fleet closer to the transport ships where the Neapolitan republicans—defeated—were waiting to depart for Toulon. After Cardinal Fabrizio Ruffo invaded the city, he had it returned to the king when the republicans signed an armistice declaring surrender. But Nelson didn't respect the agreement. So he decided to place all the insurgents under the king's orders. This is why Eleonora was taken out of the transport ship where she was held. Charles James Fox, the British parliamentarian, exposed Nelson's atrocities as soon as he heard them. By then, it was already too late."

"I like Fox. He supported the American patriots and the French Revolution," Jefferson said. "He must have realized Nelson's excesses."

"The letters between Queen Carolina and Lady Hamilton sealed Eleonora's death."

"Did you read them?"

"I never saw them but I know they were auctioned in London. Lady Hamilton needed money after she became a widow, and so she sold them." I added, "In one of them, the queen says that the women who distinguished themselves during the Republic should be severely punished. Without mercy or pity. Obviously, she had Eleonora in mind."

Jefferson kept silent.

"It was the queen who, ultimately, delivered Eleonora's sentence to death." A moan escaped me. "Eleonora was the leading female republican. Carolina acknowledged that she had read all the issues of *Il Monitore* during her exile in Palermo. She wanted to know what was going on in Naples."

"Eleonora followed the fate of many of my Parisian friends and acquaintances, when the French Revolution erupted. Like her, many were sentenced to death," Jefferson said.

I stood up and moved to the pavilion's window and admired the view. "Carolina had power, and used it to demand vengeance. She knew Eleonora well, she had been her librarian. Do you know what she called the republicans? Rebellious rabble! Admiral Nelson, the most revered British naval hero of all time, made sure the queen's order was carried out. He believed in the divine right of kings and referred to the Neapolitan Jacobins as a bunch of fools."

Jefferson sipped some more water and then held out the container to me.

"One thing still bothers me about the case," I said. "There was a premonition in Eleonora's early political work, '*Il Trionfo della Virtù*.'"

"What was that?" Jefferson asked.

"She dedicated it to the Marquis de Pombal, the prime minister of Portugal for Queen Maria's father. In her writings, Eleonora ignored Pombal's worst deed: the execution of many members of Portugal's high nobility in 1759. This omission contains a prophetic irony."

"She was next," Jefferson said.

"Exactly. The records of the Neapolitan trials were burned by order of the monarchy in 1801. So, we'll never know the specifics of her trial and sentencing. The same applies to all her republican friends condemned along with her in 1799."

"The Bourbons, like so many other rulers, wanted to erase history," Jefferson replied.

"Indeed, and that is why Eleonora's manuscript is invaluable."

As we fell into another silence, I was aware I was withholding another detail from Jefferson. This made me question why I always slipped into a self-preservation manner. A few months after Eleonora's execution, I had the chance to send a friend a package with botanical samples by ship. For a moment I hesitated, for the ship was named *The Hero of the Nile*, after Nelson's naval victory in Egypt. The British were renaming their fleet and it troubled me to send the samples on a vessel named for Eleonora's enemy. But in the end, as usual, I came first—I was only glad no one else knew this detail from my past.

Looking out the gazebo, I let the soft breeze waft over my face again and enjoyed how it rippled over the distant meadows. How peaceful those Virginia hills were! I wanted Jefferson to understand my position, so it didn't take me long to say, "When the French Army reached Portugal in 1807—ready to depose our sovereigns and install a republic—the royal family fled to Brazil, escorted by British ships. Like Ferdinando and Carolina in Naples, our monarchs didn't accept either French ideas or foreign rule. And I agreed. I didn't want a republic in Portugal under French jurisdiction. So I've always maintained a different viewpoint from Eleonora. If she welcomed the French into Naples, she would have welcomed the French into Portugal as well."

"I understand your viewpoint but I'm a republican like Eleonora. I hope, nevertheless, that through help from cosmopolitans like you, the Portuguese crown succeeds in bringing reform from within," Jefferson said.

I nodded in agreement.

My host suggested we return to the mansion, and as we walked back in the twilight, he said, "You have undoubtedly been a loyal subject of Portugal. Has there been any news about your possible ambassadorship? Or can I still hope to have you at the university?"

"I have no news, my dear Sir. Letters from Brazil continue to take as long as before. Ships are unreliable, it's impossible to predict times of arrival and departure from any port. Sometimes I doubt my appointment will ever come through."

"Well, I'll keep hoping for my lucky day!"

"If only Virginia was located at the gates of Paris or Rome!" I said with a smile but then, afraid of offending my friend, I added, "I love Virginia, its landscape and lifestyle. I wonder, though, if I'd feel too removed from civilization."

"Why do you say that? You would have an excellent library and, I'm sure, disciples from Philadelphia would follow you here. Students provide stimulation. You would have me. Beyond that, you have a host of international contacts."

"I know you are right," I frowned as I said this.

"So, what explains your hesitation?"

"Several personal matters that I might need to attend to in Europe." I answered vaguely on purpose. This would have been the perfect moment to open up to Jefferson. But I didn't feel able to.

"Keep in mind that, as a professor, you'd be able to continue with your 'botanical rambles.' Plus, you would travel whenever you needed," Jefferson said.

"My situation is different from yours," I answered dispassionately. "You were born in Virginia, and Monticello is your life's project. You'll never be bored here."

Jefferson spoke with a youthful buoyant tone, despite his years. "Nor would you. Re-invent yourself here. This is what everybody does when arriving to our shores."

"Interesting way to put it."

"Well, botany is still at its infancy in this country. Virginia needs you, I need you."

"You flatter me once again. But for the record I must be frank and let you know that if my diplomatic appointment comes through, I'll accept it. I've worked hard for that goal." I explained that in the last few months I had come to the conclusion that that assignment was the recognition from Portugal I had always craved. I advanced what Jefferson already knew: from Rio de Janeiro, the prince regent of Portugal commanded a vast empire that stretched from South America to Macau in the Orient. I would be thrilled to serve my nation if the opportunity arose.

"That settles it, then," Jefferson said.

I was able to segue into a description of the lectures I was giving at the American Philosophical Society. They related to my field-work in a few states—Kentucky, North and South Carolina, Tennessee, and Georgia. I had been assessing the country's natural resources and passed on the information to Jefferson. The reception to my ideas had been positive in Philadelphia. My results, if well used, could contribute to the financial and political independence of the young nation.

Back in my room in Monticello, resting on my bed, I again thought of Eleonora. I recalled how she and her fellow revolutionaries had visited the *Languedoc* when the French fleet had arrived in Naples in early 1793. The fleet was under Rear Admiral Latouche-Tréville and, as an act of provocation to Ferdinando and Carolina, the Admiral had invited all the Neapolitan Jacobins for a celebration aboard the vessel. All those who had attended it had been executed in 1799. I still felt a pang of jealousy remembering what I had heard about Eleonora meeting the French admiral. Rumor spread that they had fallen in love.

A few weeks after my return to Philadelphia, Jefferson and I resumed our correspondence. I regretted that I had been unable to open up about the intimate details of my personal life. One of my letters was followed by a small package that included a container with sweet chestnuts that I had collected near Philadelphia. This was one of my enjoyments, to go out in a gig every morning to gather plants in the countryside. I had never seen this species before. I gave Jefferson instructions on how to plant the chestnuts. First, he must put them in small pots to germinate; later, he should transplant them to a place where deer or cattle couldn't reach them.

As I wrote this note to my closest friend in America, I felt eager to return to Monticello as soon as possible. We had such myriad of issues still to share. Would I dare approach my personal matters on my next visit? I hoped so. I found myself wishing that the magnolia seeds we had planted, would grow into something as flourishing as our friendship.

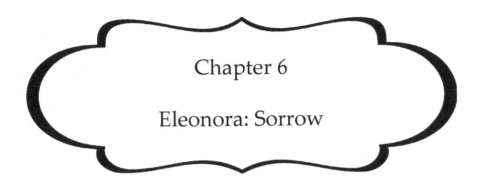

Chapter 6

Eleonora: Sorrow

At the Vicaria Prison, Castel Capuano, outskirts of Naples, July 14, 1799

My marriage to Don Pasquale Tria de Solis was a catastrophe. Shortly after I ended my engagement to Michele, my father thought I was already an old spinster. My mother had died in 1771 when I was nineteen. Now I was twenty-six. What would happen to me when he perished if I didn't have a husband? My brothers, Miguel and José, intended to pursue military careers that would station them outside of Naples. My third brother, Girolamo, had sadly perished young, but after my mother's death. My dear uncle António had already been bedridden for many years. My independence of mind, my father said, exempted me from religious vows and life in a convent. Without a husband, I would be unprotected, alone in the world. And what kind of a fate was that for a woman?

Thus, once again, my father sought a suitable husband for me through his network of contacts. His task wasn't easy, for my age was against me. Our family was, despite being aristocratic, of foreign origin. I had a dowry left by my mother—but so did other noble women. To my benefit, was my position as the queen's librarian, a worthy connection. Married, I would keep my assignment. That I was a member of various well-established literary circles was also auspicious. Finally, my uncle António had always been a respected member of the enlightened clergy in our city.

In retrospect, my erudition was actually a liability. I had found a privileged refuge, but it was something that came at a high cost.

As if the power of my mind were a masculine trait, something only men were permitted to have. I was considered a *donna virile*, a masculine woman. I was never in the habit of flirting in the salons I frequented. I didn't find it natural or honest to pay compliments to men if I didn't find them worthy. I didn't smile without a reason. Our family friends complained, at times, about the severity of my expression, something that grew fiercer as I got deeper into an argument.

I was robust and of average stature for a Portuguese woman. My hair was curly and full, which some men might dislike. I think these characteristics of mine might have diminished my femininity. Yes, I had dark, piercing eyes, and they reflected the depth of my soul. But husbands-to-be might find them frightening, capable of seeing beyond their own reach.

Men, even as civilized as those in Naples, are the weaker of the two sexes, in my view. They easily feel uncomfortable in the company of a young woman who displays intellectual curiosity and acuity, attributes they consider their exclusive domain. And a woman's physical beauty stands above all other qualities in Naples. Go for the outer layer, elect charm over mind, seems to be the male dictum.

My father's search for my husband took many months, but finally he succeeded. If only he could have anticipated the disastrous nature of his selection! Don Pasquale was a member of the lower Neapolitan nobility. At forty-four, he was still a bachelor, a captain in the army, and a small landowner with five sisters. I know my father believed that with his own sons in the military, we would all become a big, happy family of men in uniform.

I confess I was impressed the first time Don Pasquale came to visit us accompanied by his father. That he was older and had never married didn't signal a warning. He arrived wearing the impressive full uniform of the king's military officers. His imposing figure captivated me; the uniform gave him an air of authority. Don Pasquale seemed used to engaging with women and talked to me easily. His manner was that of a *bon vivant*, and he appeared entirely satisfied with the marriage prospects. I had always been a dedicated daughter, and I didn't wish to disappoint my father in his choice. Deep down, a part of me preferred to stay single and proceed with my literary career. However, my father constantly pointed out that one day he would be gone and I would remain alone. So I ended up agreeing with him. I saw Queen Carolina was a contented woman, and she must be right—it was good to be a wife and mother. She had a lot of leeway for her personal interests, and I intended my life to be the same, to proceed with the learning I enjoyed so much.

The details of the marital contract took some time to finalize. Since Don Pasquale was stationed outside of Naples during our courtship, we hardly saw each other. I found this arrangement rather agreeable. After Joseph—whom I had passionately loved and lost—and after Michele—whom I had secretly despised—I was glad to see so little of Don Pasquale. I also wanted to savor the precious last moments of my independence.

The wedding ceremony took place in the church of Sant'Anna di Palazzo, the location of my mother's funeral. We received many gifts, including one from the king and queen—the couple was painted in a porcelain tile, framed in exquisite gold and mother-of-pearl. I was now moving into my husband's home, and my mother's dowry would help take care of our expenses. As was customary, the dowry was given to Don Pasquale to administer, and from it, he would regularly provide me with "*nastri e spille*," literally, "ribbons and pins."

My mother's father had been a pensioner of the Kingdom of Portugal and my mother had inherited his income; this provided a good yearly allowance, ample savings, and property in her name. My mother's will had left my brothers only the *legitima*, the minimum required by law. King Ferdinando was planning to pass a decree giving royal prerogatives to the children of aristocratic foreigners residing in Naples. Therefore my brothers' military careers were secure. The largest part of my mother's wealth went to me, so that I'd have a dowry for a good marriage.

My mother doted on me with an affection that brings tears to my eyes. Always delighted by my accomplishments, she sought to protect my well-being through her property. She addressed me as her talented daughter, wishing me to pursue my career as the *literata* she had always envisioned. She wanted me to be able to continue circulating in the literary salons I enjoyed. She instructed me to obey my father and follow his advice. She asked that I always invoke her in my prayers. As a devout Catholic, she was certain our family would reunite in paradise.

My new household with Don Pasquale included his four sisters. A fifth sister had already entered a convent. We lived in an area called Vomero on Naples's outskirts. My father had mentioned that this might be a very nice arrangement for me, to have my sisters-in-law in the same villa.

Nine months after the wedding, I gave birth to a boy we called Francesco, named after Don Pasquale's father. I was pleased with the name for Joseph's middle name was also Francesco, Francisco in Portuguese. So no one knew I had brought a piece of my former passion to my new family. Secretly, I rejoiced in this detail as much as my fulfillment of becoming a mother.

The period of my happy married life was short-lived. Soon after my darling Francesco's birth, my life turned into a nightmare. At eight months old, Francesco died in my arms. His last few days, I bathed him constantly with rose water to comfort him. I could see he enjoyed it, for he smiled.

My despair after his death found no solace. I felt my husband and his sisters were unable to comfort me, as if we lived on different worlds. I turned to my poetry for consolation. In a classical Petrarchan style, I spent many nights writing sonnets to honor my dead son. These verses were, and remain, a hymn to any mother who similarly lost a child. I used my Arcadian pen name to describe the most profound sorrow a mother can experience. The first lines of my first sonnet began:

> *Son, you reign in Heaven and here I stay*
> *Miserable, afflicted, deprived of you;*
> *But if you reign my joy is this,*
> *Your life is gone but my hope is alive*

My troubles didn't stop here. I had more pregnancies, but they resulted in miscarriages. It was as if my femininity was slowly eroding, deserting me. After the final miscarriage, I knew I'd be unable to conceive again. And so did Don Pasquale—who had counted on having a son and heir. Embracing my suffering, I continued to write elegiac odes to these personal losses of mine. In one of these, I praised Doctor Renato Pean, Queen Carolina's doctor, for saving my life.

Don Pasquale's cruel treatment of me contributed to these unhappy times, his maliciousness had no end.

Everything I share here can be found in the records of the Neapolitan family court where the case of my married life is archived. Don Pasquale deprived me of my dowry financial means, down to the "ribbons and pins." He used it for his own pursuits. I had expected to live in the same way I had been brought up—surrounded by books, servants, and a carriage for my outings. We had lived parsimoniously, but I had always enjoyed the same kind of life and amenities of the Neapolitan elite.

Feeling ashamed of my lack of funds to even dress appropriately, I didn't go to the Royal Palace as often as before. Carolina seemed indifferent to my absence, even though I had confided in her my difficulties. She was compassionate about my problems, and to this day I am thankful for that. Living on Naples's outskirts also made my situation a bit easier, for I didn't want my *literati* friends to know about my *infortunio,* my unhappiness. Correspondence became our usual means of communication, and I excelled in it as never before.

Don Pasquale pawned the jewelry I had inherited from my mother, which had belonged to her mother. When he couldn't pay a debt on time, I lost those precious jewels forever. Worse, he started beating me often and violently. He hired a detestable maid, Angela Veronica. With his sisters, I felt I had yet another spy in our household. Then, the maid's daughter moved in with us.

My life became a living nightmare. Don Pasquale true self emerged—he was a southern brute, a delinquent, a grotesque creature. He belonged to the Naples *profunda,* a cultural designation for those who were born and raised in the deep south. Compared to him, my cousin Michele had been harmless. If I had married Michele, he wouldn't have treated me abusively. He might have been indifferent to my feelings, but he didn't have a violent disposition.

I've often asked myself, what was at the root of Don Pasquale's behavior? I feel that most of all, he detested my life of the spirit. He called me bookish, and was envious of my knowledge. This was something he couldn't take away from me, even if he took my dowry. He burned the books on my nightside table. He prohibited me from attending the salons with my friends and colleagues. He said they were too avant-guard, too modern, and bad influences. The law protected his behavior: a husband had authority over his wife. How I reviled him when he claimed he was acting out of necessity to save my conscience from evil. Unlike my mother, I had never been very religious, but Don Pasquale's treatment made me stop praying.

It was also an outrageous situation with Don Pasquale's less-educated sisters. They abhorred me. They saw me as a refined European, and therefore eccentric. I tried to be gracious, but they were provincial to an extreme. They were also conservative, while I was progressive. They may have looked genteel but, behind that surface, they were ignorant and boorish. At times, I felt so downtrodden that I blamed the Neapolitan climate for their weak brains and vile temperament. It seemed they sought to destroy me; I hadn't met anyone like them before. At Don Pasquale's request, the sisters intercepted my correspondence. He told them they were secret love letters. Since I often corresponded in French, he didn't believe such letters were a part of my intellectual life. In all, he wanted to end my contact with the outside world. I still enjoy thinking of the letters Abbé Alberto Fortis and I exchanged; I needed their flirtatious tone, it was nourishment for my ailing soul.

One time, I dared to mention my private situation to Carolina, for she had seen a bruise on my face. With kindness, she advised me to go to Acton, the prime minister, and file a complaint about my husband's dishonorable conduct. Queen Carolina got embarrassed: as an officer in the king's army, my husband was required to behave. When I talked to Acton, he took action on my behalf. For a while, Don Pasquale behaved. However, the best outcome of his intervention was that my sisters-in-law voluntarily moved to a convent.

I recall a phrase of mine during my separation proceedings in court, "I agreed to have Don Pasquale Tria de Solis as husband… thinking that I would enjoy his affection, if not the love that so many times has escaped me."

I gave a lot of thought to this statement before making it. It's true to this day: sentimental love has always escaped me. While young, my body was full of desire for Joseph. But he fled from me. Michele and I never enjoyed a romantic relationship during our long courtship. Our parents, not we, wished us married. And Don Pasquale never enjoyed my company.

What kind of love did I experience from men? I suppose the love of family members: my father, brothers, and Uncle António. But it started and ended there.

One night, during my ill-fated marriage, close to its seventh year, my life took a turn for the worst. It was summer, and I woke up swimming in sweat. The day had been sweltering warm, and the heat didn't die off during the night. I kept tossing and turning in bed, but nothing could calm me. Don Pasquale wasn't in bed with me, but that happened frequently. Many times, I got up to find him seated on the dining room balcony, smoking a cigar or drinking limoncello, his favorite lemon liqueur.

I thought a glass of water would do me good, so I got up to go to the kitchen. Even in the dark, I knew where the large, clay pitcher was. Angela always had it filled to the brim, Don Pasquale insisted on that. As I got closer to the kitchen, I heard sighs, moans, and whispers. They didn't stop me from entering the room, as I intended. The horror of the scene that ensued was inconceivable then and continues to be today.

"What's going on?" I shouted in the dark, confused.

"Get out of here!" Don Pasquale hissed.

I saw two silhouettes moving in dawn's dusky light. Angela lay on her back on the kitchen table, with her legs open. Her long blond braid fell nearly to the floor. Don Pasquale was standing next to her, naked. The bodies, fused together only seconds before, had separated when they heard my voice. Don Pasquale's erection still showed.

"I said, get out of here!" he repeated. "Or do I have to push you out?"

Already he was on me, shoving me out of the room. In the corridor he slapped me viciously. "Why did you go to the kitchen in the middle of the night?" he shouted. I managed to escape, and stumble to my room. Inside, I locked the door.

The suspicions I had been having turned out to be true. The woman my husband had brought to our house to be our servant was actually his mistress. The little girl was probably their daughter.

Alone, in pain, and shattered, I wept in silence. The sordid affair going on in my own house debased my soul. The following day, I went to my father, showed him my swollen face, and told him I wanted a separation from my husband. My father agreed to ask the court of Naples that I be returned to his home. The judicial proceedings that followed filled more than one hundred pages.

Shortly before the court granted my legal separation, my father died a broken man. He realized how he had erred in his choice of a husband for me, and agonized about my future. He knew that his intentions, even if admirable, had been disastrous to my life.

These were heartbreaking times, but there was no going back. I saw myself as a failed wife and mother. Separated by law, Don Pasquale remained my husband until one of us died. Heavily in debt, he never complied with the court ruling to support me. It was during this period that I decided to wear black forever, as if I were a widow. When Don Pasquale died in 1795, ten years after our separation, the relief I experienced was indescribable. I was now free from the worry that he might reopen our separation case. He had made exaggerated accusations in court about my progressive views and my character, and I always feared the consequences.

Finding myself in financial distress, I was able to secure at this time a monthly royal grant of twelve ducats, which greatly helped me. Later, I was able to recover a small amount of my dowry through Don Pasquale's brother, Monsignor Nicola Tria de Solis. A priest, he was in charge of administering the family's holdings after Don Pasquale's death. What I got back didn't come close, notwithstanding, to the amount I had lost. That a member of the clergy could behave on such a way, ended my Catholic faith forever.

With no husband and no parents, I found comfort moving in with my paternal aunt and uncle for a while. Don Pasquale hadn't succeeded in his court appeal that I be confined to a convent. I missed not only my honorable parents, but the rewarding life we had enjoyed together. They had been aristocrats in the true sense of the word. Now, my life in Naples—the city I had embraced so joyfully in youth—had brought me to my knees. Still finding myself with a modicum of luck, I wrote at this time a eulogizing piece,

Il Vero Omaggio, True Homage, celebrating the return of Ferdinando and Carolina, who had been away from Naples. It was only when Don Pasquale died, and I felt freer, that I moved to a modest place of my own in Piazza Sant'Anna di Palazzo. I wanted to be near the church of the same name, where both my mother and son had been buried.

So much happened as time went on. I might be naive, but I felt in the subsequent years of my separation that evil had triumphed over good. I thought it then—and I still think it now.

I still do not know how long I will be imprisoned here at the Vicaria. My mental and physical states are deteriorating. Today France celebrates Bastille Day, the start of the French Revolution. A captive like the Bastille prisoners, how I wish I could celebrate the cause of liberty! France enjoys a Republic now. What will happen in Naples?

I've had too much time on my hands for self-reflection. So here are my thoughts: I must confess to a moment of weakness after my father's death. I desperately wanted to know what Joseph was doing in Lisbon. And I felt I had nothing to lose by asking, provided I was careful. Many years had passed, and Joseph and I had never again communicated. He remained, though, just as alive in my heart, no one had replaced him. I wondered if he would reciprocate if I got in touch. I came up with a plan. I wrote a letter to the celebrated friar D. Manuel do Cenáculo for I knew that when Joseph had returned to Portugal, he had lived briefly at Cenáculo's house in Évora. Toward the end of my letter, I ask the friar casually: "What is the Academy of Natural History, in Lisbon, doing under the auspices of the Duke of Lafões? With such an illustrious president, it is certainly not idle; to honor my maternal country, I would like to know about its public ceremonies, or about particular memoirs that might have been generated…"

Cenáculo never answered me and Joseph never approached me. So I don't know whether he ever knew that I asked about him.

I was sad, I was solitary, and I was hurt to the core—but I returned to my literary work and this gave me a renewed sense of purpose. My translation and introduction to Nicolò Caravati's treatise on government showed my commitment to the crown. Its title was long, *Niun diritto compete al sommo pontefice sul Regno di Napoli,*

No right pertains to the Supreme Pontiff over the Kingdom of Naples. It took me several years and much dedication to interpret Caravati's philosophical thinking. My essay received royal favor and praise, as its theme touched the Neapolitan sense of pride. Much *en vogue* at the time in Naples was the call for the separation of church and state—which I supported. I stated that the Bourbon monarchy should not pay the yearly tribute, the *Chinea* tax, to the Papal States. This involved a ceremony where a white horse, decorated with gold and precious stones, bowed its legs with offerings to the Pope in Rome. I saw this event as a medieval ceremony. The horse was trained to bow—*inchinarsi* in Neapolitan—as a sign of the kingdom's allegiance to the supreme pontiff, the Church of Rome.

My argument showed a keen interest in political issues, the same I would later display as editor-in-chief of *Il Monitore Napoletano*.

My personal joys in Piazza Sant'Anna di Palazzo were trifling but pleasing. I acquired a yellow canary that sang incessantly. In its small wooden cage by the windowsill, the bird loved the morning sunshine as much as I did. When it sang, time seemed to be suspended; as if the bird sang for the two of us alone. Such a small consolation: and yet a ray of hope amidst the desolation of my life. How I miss that tiny creature now!

I ate Portuguese food to keep my parents' memories alive in my new surroundings. I enjoyed going down to the fish market along the bay early in the morning to buy *bacalla*. My mother always called *bacalla* the Portuguese people's most faithful friend. I cooked it with small tomatoes and onions, and then sprinkled it with parsley. I served it with olives on the side. I ate it both to build strength and honor my memories. I always went to the same vendor, and she sang in Neapolitan dialect "Tarantella del Gargano." Sometimes young boys accompanied her with castanets or tambourines. I treasured hearing that love song of passion and jealousy.

Having abandoned the notion that aristocratic women shouldn't walk the streets alone, I strolled the city freely for pleasure. I liked the *pedamentina*, the streets that were made of stone steps taking you up or down. My father had once told me how Lisbon had the same shortcuts for those on foot. Naples was lively, entertaining, and full of activity all day long. Once in a while, if lucky, I got to see the Commedia dell'Arte, often performed by traveling troupes. These spectacles had a civic purpose I very much admired. The actors enlivened the streets and were an important educational source for the *lazzaroni*. Actors placed their four-legged podium in the city's piazzas, and depicted simple stories that expressed the variety of human sentiments: love, greed, jealousy, disgust, surprise, or grief. Pulcinella was a favorite character, quick-witted and sharp tongued. He was an amicable buffoon, a *provocateur*, a clown; in short, someone with whom the poor and illiterate could identify through the heart. Pulcinella played the same old tricks on people —and always acted oblivious to their negative impact. He would make someone look the other way, while stealing the pasta from his or her plate. The funny routine made the *lazzaroni* momentary forget the harshness of their lives. I loved watching the awe of the children, many of them holding their mothers' hands. I often found myself looking at boys who were my Francesco's age, had he lived.

Inside a labyrinth in these thick prison walls the past few weeks, I hope to be able to preserve a sense of time. The lyrics of "Tarantella del Grazano," I just recalled, made me think of the love that, as I said in court, had always escaped me. What would have been my fate had I been happily married to Joseph, surrounded by healthy children, and able to pursue a literary career in the sanctity of our home? Had I married cousin Michele, even knowing we were mismatched, wouldn't he respect the woman in me? Had Don Pasquale been more sophisticated, had he allowed me to pursue the life of the spirit, would I have become a full-fledged Jacobin?

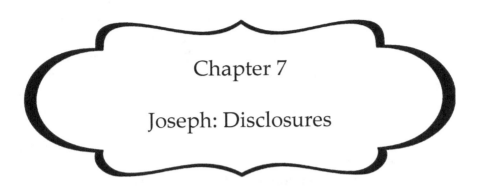

Chapter 7

Joseph: Disclosures

True, we cannot offer you the scientific society of Paris…From others you can get nothing new, and the pleasure of communicating it should be greatest where it is most wanting. Stay then with us. Become our instructor.
—Thomas Jefferson's letter to Joseph Correia da Serra, January 1, 1816

❦The last time I was here, I said that I had private matters to attend to in Europe, and that this was a reason for me to decline your kind offer to teach at the university. I didn't explain further and would like to do that now. I think you'll understand my disclosure, we're friends," I said to Jefferson.

Jefferson followed me to my room, where we could talk undisturbed. I shut the door and offered him the room's only armchair. When he admired my valise standing next to it, I opened it to show him the inside. It had separate compartments for different pieces of clothing, a novelty when I bought it in Paris a few years earlier. I had arrived in Monticello before Easter and it was still very cold. The fireplace in my room was lit, and I warmed my hands before sitting on the edge of the bed.

"During our talk last spring, we touched on my personal life, and now that I'm back, I'd like to share more with you. May I, my dear Sir?" I paused, waiting for Jefferson's assent.

"Please do, go ahead," Jefferson caressed his right wrist, the one that he had injured in the Bois de Bologne long ago.

"You've described how tempting Parisian women were and how, at the start of the French Revolution, many abandoned social conventions. Well…a main attraction for me in the French capital was one of these women. I had a love child the year after I arrived in Paris," I said.

"Another Catholic priest bound by vows of chastity with a child. You're not the first, and you won't be the last." Jefferson leaned forward in his chair and continued rubbing his wrist.

"I lost my mind in Paris. Few of my Portuguese friends know of this secret of mine. Edward, my son, might join me here in America. His mother, unfortunately, is very sick."

"I'm sorry to hear that and I look forward to meeting Edward some day. I myself had a romantic attachment in Paris," Jefferson said.

"Oh?" My brows rose in curiosity, inviting him to continue.

"She was Maria Cosway, an Anglo-Italian painter." Jefferson expression was innocent. "Her self-portrait with arms crossed and looking directly at the viewer is a rather unusual pose for a woman. She wanted wings to fly."

"I wonder if that's why you assume the pose so often when you talk," I said humorously.

"It's quite possible, no one has ever mentioned it. Maria and I had a fascination for each other. But she was married. Unlike my dear compatriot Benjamin Franklin, I feared a sexual scandal would damage my career."

"Were you in love?" I asked.

"So much so that, for a while, we saw or wrote each other daily. I debated the issue in a letter to her I titled 'Head and Heart.' But, unlike you, my head won over my heart," Jefferson said.

Then, abruptly, Jefferson's expression became distant. He asked, "How old is Edward now?"

"Almost sixteen. His mother gave me the most enjoyable, tender moments I have experienced as an adult."

"I guess you succeeded in forgetting Eleonora," Jefferson said.

"They were very different women. Eleonora was an aristocratic intellectual. Esther, Edward's mother, is Jewish. Much younger than I when we met, and free-spirited."

"Jewish and born in the Court of Versailles?"

"Yes. Her father died when she was a child and her mother ran the family apothecary business. They prepared and dispensed medicinal herbs."

Jefferson brought his hand to his nostrils, as if inhaling exotic scents. "Where did you two meet?"

"In the Jardin des Plantes. Besides writing entries for the *Biographie Universelle* in the library, I attended many lectures in the main building. I spent the rest of my time in the garden, and this is where I met Esther."

"I know that building well. It's where I developed my knowledge of horticulture."

"Esther came to talk to the gardeners every morning. She enjoyed a degree of patronage from them: seeds, clients and what not. After Edward was born, she trained in aromatherapy. I loved the smells that spread throughout the family shop: fennel, mint, garlic, hazelnut, and others. I was seduced by her wonder of the natural world; it was love at first sight."

Jefferson's intent face encouraged me to continue.

"We never lived together, her apartment was too small." I got up from the bed and began pacing the room; once in a while I returned to the fireplace to warm my hands. "The minute she opened the door and Edward came running into my arms, all my worries vanished."

"What worries did you have in Paris, my dear friend?" Jefferson asked.

"I was always short of money. My revenue from Portuguese religious institutions and the crown has always been paltry. I didn't inherit anything, and I never had any savings."

"A savant like you needs family funds," Jefferson said.

"My meager resources have always had dire consequences. And they affected all my relationships."

"Lack of money is, really, a *maladie*, a disease. I have had my own share of difficulties in that regard. My agricultural enterprises do not produce as much return as I need. I have no pension for my services to my country. Nevertheless I feel lucky, I've been able to rely on credit."

"Life is different if you're rich. If I had been, I might have fought for Eleonora. Or I could have supported Esther at the level she deserved."

"Did Esther ask you for help?"

"Never, and for that I'll be eternally grateful. But I helped her with Edward's upbringing. She also needed a constant supply of merchandise to maintain her business—glass or ceramic pots and jars to keep the seeds fresh, and mortars and pestles of all sizes to crush them," I said. "I can't recall the number of times I've asked friends for financial assistance, even though I never disclosed that the funds were to support my family."

"Being a priest has had its burdens for you. Your life hasn't been just about studying and enjoying leisure, as you might have anticipated before joining the church," Jefferson said.

"I've led a double life for too long. I'm Jewish and became a priest. I should be celibate and instead I have a family. I love botany above all, but I'm considering a diplomatic assignment. This explains my moods, my inner turmoil. Sometimes I call myself a lunatic."

"Well, as I said earlier, you can reinvent yourself here. Virginia suits the tranquility of your character. Bring your family here, start a new life. Move to Monticello for as long as needed until you settle in somewhere. I'm full of respect, admiration, and affection for you," Jefferson said in his suave, genial way.

"Your offer is tempting, as always. There's a major difficulty, though. I would like Edward to be legitimized. For this, I need to be closer than I am now to the prince regent of Portugal." My old anguish was sweeping over me. "I didn't move a finger to save Eleonora, which I bitterly regret. But if Edward is legitimized, his future will be safer, brighter. I need to accomplish this, somehow; I will do for my son what I should have done for Eleonora."

Jefferson nodded, I knew he had understood my thoughts. There wasn't much he could add to my disclosures, anyway. Time to end our conversation, I thought. The fireplace had only a few logs left, so I got up and stirred the fireplace. Jefferson also got up and said he would meet me later, he was going to do some work.

Then, I took my shoes off and placed them under the high chest of drawers. How I loved my alcove bed, so tidy, the perfect size for my small build. I removed the blue damask spread slowly and noticed, for the first time, how it matched the window curtains. I went to the window and closed the shutters, a refined decorative detail. I lay down on the bed, and closing my eyes in the dim light, settled in to enjoy the liberating feeling now coursing through me. I felt lighter for having disclosed to my American friend the secrets I had lived with all my life. Eleonora's memory, the love of my youth, had not been enough to sustain me over the years. Earlier, I had thought that I didn't need the love of a woman to feel a complete man. My vows to the Catholic Church, in addition, prevented me from expressing my sexual appetites openly. But, after Eleonora's execution, I had a change of heart. My silence before her impending death—and my burning of her last letter to me—had been a betrayal of our love. I wasn't proud of my conduct—my instinct for self-preservation had had cruel results.

I might appear callous, heartless, and calculating to those who never realized my financial difficulties. My birth was not like Jefferson's, or my situation comparable to the privileges he enjoyed all his life. I needed to be vigilant, and not jeopardize the occasional opportunities that came my way.

The aromas of Esther's shop had filled the fibers of her clothing—and Edward's—and had been a vital part of my spiritual nourishment in the French capital. They reminded me of my father's storeroom in our Naples home. Although a priest, I hadn't found the solace I needed from reading the Bible or even attending Sunday Mass. The smells embedded in the clothes of those I loved, and their trusting gaze, had been the foundation that sustained me in Paris. The sensation was similar to the one I felt planting the magnolia trees in Monticello's grove: a way to feel closer to my true self.

I had cared for Esther—and Edward was my own blood—but I'd felt incapable of leaving the church to marry her. I couldn't imagine myself involved in the responsibilities of conjugal life. If I abandoned my vows and left the church, I'd lose my income from Portugal, regardless of how small it was. And my status as a man of the cloth would be gone. Moreover, I couldn't be certain of getting a permanent position in Paris, or anywhere else. Marriage—and financing a family—was too risky. When Edward was born, I was already in my fifties, too old to start a new life.

Popes had courted women and enjoyed fathering children—why shouldn't I? I too needed a woman, someone to hold in my arms. True, I had had occasional peccadillos before Esther, and I knew how to behave with women. Like others, she enjoyed my conversation, and she found me urbane. Our common Jewish ancestry was an added bond. When she got pregnant she was in her late twenties, beautiful, and audacious. I wanted our child as much as she did. My whole body—my head and my heart, as Jefferson had put it so well—wanted to embrace that future. After Edward's birth, I felt a life-long commitment to mother and child—but one that didn't require what I couldn't offer, the bond of marriage. The financial difficulties would have compromised my intellectual freedom.

Edward has been a constant blessing in my life. He is a good young man, thoughtful, and I'm hopelessly proud of him. His Parisian education has been first class. Our bond is close; we've always been in the habit of sharing long, loving letters. I'm forever eager for the news of what he and his mother are doing in Paris.

Jefferson told me the mail will be here tomorrow. I feel like opening up again, as I did with my friend—I admit this is rather unusual. Could it be that the comfort of Jefferson's friendship relieves me, somewhat, from my past? Or, is it his grandchildren's laughter and games that I hear upstairs that I find so gratifying?

Whatever it is, I've decided to share with Edward a secret that I haven't even shared with my dear Jefferson. At sixteen, Edward might be still too young to fully understand my letters. But, one day, he'll reread them and perhaps appreciate my failings in life—something to learn, to grow from.

I sat down at the Sheraton card table, took out a sheet of parchment paper and, after dipping one of Jefferson's elegant yellow quill pens to a small jug of ink, I begun to write. I noticed with pleasure the fire was still going.

> *My Dear Edward,*
> *I am visiting Mr. Jefferson, and I would like to share with you something that crossed my mind as the two of us talked. While exchanging our Parisian experiences, I revealed to him that I had a son and that your mother is seriously ill. My disclosure was cathartic.*

As you know, I'm hoping to be appointed ambassador from the United Kingdom of Portugal and Brazil to the United States of America soon. Mr. Jefferson has reiterated his offer of a position at the University of Virginia, as soon as the institution opens. But, if I get the diplomatic assignment, I will accept it. The high status of this position is, as I've told you before, my life-long ambition.

Here follows a lesson I hope you'll take to heart, my son. In Paris, I published an article entitled «De l'état des Sciences et des Lettres Parmis les Portugais.» It is my thinking behind this text that I would like to share with you today, hoping you'll then understand the compromises I've had to make all my life.

I mentioned previously how unhappy I was before you were born, when I left Lisbon in 1795 to avoid persecution and incarceration. Well, the truth is that I deliberately implied in that article that our Queen Maria was the intellectual heir to our Marquis de Pombal's enlightened views.

This is far from the truth. It was only my instinct for survival that made me express that view. With my hoped-for appointment, this deception of mine will have paid off. Had I done otherwise— had I disclosed how backward and conservative our kingdom had become after Pombal—I could never have expected a future worthy of my talents.

As you know, I grew up in Naples, and when I returned to Portugal I was considered an estrangeirado, *an Europeanized intellectual. Even though the Duke of Lafões always protected me, the ruling elite was still suspicious of my contacts abroad. Thus, when I wrote that article, I had the perfect opportunity to expose the constant persecution I had suffered in Lisbon. However, the chief of police—remember this name, Pina Manique—was the queen's appointee. And so, I kept quiet; I sacrificed my better judgment to the affairs of the state.*

Our kingdom was paralyzed when I ran away; people were terrified to speak out. But the French Revolution had galvanized me. I knew I had to live in a more open, liberal society. I believed that our monarchy could be rejuvenated from within. But I was misunderstood, the police took me for a Jacobin.

Thus, again, praising our queen was a deliberate act on my part. I knew that, one day, I might seek a position the crown might give me abroad, or even desire to return to Portugal.

I hope an official appointment becomes a reality soon. If it does, I'd like you to join me in America. Your mother and I have already agreed on this. It grieves me that her health is failing, and I'll send money as soon as I can. Please give her my love, and let her know I'll write again soon.

I miss both of you very much. Your loving father, Joseph

I sealed the envelope with wax. Then, I ran the quill pen's yellow feather over my forehead; I enjoyed the light touch. After I did this a few times, I put the pen down and admired its intense color. Edward now knew the truth—I was satisfied. I felt I had done what I had to do. I had benefited from the Duke of Lafões's patronage for many years, both in Portugal and abroad. When he died, others in the royal entourage had come to my rescue. I felt proud of all the Portuguese friendships I had cultivated over the years. If only now they would come through with my ambassadorship.

When I left my room to see what others were doing in the house, I found Jefferson in the family's sitting room. The room doubled as a classroom, and I loved the celestial blue of its walls. Jefferson was showing his grandchildren Thouin's calendar. The book seemed an all-time favorite with them. I recalled how they had mentioned the pictures on my first visit to Monticello. And I appreciated how learning played such an important role in this intimate space of my friend's house.

As an ardent republican, Thouin had been chosen by the French government to replace the Gregorian calendar in 1793. The new text was so successful that it remained in place for over a decade. Instead of celebrating royal events or the life of Catholic saints, the calendar celebrated herbs, animals, insects, vegetables, and fruits. The week had ten days instead of seven, and the months varied from three to four weeks. Best of all were the pictures.

Jefferson encouraged the children to repeat the French words that accompanied the drawing for each month: *Brumaire,* for mist in Autumn; *Floréal,* for blossoms in Spring; *Thermidor,* for heat in summer; and so on and so forth. The children repeated the words with an impeccable French accent.

I took advantage of my didactic vein and entered the conversation. I told the children that the words they were pronouncing had been repeated by thousands of people throughout Europe during the past decades. To show their pride in the French Revolution, the French had enforced the calendar's use in all its conquered territories. Turning to Jefferson, I added that all of Eleonora's *Monitore* issues had used the French designations.

Since the children's lesson with Jefferson would continue for the next hour or so, he kindly offered me his carriage to visit the site of the university near Charlottesville. I was glad for the opportunity to see it in person—not just a view from Monticello as I had seen before. Shortly afterwards, I set out with Wormley, Jefferson enslaved coachman. It had rained the night before and, as we drove rough and muddy roads, I had plenty of time to think while looking out the window. Overall, Albemarle County was far from "pastoral." I found the area desolate, barren, and inhospitable. Farmers, their wives, and children, appeared poor and overworked. They lived in log cabins and wood huts along the roadside; how cold they must feel throughout the long winter. What a contrast to my host's mountaintop estate!

We soon arrived at the university's location. The area was very large, but flat and totally empty. I thought how only a genius like Jefferson would conceive a university in such a place. It struck me how my friend believed wholeheartedly in his project—I found that moving, and also courageous. Wormley knew the boundaries of the site, and he went around to show me.

My friendship with Thouin in Paris came to my mind—it continued to be alive despite the distance! He had said that I considered botany a mystery, a form of divinity—not a *métier*, a trade. This was, indeed, something I agreed with in my very core. My work with scholars we both knew well—naturalists like Augustin de Candolle to name only one—consisted in naming, analyzing, and classifying the species that the emerging science was unveiling. We all sought to understand the laws governing the natural world. Botany was far from the rhapsodizing about nature that *philosophes* like Rousseau perpetrated.

Part of the delight I took in the new science was, however, undoubtedly related to fieldwork. I loved the sense of freedom that the open fields, the fresh air, and the birds chirping provided. I felt alive in those moments, joyful, and my existence made sense. The moments of exquisite *far niente,* doing nothing, that the new science afforded me were plenty. For me, nature and mankind formed a single unity that allowed for crops, the feeding of the species, and the climate to be one, to be in synchrony.

Wormley didn't dare to interrupt my philosophizing and I was grateful for that. When we returned to Monticello, he helped me to descend the carriage steps and to remove my dirty boots on the front terrace. I placed a few pennies in his hand. I knew my small courtesy meant a lot to him; he bowed to me with a grin.

It continued to disturb me that Wormley—as well as all the negro men, women and children I had seen around Jefferson and his family—were slaves.

For many months now, I had been thinking of Jefferson's plantation and the gratification it obviously gave him. The gratification also pertained to me, his guest. The slaves worked for Jefferson's benefit. All the time. How did he feel about it? Feeling our friendship solid, the discussion would have to take place sooner rather than later. My way to start might be to ask Jefferson to show me Mulberry Row, the slave quarters near the main house. I must find the words to introduce the topic.

Back at the house, Jefferson brought me to the parlor, suggesting we talk first and then play a game of chess. "My dear Abbé, I need to ask a favor of you, when you get back to Philadelphia. The greatest achievement of my presidency was the Louisiana Purchase in 1803. With this acquisition from France, the United States more than doubled its size."

"It was quite an event!" I said.

"We got it only because Napoleon Bonaparte needed money for his conquests in Europe. What timing!" Jefferson had a smile on his face.

"Yes, he wanted to rule an empire and his need for financial resources favored America. Sending the French Army to Naples in 1798—following the conquest of the northern Italian peninsula—was only the beginning. But even then it was clear, the French didn't have the means to hold on to an empire. The troops in Naples were ill fed, unpaid, and their military uniforms in pieces," I said.

"I'm proud to have negotiated Louisiana." Jefferson continued. "I led secret talks with France for a while and, suddenly, the right moment to agree on the price came along."

After a pause Jefferson added. "The favor I need from you in Philadelphia is related to this matter. Could you help me secure the documents pertaining to the Lewis and Clark expedition? I commissioned the voyage as soon as I could, following the Louisiana Purchase. As you might have heard, Captain Meriwether Lewis, unfortunately, died under mysterious circumstances."

"Yes, I heard of that," I said.

"Captain Lewis left sketches, maps, drawings, and many other documents. These papers need to be retrieved and properly archived. They are of immense value to the geographical study of this country. All of these materials are currently with the widow of Dr. Benjamin Smith Barton in Philadelphia. He also died recently. Dr. Barton, a university professor, was helping Captain Lewis to classify the specimen to be introduced in his journals. The expedition was funded by Congress on my request, therefore these papers belong to the public."

"I see."

"The Corps of Discovery was a monumental expedition, comprised of a crew of four-dozen brave volunteers. Imagine how for two and a half years these daring men chronicled and mapped out our wilderness. They travelled up the Missouri River intending to reach the Pacific Ocean. The journey had a human toll for all involved, but only one man died. Thanks to their heroism, we established an American presence in those uncharted lands."

I listened to Jefferson's description in silence. I had heard members of the American Philosophical Society talking about the event. The dangers these indomitable men had faced confronting wild animals and hostile Indian tribes had made horror stories.

Jefferson continued, "The group made observations of soil, climate, animals, plants, and the region's native peoples. Obviously, their findings are invaluable."

"Just a detail, if I may," I said. "I've seen drawings of the unique bow-wood—also called osage orange—done during the trip. The beauty of this species is extraordinary. The botanist in me was forever coming out.

"So I have heard," Jefferson said.

"It will be an honor to be of help, Sir." I said. "My service will give us more opportunities to correspond, something that has given me so much pleasure over the years."

Jefferson agreed and said, "I'll give you the contact information for Dr. Barton's widow before you leave."

Together, Jefferson and I moved to the chessboard to conclude another memorable day at Monticello.

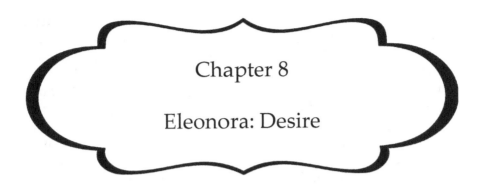

Chapter 8

Eleonora: Desire

At the Vicaria Prison, Castel Capuano, outskirts of Naples, July 26, 1799

Late in 1789, the year that marked the beginning of the French Revolution, I was dismissed from my position as royal librarian. Carolina summoned me, and when I stood before her, she said she had been informed I had become a Jacobin. I knew the term had dreadful connotations in her mind: it meant I had become a full-fledged supporter of French revolutionary thinking. She said as much, and as a result, she had no place for me at the Royal Palace; I had betrayed the high honor of being in her service. She had allowed my long absence from the library due to my ill-fated marriage and illness. She thought my work had been, nevertheless, valuable and, after all, my husband belonged to the king's army. On the occasion, she accused me of personal treachery for which I might well pay dearly one day. She reiterated I knew that reforms were being implemented in the kingdom, albeit at a necessarily slow pace. As an example, she mentioned the poem I had written earlier that year celebrating the San Leucio colony of workers. This was a royal experiment where about two hundred families of silk weavers lived and worked in complete community; the king was personally involved in the dream project. Not only was I dismissed from my position, she said my royal subsidy had also been terminated.

I stood before Queen Carolina trembling inside but appearing calm. Why give her the joy of subjugating me? Hadn't I been humiliated enough in the preceding years? I was too proud to deny or confirm her charge. I asked only who had informed her about me, and she replied with a short, wicked laugh. She said that was nothing of my business. Which, of course, was true. Deep down, I was only trying to figure out who were my friends…and my enemies.

Had I cared to admit it to myself, my dismissal was a powerful sign of the troubles I would soon face. The Carolina I had known earlier on had vanished. Since hunting and partying—not governing—had been Ferdinando's life pursuits, she had succeeded in dominating him. It might not have been terribly difficult: he was weak, ignorant, and superstitious. She was now the kingdom's most effective ruler. As such, she made sure the crown instituted the *"crimine di opinione,"* crime of opinion, a designation that applied to anyone who criticized the monarchy. That Carolina had ever supported Freemasonry undoubtedly became an embarrassment to her. She probably even agreed with her husband, who had described Freemasons as "renascent hydra." She cleverly manipulated Acton, Naples's prime minister, into her camp, cutting her husband from involvement in key decisions. Some thought the prime minister was even her lover now.

I marveled at Carolina's political acumen and foresight. The Mediterranean Sea—with Naples at its center—had become the stage for the fight between the two most powerful nations on earth: England and France. Control of the Mediterranean allowed England easy access to her colonial empire in the Far East. France wanted to curtail that possibility and pursue its own expansion. The queen had once confided in me that her friendship with Emma Hart might forge, with the diplomatic assistance of Lord Hamilton, a close alliance with England. If the French Revolution succeeded, her closeness to Emma might, in due time, save the Kingdom of Naples from republican ideas. I had listened to her views but remained silent. Moreover, I had always feared Carolina's revenge for my accidental discovery of her intimate life with Emma. Surely she wondered if I would ever gossip about it.

As each year passed, and we *literati* paid close attention to events in revolutionary France, we came to realize that our monarchy would never be rejuvenated from within. Secret meetings took place throughout Naples, with candles lit in front of portraits of Voltaire. We read the French Encyclopedists, the works of the recently formed French National Assembly, and the Parisian newspaper *Le Moniteur*. Freemasons and Jacobins exhorted each other to imitate the good French brethren and shake off the yoke of tyranny. French ideals of liberty and equality for all dominated our discussions. Equal rights, regardless of birth, was the topic of the day. To the dismay of the king and queen, the recently appointed French ambassador to Naples, Baron Armand de Mackau, had been printing and distributing pamphlets inciting Neapolitans to rebel.

During this time of revolutionary ferment, a dramatic turning point took place in my life.

It happened the day I had the chance to meet the French Rear Admiral Latouche-Tréville. He arrived in Naples in December of 1792 commanding his fleet, and at the helm of his flagship the *Languedoc*. Each and every one of the admiral's ships displayed on its masts the new flag of the French Republic. What a sight! Enthralled, my Jacobin friends and I now had renewed hopes for significant changes in our kingdom. Meeting the admiral not only solidified my Jacobin ideas, but also shaped, inescapably, my future.

As always happened when foreign ships arrived in our harbor, Naples came on shore to see the events. One by one, small boats surrounded the newcomers in the bay. Neapolitans loved the ritual of approaching large vessels in their tiny dinghies. The scene reflected well the dominant division between our opposing political camps. We Jacobins were hoping to fraternize and get firsthand news of the latest events in France. Sailing close by the squadron, some of us waved to the French, shouting out wildly: "Brave Frenchmen, persevere!" The *lazzaroni*, on the other hand, forever faithful to the decaying monarchy, made obscene gestures telling the French to leave. As royalists, they yelled: "Long live our king!"

Latouche-Tréville was a legendary figure before arriving in Naples. Not only was he an aristocrat, but he was also a well-known Freemason. In March of 1780, his warship *L'Hermione* had crossed the Atlantic carrying a distinguished passenger ready to help the American patriots fight the British colonizers: the Marquis de Lafayette. Upon delivering his passenger, Latouche-Tréville had gone on to command his vessel in the American Revolutionary War for more than eighteen months.

To us, those were credentials!

Earlier, the admiral had been one of the first French noblemen to join forces with the common citizens of France, the so-called *Tiers*-État, the Third Estate. In 1789, he had been a deputy at the National Constituent Assembly, the first parliament that France ever held. The post had established his celebrity as a liberal aristocrat.

Several of my Jacobin friends had enjoyed running into Admiral Latouche-Tréville as he freely strolled the town in the company of his sailors. I had that possibility only later. The French vessels had been damaged at sea, and Ferdinando and Carolina had allowed them to be repaired in our port. The admiral—very close to his crew as we all knew—was now allowed to roam the city around, for public viewing. Ferdinando and Carolina had given the orders because they were afraid of antagonizing the French. War with France was to be avoided at all costs. So, after settling the diplomatic incident that had brought the French fleet to Naples, the best course of action—they thought—was welcoming the French foreigners. This tactic guaranteed, they thought, the easiest way to find out what they were up to. As a result, the admiral was frequently seen doing exactly as he pleased. He visited the widow of Gaetano Filangieri, someone he described as the *"philosopher-legislator,"* and who had been a leading proponent of reform in Naples. Filangieri was famous for writing *La Scienza della Legislazione,* a text evoked often by French republicans. He had been Benjamin Franklin's penpal and had considered moving to America with his family in the aftermath of the American Revolution. The admiral also attended the San Carlo Royal Theater, addressed and participated in debates at the Academy of Chemistry, and accepted invitations to the homes of well-known Jacobins. He wore in his lapel the tricolor cockade: a circular rosette-like emblem, the very symbol of the French Revolution.

My turn to meet the alluring admiral arrived, at last, when he hosted a reception for the local Jacobins aboard the *Languedoc*. The invitation was a provocation directed at the monarchy: mighty France was fraternizing with the city liberals! The date chosen for the event, undoubtedly on purpose, was January 12, 1793, Ferdinando's birthday. The admiral presumed, probably, that the occasion would draw less police surveillance. With the Royal Palace's festivities taking place, officers would be occupied and less likely to pay attention to what was happening at sea. Since I had become ever more daring—less willing to compromise with the established order—I joined my friends as the first group to board the *Languedoc*. To go unnoticed, we traveled on a small boat from one of the city's minor quays. Other Jacobins departed from different quays at prearranged intervals. For January, the weather was not too cold; or, maybe, I didn't notice it because I was so enthralled with what lay ahead. A full moon was shining on the calm sea, a promising sign for our safety. No boat carried lanterns. The *Languedoc*'s illumination was enough to show us the way.

Later, rumor spread that I had gone aboard the ship disguised as a man. But it wasn't true—that is not who I am. I went as myself; as a woman taking action. I wanted to bear witness to my sex, to feel inspired. And I wanted to know, firsthand, the details of what was happening in France.

My excitement grew as we approached the warship. Latouche-Tréville stood in uniform on the ship's deck surrounded by his principal officers. Ambassador Mackau was already present. Sailors helped us climb aboard the ship by way of a narrow ladder on the boat's side. The choppy water next to the ship made the ladder sway around and a couple of sailors had to come down and hold it still. I needed a bit of resolve to step onto it and climb up. And so it happened that Latouche-Tréville showed surprise to see a woman arrive on deck. My long hair rippled back freely, as the shawl that had covered my head had fallen to my shoulders. The admiral stepped forward and extended his hand in a gallant greeting.

Once a majority of us were aboard the frigate, sailors passed around the liberty cap—also called the Phrygian cap or the *pileus*. The French addressed us as partisans of liberty, the same designation given to republicans in France. The Liberty cap was a small, brimless felt hat, conical in shape, with the tip pulled forward—and it felt good to touch one for the first time. The sailors had rosettes, the cockades, sewed to their lapels—a treasured symbol of the American Revolution. These emblems were the so-called "Tricolore," in red, white, and blue, the same colors as the American flag.

The ship's deck had been decorated with small elm trees in vases, another charming symbol of liberty. After the sailors sang "La Marseillaise," shouts of welcome and applause erupted. A few scattered fires burned here and there to keep the guests warm. Kerosene lamps provided light, adding to the magical atmosphere. The ship's damaged mainmast had been repaired, and a combination of Neapolitan oils, resins, and glues spread the piquant scent of eucalyptus. I rubbed my hands together. More than a way to keep warm, it was a gesture of my pure joy.

Latouche-Tréville greeted me in French with an all-encompassing smile and sparkling eyes.

"What an honor to receive you, milady," he said.

"The honor is mine," I replied.

"I'm delighted to visit your city."

"You're a world traveler. How I wish I had seen as much as you have."

"Your literary works are, no doubt, a voyage of the mind."

"How well you speak," I replied, flattered that the admiral knew about my work. "We've all heard about your victories in America fighting with the colonists for their independence."

"If I hadn't been part of the American Revolutionary War, the brave people of the New World would have won anyway."

"You're too modest, Admiral, like all eminent men," I said.

"It is I who find your daring most commendable."

"I left my fears behind a long time ago."

"You bear honor to the new French Constitution. It grants equality, liberty and fraternity to all. Women and men alike, regardless of gender."

"I wish the same for the Kingdom of Naples."

I knew my statement was audacious, but I couldn't refrain from saying it. If it reached Carolina's ears by word of mouth, it could lead to my immediate arrest.

I looked around at the crowded deck—more than two hundred Jacobins were now on board. Food and wine had been set out on small tables; the French had procured generous supplies from Naples. After a short welcoming speech, Latouche-Tréville invited me to sit with him at the center of the main table. When he indicated his right side, I graciously sat down, delighted with his exquisite manners. He was both carefree and elegant at the same time. Our conversation flowed naturally, as if we were old friends. He was forty-eight at the time, and I forty-one. I found myself unreservedly attracted to him, despite our age; and I'm not ashamed to say that I loved his wavy white-blondish hair. He didn't wear a wedding ring. I had heard he was a lady's man—scandalous stories circulated about his having a hidden mistress on board while fighting in America.

"You know Lafayette well. What is he like?"

"He's the progressive individual who drafted our Declaration of the Rights of Man and the Citizen. Like you, he's fearless. He was a close friend of Thomas Jefferson, when the latter was ambassador to Paris. The Americans were a great inspiration to our progressive work in France."

"Ours is indeed a worldwide revolution," I said. "I've always loved Jefferson's notion of public happiness. I mention it in my own work."

"Happiness has many shades, and I think Jefferson knew it."

"His Declaration of Independence is a masterpiece. What a gift to the world!"

"I agree. The warm reception I've gotten from the Neapolitan Jacobins has made me—this Frenchman—very, very happy." The admiral pointed to himself as he said this. "A private but very enjoyable feeling."

"We're so happy you came!"

"How about you?" The admiral leaned toward me with a piercing gaze. This gave me the chance to smell the sea salt permeating his uniform.

I blushed with his enticement but didn't lose my composure. "I feel very pleased in your company," I said.

Latouche-Tréville smiled cheerfully. His fingers skimmed the red silk fringe of my shawl, as if he were caressing me. I wondered why he did that. Was I his conquest now?

Our conversation was interrupted when a group of sailors started singing hymns to liberty. They were accompanied by many playing harmonicas, small wind instruments. Then, something unexpected happened. One of the performers stopped and shouted to his admiral that he should invite me to dance. Neapolitans stopped talking at once—no one knew how to react. Other sailors joined the chant for their commander and milady to dance!

Latouche-Tréville stood up, collected himself, and addressed me. "Milady, I always follow my crew's advice. Would you give me the honor of this dance?"

To deny the admiral's invitation would have been impolite. And the truth was, I was dying to be in his arms. Flushed, I rose from my chair and placed my fingers on the hand extended to me. I was going to follow his lead.

With the sailors gathered around us, we danced and danced, their clapping and singing in our ears.

I felt so young! So silly! Moonlight bathed us on the deck the same way it had when I had met Joseph alone for the first time on the Serra di Cassano's terrace. I had drunk a bit of red wine and was feeling carried away. Latouche-Tréville looked me straight in the eyes, as if I were the first woman he had ever met. Unaccustomed to such an adoring gaze, I kept my eyes down with a smile on my face. I felt transported to a place that I knew existed but had not experienced in a long time. For me, Vesuvius and the sky had melted into one cosmic canopy. The moon and its reflection on the water had also melted into one divine expanse.

I was enchanted.

After several dances my eyes and the admiral's met up close one last time. We seemed to be searching for each other's souls. *Citoyen*, citizen Latouche-Tréville and me, the Jacobin marquise, faced an indescribable attraction for each other. We felt as if we were by ourselves, even if surrounded by a large crowd.

Needing to return my attention to the deck scene, I looked around and saw that a thin layer of fog was now shrouding the *Languedoc*. As if we had become suspended from the clouds, as if the white mist announced the end of our festivities. Everyone was jolly, but we must return to Naples. Later, the wind would be too strong, making the crossing bumpy.

As we said good-bye, Latouche-Tréville made a chivalrous bow, showing his pleasure. "I take it you'd like to visit France one day. Paris," he said.

"It would be a delight."

"When we meet again, I want you to address me by my first name: Louis-René. Promise you'll do that."

"I will," was my simple answer.

We began descending the wobbly ladder and loading ourselves into the small boats awaiting us. I found going down harder than going up. When I glanced up, the admiral was watching me. He smiled, while waving. I got into one of the boats, the sea was much rougher now.

I shivered in the cold, biting wind all the way back to Naples.

The evening had been a turning point for me. Poetry had always given me dreamlike moments. But the *Languedoc,* its admiral and crew, had conveyed a sense of community for a joint political cause. I had lost faith in my ability to get personal satisfaction in marriage and family. But other dreams—revolutionary ones—were well and alive in France. It was obvious Admiral Latouche-Tréville believed in them. I had followed his lead while dancing; I was now ready to follow his lead in rebellion.

Did I feel whimsical? Did I feel fanatical? I really don't know. But I had entered a place where self-sacrifice for a higher cause was possible, even desirable. If I had failed individually, I could succeed now by working for a cause that seemed larger than my own life.

Enough of talking, fraternizing, and reading about revolutionary theories in newspapers like *Le Moniteur,* whose news arrived in Naples too late. These times required a concerted and subversive movement. France led the way. A progressive form of governing, closer to the people, was the only solution for Naples. Uprising was the new word of the day.

Soon after that evening, I found out that there had been royal spies on board, disguised as Jacobins. The monarchy suspected a conspiracy was brewing to overthrow them. As soon as Latouche-Tréville left Naples, the crown declared that those who had attended the reception had committed an act of high treason. That Marie Antoinette was decapitated a few months later—following her husband's execution—didn't help allay Carolina's fear of insurrection. Word of my warm communication with Latouche-Tréville confirmed to the queen that I was a Jacobin conspirator. And indeed, that is what I had become.

During this period, the salon I held in Piazza Sant'Anna di Palazzo gave my fellow revolutionaries the chance to solidify our ideas. What form would the Jacobin movement take if and when the

French marched on Naples? Without the help of the French Army, we wouldn't be able to overthrow the monarchy and establish a republic. This, we knew for certain. At those gatherings, I always served Neapolitan coffee in demitasse; its scent, I felt, gave everyone a renewed capacity to face the emerging challenges. Our evenings often started with singing and music, followed by verses or plays recited by well-known poets. We all enjoyed Vittorio Alfieri's tragedies. His main characters were heroes of liberty, protagonists whose revolutionary ideas pushed them into fighting oppression and tyranny.

Once the French Army conquered parts of the northern Italian Peninsula, we knew it was possible for them to reach us. They had established what the French called sister republics in the region, they were all modeled after the French Republic. And as soon as they conquered the Papal States, it was easy to enter Naples by land; we shared borders. The Directory, the five-member committee that ruled France, had given orders for the army to advance into Naples in 1798. Napoleon Bonaparte—an intrepid twenty-six year old artillery captain—had chosen Commander-in-Chief Jean Etienne Championnet for his advance into the Kingdom of Naples.

As we discussed these incendiary events in my salon, I shared my worries with my friends. Earlier, the Jacobins had congregated in the Patriotic Society. But now, as our group enlarged, we had split into two factions. Some of us wanted a constitutional monarchy for Naples while others, myself included, wanted a republic modeled after France. I believed the lazy king and his shrewd Austrian queen would be forced to either resign or flee into exile. Only radical change could transform the lives of those wretched *lazzaroni*. Education was the means for such change, but it would require resources. We needed to prevent the monarchy from emptying the city's banks if it fled.

One evening, after my guests had departed at dawn, I sat down in my bedroom's old velvet armchair to collect my thoughts. I needed to adjust to the transition about to take place in the city I adored. On top of my chest of drawers lay a few objects I had inherited from my mother. The woman who so wholeheartedly, so lovingly, had believed in me all along! The objects now seemed to belong to someone different from me, someone living in another era. Seated, I admired my row of Murano glass jars. Each contained a colorful powder derived from the amalgamation of dried flowers from Portugal. The colors ranged from dark violet, to silver blue, to glowing green. I admired those colors, I always found them soothing, nurturing, and appeasing to my heart. My mother had kept those jars in her bedroom throughout her life, once in a while replenishing their content. As a young woman, before composing a poem that I anticipated and could not yet put down on the page, I would open one of them. I enjoyed smelling the dried flowers and chose the fragrance according to my mood. I loved to inhale the aromas slowly, softly.

Now, at this crossroad in my life I didn't know which scent to choose, as if my old ritual didn't make sense anymore. I was in *terra ignota*, unknown territory. The memory of the sea salt scent emanating from Latouche-Tréville's uniform now superseded my former sensations from the powered flowers. As if I were still aboard the *Languedoc*, as if the admiral still gazed into my eyes while we danced. I was certain of only one thing at that moment: I wanted to play a role if and when the French Army entered Naples.

As I continued to contemplate my new inner self, I felt confident and ready to build my own destiny. I had only felt completely free from my unhappy marriage after Don Pasquale's death. Now Latouche-Tréville had become an inspiration. These new romantic sentiments were a stronger version of my excitement with the Joseph of my youth.

I had sided with the more radical Jacobin camp. I recalled how, under the Marquis de Pombal, heads had rolled in Portugal. During the French Revolution, many others followed; men and women alike were sent to the scaffold in mere seconds. Louis XVI and Marie Antoinette had been beheaded.

Here at the Vicaria now, will I be next? Regrettably, I must admit it is possible.

At the juncture I am describing, another major event took place that changed the lives of the Neapolitan Jacobins forever. It was the arrival in Naples, on August of 1798, of another maritime figure, Horatio Nelson. Now promoted to British Rear Admiral, Nelson had just won the Battle of the Nile in Abukir Bay in Egypt. This was a major victory against the powerful French fleet. Not only did it curtail French activity in the eastern Mediterranean but it also allowed England to sail the seas safely. Only a captain at the time, Nelson had stopped in Naples in 1793, on the *Agamemnon*, asking the kingdom for supplies to fight the French. The arrival of the admiral was of a very different nature this time around. He was now received by our sovereigns as a war hero, Queen Carolina calling him "*Il Nostro Liberatore*," Our Liberator. Covered with glory and needing medical assistance, Nelson was invited to stay at Villa Sesso, the home of Lord Hamilton, the British Ambassador. It was here that Emma Hart, now married and addressed as Lady Hamilton, took care of Nelson's recovery.

In time, Lady Hamilton became Nelson's lover. Naples, thriving on gossip as always, talked about little else but the new Trio, with a capital T. If Lord Hamilton minded his much younger wife's affair, he never showed it. Everywhere the threesome went, their lovers' eyes spoke the truth of their hearts.

From this date onward, we Jacobins were unaware of what the enemies of our cause were preparing. As it happened, Nelson's victory in Egypt changed the course of history in the Kingdom of Naples. And mine. Two powerful triangles—atrocious and formidable at the same time—ensued. A personal one was formed by Lady Hamilton, Admiral Nelson, and Lord Hamilton. This was of a personal nature, with sexual overtones. The second was formed by Lady Hamilton, Admiral Nelson and Queen Carolina. This alliance, political in nature, allowed Nelson to solidify the friendship between the two women. A few days before we established the Neapolitan Republic and the French entered Naples, Nelson commanded the *Vanguard* and escorted the royal fleet carrying Carolina, Ferdinando, their children, as well as the royal entourage southward in the Mediterranean Sea. The British were now offering the protection Carolina had sought all along. To escape unseen, the fugitives went through the long tunnel that connected the Royal Palace to the Bay of Naples, used for emergencies only. They left during the night, and carried with them all that they could amass in just a few days: money from the royal banks, art treasures, jewelry and furniture, and other valuables.

The group stayed in exile in Palermo—Naples's sister capital in Sicily—during the five months the Neapolitan Republic lasted. The implications of these events for my own life—and those of so many other Jacobins—were profound.

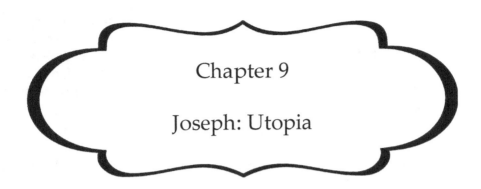

Chapter 9

Joseph: Utopia

No one could receive greater pleasure than I did at the proof that your sovereign set a due value on your merit, as manifested by the honorable duties assigned to you with us.
—Thomas Jefferson's letter to Correia da Serra, June 14, 1817

"Ambassador, congratulations on your appointment. You must feel happy, your dreams came true," Jefferson said, as soon as I arrived back in Monticello that late summer. "This appointment will undoubtedly settle you in America forever." Jefferson smiled, always the loyal friend and ultimate optimist.

"My appointment is like persimmon fruit, bittersweet. It came too late, I'm already sixty-five," I said, but I was obviously pleased with Jefferson's blessing. "After I presented my credentials to President Madison and Secretary of State Monroe, it took me a while to take up my duties. As you recall, I was appointed in February of 1816, but I wanted first to finish my botanical work at the American Philosophical Society."

"You know how much I hate newspapers, but I've decided to keep my subscription to the *National Intelligencer.* Your news gave me such pleasure that I want to stay informed. You should have visited us earlier—but I excuse you, I know how busy your last year must have been." Jefferson's voice had a hint of cynicism.

We were in Jefferson's office space, which he called his cabinet or his *sanctum sanctorum.* He had shown me into his private quarters since the first day we had met, a sign of friendship I had deeply appreciated. His camaraderie with me had grown consistently, something that had surpassed all my initial expectations. Always the exceptional gentleman, he now placed my desires for fame as ambassador above his own plans for my teaching at the University of Virginia.

I continued. "It was impossible to come earlier, my dear Sir. Let me start with personal news. I've already taken steps for Edward to join me in America, and he'll be here soon. I can't wait to see him again!"

"Your eyes are shining with delight and anticipation. Is his mother coming too?"

"No, Esther isn't well, unfortunately. Moreover, she cherishes Paris too much to have an interest in America." I paused for a moment and then added, "With my new appointment, my dream of Edward's legitimization might, one day, become true. This validation means the world to me."

"Would Edward's royal endorsement alleviate public condemnation were your secret disclosed?" With Jefferson positioned at his revolving armchair, I noticed that the chair's side arms had candlesticks to provide light for reading at night.

"Indeed," I replied, taking a seat across the desk from him. Not only would my reputation as a priest be safeguarded, but Edward would also have rights as my heir under the law." I felt so thrilled to share this information that a belly laugh escaped me. With a light chuckle of his own, Jefferson seemed to understand perfectly what I was feeling.

I looked at him, still caught up in my own feelings. To regain a sense of peace, I then examined the gadgets in the room. The office was situated between Jefferson's library and bedroom. His inventions were everywhere and thoroughly captivating. To my right was a polygraph machine where, as Jefferson wrote his letters, a copy was produced. Nearby, stood a revolving bookstand whose shelves had different heights. *The Four Books of Architecture,* by Andrea Palladio, was opened to a page that had the design of a rotunda.

Examining these objects, I now felt a gravitas I hadn't experienced before at Monticello. Jefferson had been ambassador to

France, he must appreciate my new state of mind. I decided to turn our conversation to public matters.

"I'm proud to represent the Luso-Brazilian Empire in America. We're now the United Kingdom of Portugal and Brazil; Brazil is not a colony of Portugal anymore. Our nations are the two greatest powers of the Western Hemisphere. I'd like my work to be auspicious to both sides."

"I'm sure it will be. I just hope your new position leaves you with enough free time for your botanical rambles. Botany is your passion," Jefferson replied, seemingly more interested in continuing with personal issues.

I ignored my friend's remark. "We're the first European monarchy of the New World. As such, our new geopolitical entity is problematic at best. Despite the changes put in place, Brazilians continue to talk about becoming independent. The Portuguese in Portugal, on the other hand, are lobbying for the royal family to leave Rio de Janeiro and return."

"I'd say that exceptional circumstances might require exceptional measures." Jefferson grabbed a small telescope on his desk and fooled with it.

"The site of Portuguese sovereignty is at the center of this debate. I want our former prince regent, now King João, to remain in Rio. But this requires a change of mentality in Portugal; also, massive incentives for Portuguese to move to Brazil and work the land. Too many Brazilians are saying, however, that the Portuguese have no right to govern the former colony."

"What's your opinion, may I ask?" Jefferson stopped his hand game.

"I want the United Kingdom of Portugal and Brazil to prevail. As I wrote recently to one of our cabinet members, 'The old cradle is too small for the grandiosity of our current monarchy.' The separatist movements in Brazil must be halted. Now."

"Time will tell whether your view is feasible. Brazilians are watching insurrections in various Latin American regions that still belong to Spain. And they look to us for clues on how to proceed for obtaining independence."

As Jefferson played once again with his telescope, I found the silver and mahogany combination truly beautiful. The object made me want to predict the future as if looking through its powerful lens. "I remain a reformer," I said. "Social change must be continual and orderly; it doesn't need to be revolutionary. One thing I'd like to do is to strengthen the ties between our South American–based monarchy and your American republic."

"We can certainly bolster political ties and establish new alliances; we inhabit twin continents. We could call the pact-to-be the new 'American System,'" Jefferson said.

"I like that. You remain a visionary!" I clapped my hands, applauding the idea.

"Such an alliance requires political will on both sides. Imagine us diving the Atlantic Ocean in two spheres of influence, with our two fleets commanding its waters! Our republic could dominate the North Atlantic; your monarchy could dominate the South."

"Let's pass this argument on to our respective governments," I replied, elated. "Hand me that telescope, I want to see our nations' bright future." I placed the instrument in my right eye and pretended to examine the landscape through the nearby window.

"I would rejoice if the fleets of our two nations rode together as brethren of the same family, pursuing the same objectives in that immense ocean. The Atlantic waters would be protected forever, reducing piracy in the American seas." Jefferson wore a broad smile. "Our alliance would be based on two distinct but complementary spheres of influence. A magnificent dream, for we are indeed the two most powerful American nations," Jefferson reiterated. "I also see a hidden advantage here."

"Which is, my dear friend?"

"We would keep Europe at bay. "

"This is certainly viable—particularly if the current site of Portuguese sovereignty remains in Brazil."

"The dreams of the future are so much better than the history of the past." Jefferson leaned back in his chair and stretched out his legs, pleased. As for myself, I wholeheartedly approved his ideas. The telescope in my hand appeared to symbolize the future we were free to pursue.

"We should proceed with this alliance. I need to talk to my friend and neighbor—our new president—Mr. Monroe."

We fell into silence. Even if I approved of Jefferson's theory of the 'American System,' it remained to be seen if the American president would back it. Jefferson seemed to believe now that a pact with Portugal to protect American waters might be more productive than backing adventurers fighting for Brazilian independence. He had given them support in the past. Would Mr. Monroe back Jefferson's plan? Even if I liked to think so, only time would tell.

But why—I ruminated—would Jefferson advise the President to seek an alliance with a southern-based monarchy? True, Portugal had recognized the United States of America in early 1783, half a year before the country's peace treaty with England. This had opened Portuguese ports to commerce with America, a matter of significance to both nations. Jefferson's idea for a new alliance between our countries was great. I was now eager to address the subject with our king—not any more with the friend who was sitting in front of me. He himself had once said that silences were golden. Retired now, Jefferson had no official power to carry out his views even if his eminence gave him a great deal of influence.

Jefferson broke our silence. "I still haven't lost hope that, after you retire from your ambassadorship, you might come to the university," he said with a warm smirk. "Allow me to show you the new drawings I've completed for its buildings."

My friend took his sketches from a large folder, and I realized how many of the details he had added to the Rotunda were influenced by Palladio. He loved European neoclassicism and wanted his country to benefit from his worldly knowledge. His drawings showed how he was enamored by light as well as form.

After we discussed a few details—my friend said the Rotunda was the jewel of his plans—I noticed the folder also contained the outline of a curious appliance. When I asked, Jefferson explained that he had drawn a new machine to make macaroni. My chin dropped; the man in front of me had an ingenious mind, he was the Leonardo da Vinci of modern times!

Besides stately buildings, Jefferson loved designing objects for daily use. The macaroni machine, he said, had been perfected after several attempts. I smiled, delighted to learn more about his invention. The device required precision, he said, because it was fundamental to mix the right proportions of water and semolina—the best quality flour for pasta. Jefferson's sketch indicated how to insert the flour, mix in the water, and turn the central tube so that the perfect blend of dough came out. In the past, he had imported wheels of Parmesan cheese to accompany his macaroni dishes. But this was so costly that he had considered making the cheese at Monticello. He only gave up on the idea when he realized he would also have to import cows from the Italian Peninsula.

It didn't seem part of the American ethos to be such an epicurean. No doubt Jefferson's cosmopolitan experiences explained his interest. I told him that the best macaroni came from Naples—and that my mother had passed on to me the secrets of its perfect cooking. In character, Jefferson suggested that we find time to cook together, so that I could pass on the details I knew. Eating the meal afterwards would be entertaining, he added. I found his suggestion so amusing that I didn't worry the summer heat would make our work rather unpleasant.

The time was ripe now, I finally felt after all my visits to Monticello. After this conversation, I asked Jefferson if he would be free later on that day to show me Mulberry Row. I had seen it many times from the house—and I knew it was the center of the mansion's activity—but I had never seen it up close.

"Of course," he said. As tall as Jefferson was, I noticed his shoulders had lifted slightly back, a sign of confidence.

And so it was that in the afternoon we met up to visit Mulberry Row. Jefferson came out of the house wearing a large, broad-brimmed hat to shield his face from the sun. He handed me a smaller one. We walked about a hundred yards to the settlement when Jefferson, stopping, said he was glad to introduce me to the members of his extended family.

Many slaves, men, women and children, lived and worked on Jefferson's plantation. Overseers and workmen—mostly white but a few negroes—also lived in the Mulberry community. We toured the sheds where the nailery, the smithy, and the carpenter's shop were located. With construction going on at all times in the main house, these shops, Jefferson asserted, were essential. We passed the smokehouse, the washhouse, and numerous storehouses. I saw the slaughter cabin and the area where the poultry was raised. We didn't enter the slaves' quarters—some of them individual huts for families—but Jefferson pointed them out.

"Mulberry Row links the plantation's resources to the domestic needs of my home. I've built a dynamic, industrial center adjoined to the slaves' living quarters. With Patsy's large family living with me, and with visitors like you a constant flow, this spot helps keep expenses under control and servants handy," Jefferson said.

I had never seen anything like Mulberry Row; it left me speechless. Even if this seemed a privileged location to live in, I'm going to repeat myself: all these men, women and children, were Jefferson's property. He owned them, they were his chattel, his personal possessions. If I didn't know about slavery in America, I might think these mulattos were paid laborers like those I had met in France, Italy, or Portugal. Jefferson's slaves moved about freely, not in chains; they worked diligently at their crafts; and no one displayed signs of beatings. All appeared strong and healthy.

Jefferson addressed every slave we met with courtesy and affability. Here and there he paused for a moment to exchange a few words. In my view, he acted like a benevolent father not a tyrannical overlord. Some of the women were sitting outside enjoying the shade; a few nursed their babies. Children played freely among dogs, cats, and chickens. Many of the enslaved people were of mixed blood—mulattos, not African negroes.

Turning to me, Jefferson said without embarrassment, malice, or irony, "My slaves contribute to my happiness, they bring me and my family a lot of comfort. They afford us a state of 'tranquil felicity.'"

"I imagine some Northerners might be upset by your words," I said, cautiously. "I've seen how slavery's a big divide in this country."

"I inherited a lot of my slaves from my father-in-law," Jefferson replied.

"I notice the people here are mostly mulatto."

"True. Some of them belong to the Hemings family."

"Who are the Hemings, may I ask?"

"A slave family that came to Monticello after my father-in-law died. He owned them."

"Do you also have purely African slaves?" I asked.

"Yes, they work in the plantation fields further away. They're robust and hardworking. Some are originally from Guinea and Angola, your Portuguese colonies."

"Interesting. I wonder, do you ever sell slaves? And do you ever need to discipline them if they misbehave or attempt to run away?"

"Yes," Jefferson said slowly. "I've sold some, but only when my creditors demand I pay off my debt. And I only sell those who don't mind leaving Monticello. I always keep the ones who want to stay with me. Do I ever punish them? Yes, usually just the men, and those who are chronic runaways. I flog them in front of the others when they're captured, a lesson to all."

"But I think of you as a humanist," I said.

"I am a humanist. When I hire my slaves out to work for money, I always make sure they're treated benignly."

"Your experience is a lesson to me." There was no irony in my voice when I added, "Both Virginia and Brazil are slave societies dominated by whites. You live surrounded by people of a race other than your own and you treat them benevolently."

"These are the conditions we seek to have here in Virginia."

"Yes, but if you allow me to express a thought, my dear Sir, the situation is paradoxical. You wrote the most famous document in American's young history. I know the words by heart: *We hold these truths to be self-evident, that all men are created equal, and that they are endowed by their Creator with certain unalienable rights, that among these are life, liberty, and the pursuit of happiness.* You crafted the most inspiring and egalitarian promise ever created by mankind. But here in Monticello you own other human beings."

"Yes, and I have no excuse for it, although I spoke publicly against slavery during the Federal Congress in Philadelphia in 1784. And I wrote the proposal to end slavery in all newly created states by 1800. Unfortunately the proposal lost by one vote."

"I've heard of it."

"I also wrote about the evils of slavery in *Notes on the State of Virginia.* And over the years, I have often stated that slave emancipation is necessary. It was during my presidency that Congress passed the 1808 law, making the slave trade illegal in this country. But, currently, I think the issue can be solved only by the next generation."

"And why do you think that is, if I may ask?"

"I and others doubt that these people would be able to take care of themselves, if set free. They are like children, dependent."

Jefferson ended the conversation and directed our attention to the stables where old Eagle, his favorite horse, lived. We entered the stall, and Jefferson patted Eagle on the white spot on his forehead. The animal whinnied with joy at his master's touch. Then, Jefferson carefully examined Eagle's horseshoes, telling me that he always wanted them in perfect shape. All along, he used his left hand, as if he lacked strength in the right one. The damage during the outing with Maria Cosway—when he had fallen in Paris—appeared to be permanent.

While Jefferson inspected the horse, I thought about Jefferson's position on slavery. People I knew in Philadelphia considered his later-life silence rather disturbing. It was clear to me, and probably to them, that Jefferson's beloved Monticello, and its comfortable life—was only possible because of slave labor. Jefferson used his slaves—whom he called his extended family—to his heart's content; he took advantage of them to pursue his own dreams. So did his family; and so did all of us who visited him. Therefore, his extended family was composed of people that he used for his own benefit and that of those he loved.

George Washington came to my mind as our visit to Mulberry Row ended. What would Jefferson do one day? The first American president had freed his slaves in his will. From what I was seeing, Jefferson might let his family inherit his human chattel.

That night, dinner with the Jefferson clan was as entertaining as ever. The family used *service à la française*, or French-style service, a grand and varied presentation of dishes catered to everyone's possible whim. Jefferson's exquisite taste in wine and foods, prepared with herbs from his garden, was a constant source of pleasure. A lover of fish like all the Portuguese, I very much enjoyed the *bacalla*—so exotic in a plantation setting!—a fish I hadn't yet seen eaten in America. Jefferson said he had built small ponds to farm a variety of fish, especially carp and shad.

During the meal, the family talked as if they were playing games. The children constantly called their grandfather's attention to different subjects. The spectrum of discussion ranged from the art of ballooning, for which Jefferson saw a military use, to diplomatic code language. Benjamin, maybe nine, wanted to know the secrets in the wheel cipher that Jefferson still used to send and receive messages. Jefferson described to us his thinking process in building the instrument and gave examples of how to send encoded texts. He explained how each row of letters represented a different encryption of the message, and what the recipient must do to understand the sequence.

After dinner, when everyone scattered for their next activity, I sat on the tearoom's sofa and gazed out the south lawn. I recalled how Jefferson and I had sat in the same sofa during my first visit to Monticello. A lot had happened during the intervening years, and this moment of repose gave me an opportunity to reflect on those developments. I was getting on in years. And I was now an ambassador, as I had always wanted to be.

I must decide what to do with Jefferson's gift of Eleonora's manuscript. Despite its tragedy, it had remained a fundamental piece for a deeper understanding of myself. It was imperative to preserve it in a safe place, otherwise it might disappear after my death. The manuscript was written in Portuguese, so I wanted it to remain in Portugal. Even if its author had never traveled to the land of her forebears, I felt her words should remain there. Although I had taken the rosemary sprig out many times to hold in my hands, I always put it back in the little back pocket. Let posterity figure out what it meant!

One possibility for the booklet would be to offer it to the University of Évora, since both our families came from the region. Were I to deposit it in such a public institution, others might benefit from reading it. Eleonora's revolutionary zeal was not for me, but others might learn from it. Even if I had been liberal in my younger years, I had grown more moderate with the passage of time. Now, my ambassadorship might make me more conservative than I would like to admit. The proof lay in my current position. I really saw nothing wrong with my king wanting Brazil to remain united with Portugal. As for slavery, if Jefferson and my King João sanctioned it, who was I to oppose the practice?

Jefferson joined me on the sofa and asked what I was thinking.

"I was recalling my first visit here, when the two of us shared this corner. Do you remember how you comforted me after I read about Eleonora's execution?"

"I do," Jefferson replied.

I went on to thank my friend for the room I had enjoyed in Monticello over the years—how much I loved the idyllic moments of contemplation it had provided me. What privilege! At times I heard only silence and my own breathing. Certainly I had been unable to erase Eleonora from my memory; as has been said, some people never die.

Since we had visited the slave quarters that day, I wanted to bring up Sally Hemings with Jefferson now. My colleagues at the American Philosophical Society had mentioned her name when they heard that Jefferson often invited me to Monticello.

These academics were not gossiping. They feared the rumors that Hemings might be Jefferson's concubine were true, which would damage his reputation and legacy. It was a crime in Virginia for a white man to sleep and father children with a slave woman. Jefferson had been twice president of the country. In 1802, when Jefferson was president, the journalist James T. Callender had published the allegation that Hemings was Jefferson's mistress and that they had several children together. The journalist had likely never seen her, but to tantalize readers, he branded Sally "African Venus" and "Dusky Sally." Since Jefferson never denied or acknowledged the allegation, the rumor persisted. Sally Hemings also happened to be Jefferson's late wife's half-sister, both fathered by the same Virginian plantation owner, John Wayles. Strangely, Callender had been found dead the following year.

"May I ask you, my dear friend, how the French reacted to your having two slave servants in your house in Paris?"

"They might have gossiped about it, but I was never asked the question directly. So I don't know. One of the slaves was my cook, James. I wanted him to master the art of French cooking. Later, my now-deceased daughter Maria joined me and her sister Patsy. Maria was eight years old at the time and was accompanied on the voyage by her maid, Sally Hemings. She was also James's sister and though they were our slaves, in Paris I paid them."

"Wise of you. You might have a scandal in your hands if you did otherwise. They also might have tried to run away," I said quickly.

"There was no reason for them to do so, I treated them well." Jefferson had an ascetic, serene expression. "I paid them because I didn't want them to feel different from my other French servants."

"I see, you signed your own 'treaty' of Paris; you kept everyone happy," I said to Jefferson's chuckle. He agreed with me.

"You might have seen Sally around the house, she's now my chambermaid. She takes care of my wardrobe and linens."

"Yes, I've seen her often."

Sally stood apart from the other servants with her light mulatto skin. Such people were called "mighty near white." She had dark hazel eyes and long hair down her back. I guessed she was in her forties but youthful, and delicately built. She always moved gently, confidently, and at ease. I often saw her carrying piles of clothing in a straw basket into Jefferson's private quarters. She usually wore an embroidered white cap, similar to Jefferson's daughter Patsy, which I took to be a sign of her status. Patsy and Sally were only a few months apart in age.

Jefferson remained silent, so I said, "Sally and I have exchanged smiles instead of words."

My friend's eyes suddenly turned a glacial blue. How could I possibly continue and ask him about the mulatto children I had seen playing and singing outside with his grandchildren, the day Mr. Valentin gave his musical performance?

Clearly, Jefferson was not going to discuss his colored Aphrodite with me. And I did not intend to jeopardize the hospitality of this gentleman-philosopher I so admired. I suspected he considered racial amalgamation, as they called miscegenation in Virginia, a taboo. Yet, there existed a secret sexual history between negroes and whites in the South, with the whites in control. I might be a friend of Jefferson now, but I was also a foreigner, an outsider. Only negroes, as far as I had discerned, recounted these secret stories in an oral tradition. Miscegenation was a sensitive topic worldwide, not only in Virginia. As much as Jefferson, I wanted to behave like the most affable sphinx.

Secretly, notwithstanding, I imagined the mulatto children I had seen outside playing and singing, to be his—his and Sally Hemings. I knew my Philadelphia colleagues would agree with me, had I dared to ask the question.

After my friend left the tearoom, I thought how the Portuguese had always sought hegemony by encouraging racial mixing. Therefore, races mingled freely throughout the Portuguese empire. People of other nations considered the Portuguese mild, good-natured, and eager to relate with others through sex. Even Eleonora in *Il Trionfo della Virtù* had addressed the theme. White Portuguese men were known to enjoy sexual encounters with other races. They lived with negro and mulatto women, openly, blissfully. They satisfied their sexual desire with free or slave women—and without public blame or shame. Many Portuguese asserted, the more concubines, the better; procreation, regardless of race, is good for population increase. The cases of racial intermingling were so many that it was not uncommon for Portuguese men to write provisions in their last wills for their illegitimate offspring with women of other races.

My reflections that night knew no end. It was a hot evening and even if I had the room's wood shutters open, I sweated. Portugal was one of the main countries involved in the slave trade to the Americas. After 1808, no slaves could be imported legally into this nation. But even Jefferson, as he had described, owned slaves originally from the Portuguese Empire. The Atlantic trade constituted an old triangle formed by Portugal, Brazil, and our colonies in East Africa. There were other slave routes, of course, but Portugal had been a major trader.

Where did I stand on this issue? Monticello provided the first instance where I saw a family—and a plantation—taking advantage of human servitude. It had been shocking. But why did I think Jefferson had taught me a lesson with the visit to Mulberry Row? Jefferson treated his slaves with humanity. As an ambassador, I now represented a crown that not only tolerated the slave trade but also welcomed slaves in Brazil's rich plantations. Indeed the thriving Brazilian economy depended on slave-produced goods— sugar, cotton, coffee, cocoa, and tobacco—for its profits. With land widely available, it was labor that was needed. Moreover, it was well known that negroes worked much harder, and more willingly, than the indigenous Indians. Commerce in general, and the slave trade in particular, had made us a powerful, prosperous empire. As a representative of our crown, I felt proud of our standing in the world. I allowed myself to believe that if slavery was evil, it was also necessary.

Moreover, Catholicism saw the Luso-Brazilian imperial mission as bringing civilization, through baptism, to poor negroes—who were then able to enter the realm of God and his mercy. There were scattered voices that here and there denounced excesses; but, overall, the Catholic Church did not condemn the trade of humans as sinful. I could, thus, quiet my conscience by following its directives.

Later, I had had to deal with the case of the *Antelope*, which involved the trade of slaves. This had been an upsetting matter that took away many hours of my sleep. The *Antelope* was a ship found in American waters in 1820, carrying three hundred chained Africans intended for sale. After the ship was detained by the naval authorities of this nation, the Portuguese and Spanish crowns sued America for part of its cargo. I chose to view this as an internal matter concerning Portugal and Spain alone. There was no need for me to discuss this issue with Jefferson.

Eventually, I rose from the sofa to get some fresh air outside. As I paced back and forth in front of the window of my room, my thoughts turned to Dr. Casper Wistar, president of the Society for the Abolition of Slavery, a friend Jefferson and I had in common. Jefferson had been pleased when I suggested naming the exquisite Wisteria vine in honor of Dr. Wistar. I had enjoyed the lively discussions that took place in his Philadelphia home with the great minds of the society. I had recounted many of these conversations to Jefferson, either by letter or when I visited. Some members of the society were considering sending African-American slaves back to Africa, and Jefferson had agreed with the idea. Those members intended to buy land where the freed negroes could live and work. When I heard about the plan, I wrote to our king in Brazil, asking if he might be interested in freed slaves who didn't want to return to their continent. They would be sent as "escravos forros," freed slaves who had a manumission letter.

The idea for an 'American System,' my worries about my son's future, Eleonora's memoir, slavery, miscegenation, and the slave trade—how much Jefferson and I shared in common! I marveled how our relationship felt as harmonious as any true friendship could hope to be. So far, no conflict had come between us; we saw things the same way. We kept our secrets, and our silences, close to our hearts. My friend had an elusive character that met my own in a place where contradictions—and inconsistencies—vanished for the comfort of our souls. Both of us realized this at a profound level. Thus, our intimacy went beyond the words we exchanged with each other.

Looking back, I really couldn't foresee that a major disagreement would arise during my last visit to Monticello.

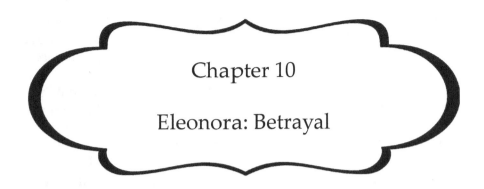

Chapter 10

Eleonora: Betrayal

At the Vicaria Prison, Castel Capuano, outskirts of Naples, August 4, 1799

The political climate was highly polarized in 1798, the year before a republic was declared in Naples. Ferdinando and Carolina, their entourage included, feared deportation if the French entered the city or, even worse, assassination. We Jacobins dreaded exposure and imprisonment. People were suspicious of each other, filled with turmoil. Freedom of speech had been banned; I was no longer able to speak or write my mind. To show determination against revolutionary plots, Carolina had already ordered the Chief of Police Luigi Medici to suppress Freemasonry, the association she had once so fervently supported.

It was the age-old struggle between conservatism and progress.

Carolina also put my name on her police force's watch list. My steps were scrutinized everywhere, as if someone were following me with a sinister intent. What was the queen afraid I might say or do? My friends were busy condemning the monarchy, but I knew I had nothing to gain by exposing her love scene with the now married Lady Emma Hamilton. My salon in Sant'Anna di Palazzo didn't help my case. The police undoubtedly saw it a seditious meeting place, where revolutionaries plotted to abolish the Kingdom of Naples and install, instead, a republic. As my parents had always been in close touch with the Portuguese Embassy, Don José Agostinho de Souza, a diplomat and a family friend for many years—he was the ambassador's personal secretary—was a frequent guest at my gatherings. An easy-going, dedicated diplomat, he frequently advised me to keep my thoughts to myself. "Above all," he advised me, "be careful. Times are challenging. You are a woman alone. Protect yourself."

I was arrested for the first time on October 5, 1798, a date imprinted on my mind forever. An army officer, a handful of soldiers, and a scribe entered my apartment, unannounced, during the early hours of the morning. With a warrant for my arrest, they could do as they wished. First, they pushed me to a corner, and then ransacked my belongings for incriminating information; afterward, they went searching my shelves. They found a pamphlet one of my *literati* friends had written that stated kings should rule by the will of the people, not divine right. They found Diderot's *Encyclopedia* and several books by Voltaire. They found the works of Gaetano Filangieri, the Neapolitan legislator whose widow Latouche-Tréville had visited. Just to mention his name in public had become incriminating. Filangieri's seven volumes, *The Science of Legislation*—now banned in the kingdom—enjoyed immense influence in a Europe on the verge of change. Filangieri wrote that the people, called citizens now, should be able to choose a government freely. He had become enamored with certain inalienable rights that existed already in republican, democratic nations like America.

My voluminous correspondence, a record of decades I kept in carton boxes, was entirely confiscated. The letters alone, I knew well, were enough to condemn me. The scene took quite a while because the scribe wrote my list of books rather slowly. Unable to move from my assigned corner and keep control over my belongings, I asked for a glass of water in order to calm down. My stomach was churning.

Neighbors heard me shouting in resistance when the soldiers wrestled me down the stairs and into their police wagon on the street. I was now a "*reo de opinioni*," guilty of opinion. All the "subversive material" they confiscated from my apartment rode in the wagon with me. Scared, but determined to keep a cool head, I wanted, above all, for my neighbors to witness what was going on. So I called out to them that I was being forced from my home against my will. As the wagon rolled away through the streets of Naples, I soon understood we were headed to the Vicaria Prison. As I had been to the penitentiary before, I knew I was going to be incarcerated. My fears had now been realized. It was only unclear how long my captivity would last.

My heart sank as I crossed the prison's gates into the large entrance loggia. I don't know exactly why—I hadn't been in touch with Suor Amadea della Valle for a while—but I expected to see her as I came in. Maybe because she had greeted me there the first time I visited, after she solicited Carolina for donated books to use with the jail's literacy program. But Suor Amadea was nowhere to be seen.

I passed long, empty corridors until I was finally thrown in the *panaro*, solitary confinement. This was a cold, dark, and damp dungeon in the building's basement. There were no windows in my cell. And how I needed the Neapolitan blue sky for solace and strength! The cubicle had moisture dripping down the walls, with mold growing on the old stones. There was a large crucifix above the dirty, gray, straw mattress as if calling the prisoner to repent her sins in the name of Christ.

As the days went by, I could see the nuns in charge of me knew I had been arrested for Jacobinism—they therefore had no reason to be sympathetic. If I were a Jacobin, then I was, by definition, against the crown, religion, and God.

The prison was crowded and the nuns overworked. I was just another prisoner to keep a close eye on, one more mouth to feed. But they knew they had in their keep an aristocrat and, on top of it, a female one. I had dared to defy the kingdom's laws! How on earth could I ask for compassion?

In the *panaro* no one was allowed to communicate with anyone, let alone to receive visitors. My fellow *literati* couldn't come to my rescue. But where was Suor Amadea? I asked myself many times. We had parted in very good terms, and it was impossible she didn't know I was in her prison. Had she left her position as Madre Superiore? This was unlikely, but I decided not to ask, I was afraid my question might incriminate her.

The court to where I was taken a number of times for interrogation was located next to the penitentiary. There, my so-called subversive activities against the kingdom were examined in detail. I knew the royal magistrates conducted their work ruthlessly, they weren't the least concerned with kindness. On those court days, I was escorted through an endlessly long corridor to reach the gilded room where a judge sat on an imposing chair. As if to epitomize what was to follow, the ante-camera to the gilded room had three monumental stucco statues. They represented the Christian virtues of justice, truth and charity.

I never saw Suor Amadea as I came in or left the *panaro*. How I wished to have, if only for a second, a glimpse of her; to know she was alive. Someone, who could, perhaps, offer me protection.

The room I was brought in was dark, enclosed, with virtually no light coming through the miniature windowpanes. They had not been cleaned in years. I was usually interrogated by one single judge at a time, and as the questioning proceeded, a scribe took notes. Every time, I wondered how the poor fellow could see what he was writing down.

At one of these sessions, a judge said that Queen Carolina wanted details of the plot against the monarchy. She also wanted the names of those who had attended the treasonous meetings at my home. As my expression became impenetrable, he added that if I revealed this information, the queen might order my release.

The interrogation went on for hours, as the judge tried to break my resistance. I remained silent. Never would I betray those like me who pushed for progressive reform.

I had been standing all this time, and I now shivered with exhaustion. Weak, I worried I might not be able to bear the questioning much longer. Carolina had indeed amassed vast powers over the years. I was powerless under her control. It now seemed possible I would be the first woman imprisoned for life. Who knows, I could even be executed. I tried to focus on the frescoes covering the walls, but they were so mediocre I couldn't look at them, even for solace.

Back in the *panaro* following each court session, I lay down on my hideous straw mattress and closed my eyes for a bit of rest. Part of me felt proud to have resisted the judge. But for how long would I be able to fight back? My health was failing—and the prison food was sickening. The winter had now set in around Naples and the cold was ghastly at night. I had only a filthy rug filled with holes to cover my body. The bucket for my bodily needs was rarely emptied, and the nauseating smell affected my mental abilities. I was losing the clear mind I had always been proud of. Lying down, with legs curled in the fetal position, I tried to shake off my despair. I imagined myself inside my mother's womb, safe from suffering.

During one of those nights, in a state of delirium, I visualized a poem that showed my scorn for Carolina. Afraid of forgetting it, I recited the poem to myself over and over again. I called this work "Revived Poppaea" and it starts out with this verse:

Revived Poppaea, impure lesbian
the imbecile tyrant impious wife
tighten our chains as much as you like
mankind is alarmed…and so is nature.

Poppaea was a celebrity of ancient Rome, the cruel mistress and future wife of Emperor Nero. I recalled her because she and Nero loved the Bay of Naples so much that they used to vacation close by. Later in the poem, I referred to the effects of "the dark cloud," and the "roaring thunder." I had in mind Carolina's adultery with Lady Hamilton, her shady character. I enjoyed my reference to the natural world—it soothed my heart. The poem ended with the idea that what happened to Maria Antoinette might also happen to our queen: her unworthy head might roll to the ground.

I certainly wanted her to be the one to face the guillotine, not me.

This poem shows how much imprisonment had changed me. Isolated from loved ones, separated from my books, and removed from the care of admiring friends, I had become a different human being. It was as if my personal survival wasn't a goal of mine anymore. I wanted to shock because I was shocked. I wanted to hold my head high, as high as I could. The poem shows a violence that I would have found unimaginable in my youth; it's full of anger and bile. The profanities I uttered in prison made me feel lighter. I had lost any sense of decorum, in particular the elevation of spirit my mother had imparted to me. I felt alive, brave, and fearless as I slowly uttered the poem's words one by one. I hoped that, out of prison one day, the poem would be read and applauded in Naples, just as my former poetry had been.

There is only a brief moment of relief when I think of my days in the *panaro*. My parents were both gone—and I saw this as a blessing. They would have been deeply hurt to witness my circumstances. My dear Uncle António had died in my care a few months earlier. How comforting it was to know he didn't have to endure my experience. His last prayers on my behalf, fearing for my future, had been extremely heartening.

Late one evening, there was a light, unexpected knock at my cell's door, and I realized a visitor was about to come in. And there she was—when the door finally opened—Suor Amadea! There was another nun behind her, and I understood my friend couldn't talk. But she smiled quickly at me, and her eyes showed a commiseration I hadn't seen in a while. She asked me to get up from the straw mattress, and with the help of the nun, shook it out. Fleas sprayed out everywhere, horrifying us. Then Suor Amadea told the nun to remove my bucket, the smell was nauseating. Another quick smile as the nun carried the bucket out, and both of them were gone.

That night I slept for a few hours. And I had the impression that Suor Amadea's visit might be the first of others to follow. Much to my relief, it happened as I predicted!

She appeared once in a while now, always with a quick smile and always in a hurry. I had the impression she only visited when she felt it was safe. Safe for her—and safe for me. She behaved matter-of-factly and stayed only a few minutes. As the weeks went by, she came in by herself a few times. She always knocked softly at the door beforehand; so I always knew it was she. We never talked to each other, we never discussed my isolation. But I often imagined she preferred me interned here, alone, instead of upstairs with the other female prisoners. Many of those women were hardened criminals: they had robbed, stabbed, and killed. I had heard of their prison gangs, how they had leaders and attacked each other by day and night. The nuns were unable, or unwilling, to keep the prisoners safe within their walls.

If I felt strong enough, I rose from my mattress to greet Suor Amadea. I understood that she worked under trying circumstances. The prison environment was full of deception and a guard might report her activities to the judges. She never talked to me; I never talked to her. I appreciated that, despite her silence, and her seemingly distance, she seemed concerned. I believed that she visited me in sisterhood and humanity. Why else would she call a nun to empty my bucket if she found it, once again, full of excrement? It seemed this was all she felt capable of doing on my behalf. If the judge were to ask her about her visits, she could easily say she was ensuring the prison's sanitary conditions, not improving my lot.

I was growing weaker by the day—inadequate food, no light in my cell, that sickening smell. And I knew prisoners had died at the Vicaria for similar reasons.

So, one day when Suor Amadea happened to visit, I begged her to help me. My *biancheria,* my undergarments, were saturated and needed washing. I felt dirty, and there was no way I could clean myself. It was both humiliating and unbearable.

I started by saying to Suor Amadea, "Please help me. You name is Amadea, it means 'loved by God.'Get in touch with Don José Agostinho de Souza at the Portuguese Embassy as soon as possible." He had been appointed chargé d'affaires shortly before my imprisonment, when the Portuguese ambassador was away. She needed to write an anonymous letter describing the conditions under which I was living. Her assistance could save my life, I said with tears in my eyes. And the letter should be written in Portuguese so that if intercepted, few would understand its content.

Coming closer to my face, she conveyed with a bowing of her head that she would find a way.

It was only the following year that I found out what had happened. As editor of *Il Monitore Napoletano,* I was very close to the republican government. Curious, I asked a dear friend to find my old files. So, I had a chance to look at the correspondence about my case.

Suor Amadea's message had been, unfortunately, intercepted and the consequences for Don José had been disastrous. He was summoned to explain why a letter on my behalf had been addressed to him. He was told a conspiracy against the monarchy was underway, with me as one of its advocates. Thus, why was I, a person "guilty of opinion"—and currently under the custody of the Kingdom of Naples—soliciting his help?

Even more damaging for Don José's position at the Portuguese legation were the subversive letters found in my home at the time of my arrest. The envelopes addressed to me were inside envelopes addressed to him. It was clear he had allowed me, a private individual, to use the diplomatic mail service, an exclusive privilege for embassy personnel. De Souza had become, as a result, part of the "vast and profound" plot against the kingdom.

What followed was, for me, an unacceptable episode in Portuguese diplomacy. Don José explained himself in writing to Luis Pinto de Souza Coutinho, the Portuguese Minister of Foreign Affairs.

Don José defended his actions by saying he had known me, and my parents, since we had arrived in Naples, so many years earlier. He had attended my salon in recent years, as a family friend in the Portuguese community. He had been a friend of my parents; when they died, he had continued to befriend me. He said he had nothing to hide about those friendly visits. He had never heard, in either my parents' or my home, any conversation that was revolutionary in nature. He added, I might be accused of indiscretions, but never of a "plot" to abolish the monarchy.

He then stated that I had misused his trust. And that he was unaware of my correspondence's content because never in his life had he opened a letter that was not addressed to him. Thus, if I had been involved in subversive exchanges that involved the embassy, they had taken place without his consent.

Don José's letters to the Portuguese minister admitted that I had extraordinary gifts, superior culture and education, poetic ability, talent in foreign languages, and a most honorable code of ethics. Answering the question as to why I had asked him for clean linens, he replied he would likely help anyone in prison—not only me. He then added in his letter, "I suppose she has gone mad; this is no cause for surprise, given her vivacity; and to whoever is willing to consider her painful and very sad situation."

Those were the words of someone trying to save his own skin: as we say in Portuguese, *um pobre diabo*, a poor devil. Don José might have enjoyed my company and that of my parents, but he did not respect us—or me. For if he had, he wouldn't have said I had gone crazy. I felt insulted even though he had advised me to be cautious. His warning showed that he knew I was fighting for a cause I believed in. Already in his fifties, Don José was undoubtedly afraid to be declared persona non grata. He didn't want to be expelled from Naples, the place where he had lived for most of his life.

Don F. Nicola Pignatelli—the ambassador from the Kingdom of Naples to Portugal—did not behave better than Don José. He also tried to discredit me. He wrote in his diplomatic correspondence, "She is as erudite as crazy, reckless, and inept." He added the Portuguese minister of foreign affairs had informed the then prince regent of Portugal, about my arrest. Don Pignatelli had all the assurances he needed from Portugal that, if necessary, Don José would be recalled from his post and severely punished.

As the correspondence went on back and forth, the now frightened Don José started to cave in. Soon, he sent another letter to Lisbon stating that if I had been incarcerated, then undoubtedly the Kingdom of Naples had a good reason for doing so. He wrote, "I will dutifully reply to all questions and interrogations asked of me in this regard." The letter reiterated that the Kingdom of Naples and the Kingdom of Portugal should continue to help each other in matters of national safety.

When I saw this correspondence, Olympe de Gouges—the French writer—came to my mind. A woman like me, she did not conform to accepted societal roles. She wrote the Declaration of the Rights of Woman and the Female Citizen in 1791 and, bravely, dedicated the work to Marie Antoinette. Her text comprised seventeen articles on women's rights: rights to liberty, progress, property, security, and freedom from oppression. She even said women should have the right "to mount the scaffold."

While others— in America and Europe—were taking advantage of slavery and the slave trade, she penned *The Fortunate Shipwreck*, the first abolitionist play ever written in France. While giving people of color voices equal to their white peers, she simultaneously portrayed women and men as equals. She not only highlighted the barbarity of slavery and the slave trade but she put a slave on stage in the hero's role.

I admire Thomas Jefferson in America, and his Declaration of Independence, but Gouge's views on slavery are more progressive than his writings, in particular those expressed in *Notes on the State of Virginia*.

Like me, Olympe was accused of "revolutionary fever." Her

contemporaries couldn't understand how she changed from a provincial housewife into an incendiary revolutionary. She was singled out as a social deviant, a hysterical fury, and a monster—all because she had wanted to help forge a new and better society.

Olympe opposed Robespierre and she was beheaded during the Reign of Terror. I wonder—I live in permanent fear now—about what will happen to me. An official accusation might well be imminent. It is not that I fear death, as much as I long to live to fulfill my republican convictions and see Neapolitans freed from tyranny.

Sadly, the Kingdom of Portugal sealed my fate by ignoring my bleak future. No one from the embassy ever contacted me or intervened on my behalf. Living abroad, I had been in touch with Portugal my entire life, I considered myself a daughter of that nation. How much I now wished I had visited the land of my ancestors while free!

After the deplorable episode I exposed above, I knew I was officially alone. My disappointment was devastating—I felt outraged, heartbroken, and betrayed all at once. The Kingdom of Naples now had complete power over my life.

I was certain Portugal could have helped me. The then prince regent—the son of Queen Maria—could have intervened on my behalf. If the cause for my actions was labeled as insanity, then the prince was familiar with the result of fierce power struggles. From 1792 onward, his own mother had been declared insane, unfit to govern. He grieved openly over the fact that courtiers forced her out of power on claims of ineptitude. Reluctantly, he had begun signing state documents in her name. He knew the label of female insanity might be true—or false—depending on whose political side one took. Thus, he could have taken steps to save the daughter of one of his noble families, especially one located in a foreign land. Aware of my predicament, as he certainly was, he could have offered me refuge in our homeland. The practice was customary.

I had witnessed how European queens reacted differently to the French Revolution. While Carolina grew vicious—like Robespierre—Maria, called the pious, was so religious that she lost her grip on events. She saw evil and degeneration in every human being who didn't agree with her views. This is why she appointed the chief of police, the cruel Pina Manique, to do the dirty work of "saving" the kingdom from republicanism. I know many good people who were forced into exile during her reign. Joseph was a liberal, and afraid of imprisonment, he was forced to flee Lisbon in 1795.

The prince had seen his mother rant and rage in the Palace of Queluz, near Lisbon, where she had been confined. It was true that the queen adored her oldest son—called José after his grandfather—and had witnessed his horrible death by smallpox. She had refused, on her confessor's advice, to inoculate him, a practice some royal families had followed. I've been through a similar loss, I know the devastation of losing a beloved child. But while the prince showed benevolence toward his mother—why didn't he show it also toward me?

He decided I was a liability—and I know why. He headed a conservative monarchy, and every one considered him an undecided monarch. Like other European sovereigns, he was extremely afraid of the revolutionary principles of the French Revolution. He feared the French ambition for expansion and empire, and he particularly feared the French Army. Thus, there was no way he could offer refuge to a revolutionary—particularly a revolutionary woman. That in 1792 I had written an *oratória* entitled *La Fuga in Egitto, The Flight into Egypt,* a poem praising the first maternity of his wife, Carlota Joaquina, didn't count at this crucial moment of need for me.

The close ties between the royal families of Naples and Portugal—in addition to their political alliance—also counted for my demise. Carlota Joaquina was a member of the Bourbon family, a niece of King Ferdinando.

Thus, it turned out to be practically mandatory for the prince regent to let me rot in a Neapolitan prison.

After three months in the Vicaria, I still hadn't received a formal indictment.

A few days after our sovereigns fled into exile but before the French Army entered Naples, an angry mob forced open the heavy Vicaria gates—a similar event to what happened at July 14th, 1789, at the Bastille in Paris. The *lazzaroni,* the people of Naples, liberated all of us! Aware of the French impending entrance into Naples, they wanted everyone at home.

My release gave me the unexpected opportunity to be on hand when the French Army arrived in Naples. I joined my Jacobin friends and we excitedly gathered and waited for them in our principal fort, Sant'Elmo. Filled with joy, I wrote at this time the *Inno alla Libertà, Hymn to Freedom,* a revolutionary poem I imagined would be read in front of a crowd if a Neapolitan republic was ever declared. I chose an adaptation of the "La Marseillaise," the republican anthem of France. The music of Giovanni Viotti, an inspiration for the melody, had moved me since my youth. And its words always inflamed my heart: *"Aux armes, Citoyens!* To arms, Citizens!"

We didn't know the exact location of the French Army; communications were difficult and sporadic. But we knew they were very close. Finally, on January 22, 1799 the French arrived in the evening, under the brilliant Commander-in-Chief Jean Etienne Championnet. We had proclaimed the Neapolitan Republic the day before; the *Grande Nation,* the Great Nation, our inspiration and model, was with us! Championnet had been appointed by Napoleon Bonaparte—a member of the Directory—to enter Naples. We established a republican government that we called provisional. These were exciting and chaotic times all at once. I filled my heart with a sense of mission for a better future for our kingdom. The possibility was now real, I wanted liberty for all.

We didn't expect developments to be as bad as they turned out to be. Upheaval spread throughout the city itself and the nearby provinces. From the start, it was clear only we, the *literati,* wanted the French among us. The *lazzaroni,* forever loyal to Ferdinando and Carolina—and despite their escape—resented the foreign intervention and what they saw as their bizarre ways.

Although I had left the Vicaria weak in body, mind, and soul, my revolutionary zeal had doubled with the challenges that lay ahead for the nascent Republic.

Chapter 11

Joseph: Melancholy

I received your adieu with feelings of sincere regret at the loss we were to sustain, and particularly of those friendly visits by which you had made me so happy. I shall feel too the want of your counsel and approbation in what we are doing and have yet to do in our University. The last of my mortal cares and the last service I can render my country.
— Thomas Jefferson's letter to Joseph Correia da Serra,
    October 24, 1820

"My dear Mr. Jefferson, I apologize for arriving here unannounced, but I trust our friendship justifies my intrusion." Burwell ushered me to Jefferson's greenhouse, where I found him working in his workbench. It was a hot, humid, August day. To the eye, Jefferson embodied contentment. Orange, acacia, and lime trees in full bloom surrounded him. The light entering the area had a bright summer quality. Mockingbirds were singing; some were inside, others outside. I had entered my friend's sanctuary without a proper invitation.

"What a surprise to see you. Welcome!" Jefferson was undisturbed by my sudden arrival. "You know the same room is always ready for you when you wish to stay."

"I know this is a breach of etiquette, please pardon me. But I didn't have the time to contact you beforehand, it would've taken too long."

"You look flustered. Shall we have some cider? Our apples are delicious this year." Jefferson put his tools aside while asking me to have a seat. He then stepped out for a minute to ask Burwell to bring us drinks.

"I'm more melancholic than flustered," I said, pretending to be calm. "It's hard to believe my last visit here took place a couple of years ago! I've missed our conversations but, as you know, my work made it impossible to find time to visit you. My letters were also less frequent than I wished. I'm leaving for Brazil. I came here today to say goodbye to you and your family in person."

"But why, my dear and good friend?" Jefferson asked, biting his lip.

"I recently sent my resignation to my king. The last four years have been enough."

"I know your work hasn't been gratifying," Jefferson said. "President Monroe was here recently visiting his plantation, and we had a chance to discuss your nation's concerns with our administration."

"My pleas to the American government haven't been heard. Despite your friendship with the president, I doubt there is anything you can do." I said.

"I'd like to hear your side of the issue, if you please," Jefferson said, as cheerful as ever, as we now sipped the delicious cider.

"Simply put, Portuguese merchant ships are unable to sail the Atlantic Ocean safely. José Artigas—the Latin America revolutionary—captures our ships after recruiting crews made up of American pirates. He is a licensed privateer—and operates under an insurgent flag—both of which your authorities sanction," I said emphatically. "Then, Artigas sells our merchandise in the port of Baltimore with the knowledge, if not the approval, of its local administrators. Your government does nothing to stop these criminal activities."

Jefferson listened to me in silence. He then took another sip from his mug, giving me space to continue. "Latin American revolutionaries like Artigas are paid by supporters of Brazil's independence movements. Please understand, these people have no love for the Portuguese!" I finished on a note of exasperation.

"If the Portuguese hadn't invaded the so-called 'Banda Orien-

tal,'—you know, the area between the Uruguay and Paraná riv-
ers—to block revolutionary contamination, Artigas would not be
so committed to this fight," Jefferson answered in a suave voice.

"But again, the port of Baltimore is amassing huge profits from
the looting of Portuguese ships under Artigas's flags. When we
bring these cases to court—and I have brought many so far—your
judges fabricate excuses. Ultimately, your government is siding
with the privateers against the Luso-Brazilian empire," I said in a
higher pitch than I wished.

"I know how difficult the Portuguese cases brought to our maritime courts have been," Jefferson nodded. "The ships sailing under
the Artigas flags usually operate outside our waters."

"But, as I said, the crews Artigas hires are American and the
Portuguese goods are sold in Baltimore," I added. "This is robbery,
pure and simple."

As if to ease the heat that now simmered between us, Jefferson's
eighteen-year-old granddaughter Virginia suddenly entered the
greenhouse. I was grateful—the interruption gave me a moment
to quiet my anger. She also brought back the fond memory of my
latest visit to Jefferson and his family; I had brought Edward with
me at that time.

Virginia addressed me with her melodic voice. "I asked Burwell
where Edward was, and he said he hadn't come with you."

"I'm so sorry that Edward couldn't accompany me this time."

"Me too. I wanted to hear more stories, his adventures were so
entertaining." Virginia's voice was so musical that, as she spoke,
the mockingbirds sang louder. "Well, it's nice seeing you again."

The young woman didn't waste another moment of her time
with us. She stepped away to the south lawn through one of the
greenhouse's large open doors. I followed her trail to the garden and watched her move through the flowerbeds admiring the
blooms. She wore a blue summer dress, and I thought how youth
was so fresh and innocent, so full of promise. Patsy, her mother,
joined her shortly with the other children. We could hear them
talking and laughing.

A cloud moved across the sky and momentarily hovered above
the group. The atmosphere changed from sunny to overcast, creat-
ing a soft filmy shade. I happened to be admiring Virginia's blue

dress, when all of a sudden, all I could see was Eleonora in the Serra di Cassano's terrace the time we had kissed.

It took me a few minutes to return my attention to the greenhouse, and when I did, Jefferson continued our conversation. "You must understand that President Monroe—and his administration—are trying to solve this issue," Jefferson said, looking down at the floor instead of me.

"But my dear Sir, President Monroe and Congress aren't enforcing the Neutrality Act of 1817. The President and I have discussed this matter in Washington several times. We are a nation at peace with your nation, and these acts at sea are acts of war," I replied, my throat hoarse in reaction to Jefferson's remark. "We know why Mr. Monroe acts this way—it's because he supports Brazilian independence."

"If our theory of the 'American System' had ever been implemented, what you're describing would never have happened!" Jefferson stated.

"Our dream failed, as often happens. Having your fleet commanding the North Atlantic and our own fleet commanding the South has become impossible. Our countries have adopted different policies as far as the Atlantic is concerned," I said.

Jefferson handed me another mug of cider as if to assuage my feelings. And although he also replenished his own mug, his hand fidgeted with discomfort.

"The Portuguese merchandise is invaluable," I continued. "Precious metals and stones, gold and silver; coffee, sugar, wine, tobacco, and spices. This is why the coastal guards, the judges, and the merchants who sell the stolen goods all remain silent."

Jefferson sipped his cider and looked out at the small group still gathered in the garden. Then, his gaze turned to the cedar trees where the mockingbirds loved to park.

"I've asked Secretary of State John Quincy Adams to establish a joint commission between our nations to investigate the problem. Portugal demands an indemnity to cover damages," I said.

"You know the high regard I have for your king," Jefferson replied, evading the subject.

"But that has not helped the situation in any way," I said hotly, unable to contain myself.

I looked again at the flowerbeds to quiet my anger and see what Virginia and the others were doing outside, but they had left. I was fuming. The *joie de vivre*, the joy I had felt all my life while studying botany, was gone in the last years. My ambassadorship had given me status and income—but no pleasure. I didn't enjoy discussing with Jefferson the state of affairs between our nations. I was tired, worn out, and disappointed. There was no point in arguing further with Jefferson. It even risked damaging the beautiful relationship we had cultivated over the years. It should be enough for me that I had expressed my views, and that Jefferson realized how trying my last years had been.

Sooner or later, I thought, Jefferson would side with Monroe and his administration—if he hadn't already. Retired for many years now, Jefferson's political influence had probably diminished, making it doubtful he could help my cause. I had to look at the situation as a fact of life: Jefferson and Monroe were Americans, planters, and neighbors. It was only natural they sided with each other. The University of Virginia filled Jefferson's days now, and he wanted the premises to open as soon as possible. The project had been chartered, and several European professors had been hired. His many plantations—not only Monticello—his correspondence, and his family were enough to fill the remainder of his time on earth.

I had come to say goodbye and to preserve my friendship with Jefferson. Always the gentleman, I was grateful he hadn't mentioned what the newspapers were saying. It tormented me that even the *National Intelligencer*, the first national newspaper, democratic and republican, supported the government's position on the piracy of our ships. They called me a *philosophe* who had become an agent of despotism. The paper's claims tore at me, saying things like: "It's inconceivable that a man of liberal ideas, a philosopher as well as a scientist, should oppose the emancipation of the people in South America." These attacks stabbed my soul with words instead of a knife. I was powerless to make these reporters understand the position our king wanted for Brazil within the community of nations.

Jefferson could sense my distress and sought to ease it by turning the conversation to Edward. He knew how much I cherished and warmed up to the topic. For a while, we chatted about my son.

The former president and Edward had related beautifully during our brief visit a couple of years back. I was pleased with my son's flawless French manners. Jefferson had gathered Patsy and his grandchildren to meet Edward. That first night at the dinner table, he had seated Edward between his granddaughters, Virginia and Mary, closest to Edward in age. Then, kindly, he asked Edward all sorts of questions.

"Are you enjoying America, young man?"

"Yes, my time at St. Mary's College in Baltimore has been superb," Edward said. "It took a bit of time to follow the classes in English, but now I'm doing well."

"Edward only spoke French when he arrived," I said. "But the Benedictine fathers are learned and demanding, a good combination."

"That's the kind of environment I had at William and Mary," Jefferson said. Then turning to Edward he added. "I've invited your father, in fact your family, to live here in my house and teach at the University of Virginia. Sadly, I've been unable to convince him."

"I know how much he honors your friendship," Edward replied.

"What are your plans after St. Mary's?"

"I'd like to study medicine like my grandfather."

"Not following in your father's shoes?"

"No, I'd like to be independent from kings and presidents."

"Wise of you," Jefferson said.

What a wonderful son I had! His words showed he understood my own tribulations—past and present—and had taken them into account when making his own career choices. I thought about the letter I had written to him about Queen Maria, years before. He must have given it full consideration and thus decided to turn away from unwanted compromises.

"In what language do you two communicate?" Virginia asked.

"Portuguese, as my father wishes," Edward said with a note of complaint.

"Could you say a few words to each other, so that we hear the sound of the language?" Virginia said.

"Of course," I replied. I told Edward in Portuguese that I loved him and that he was doing very well during his first visit to Monticello. Then I said our host's grandchildren already liked him. Edward translated this into English, and we all had a good laugh.

Virginia said Portuguese was very musical.

"It's good for Edward to have a certain degree of fluency in Portuguese. It's my wish that he read our classics in the original, particularly Luis de Camões and António Vieira. These are good writers, worth reading for different reasons. Camões was our veneered great poet; Vieira lived in Brazil and wrote about that vast region, slavery included."

I added I had found a good way to increase Edward's interest in the language. Father Pierre Babad, a Frenchman and St. Mary's teacher of Spanish and Portuguese, was writing the first Portuguese grammar in America and, whenever the two of us discussed the book's progress, I brought Edward along. Since both Father Babad and Edward were native speakers of French, they enjoyed a freer conversation when discussing the intricacies of Portuguese. I finished by saying that Portuguese was a language spoken throughout the Portuguese empire—the vast territory of Brazil included— and a useful tool for Edward in the future. He might even end up in Brazil one day. Edward made a face as if to say he certainly hoped not.

I then asked Edward to tell our friends the adventure we had just had the night before arriving in Monticello. Edward described how first our coachman had lost his way more than once in the journey from Washington to Virginia. Even worse, at one point he had plunged us to the cliff edge of a steep ravine and the carriage had lost one of its wheels. The accident had been terrifying. From there, we had to go on horseback to the nearest inn. Luckily, there had been a fiddle festival in the neighborhood that day, and the people walking along the road came to our assistance.

We stayed at the local inn—close to Fredericksburg but still in the middle of nowhere—while the coach's wheel got repaired. The fiddle festival had brought many musicians to the area and our inn was filled with travelers. Until well past midnight, everyone drank beer, talked, and some played the fiddle in the small main room. The music made a lively, enjoyable scene. Pipes filled with tobacco were passed around for everyone to have a taste. Since the pipes belonged to the inn and could be used for free, smokers paid only for the tobacco they consumed. The smoky room made it hard to breathe, but the fiddlers played beautifully, making up for the smell.

But then things took a turn for the worse when we wanted to go to sleep. As there were no single beds or free rooms, Edward and I had to share the last available bed in a room with many others. The straw mattress was hard, and before lying down on it, we inspected it carefully for fleas. We slept, of course, with our street clothing on. The following day we paid the innkeeper for our bed, the beer we drank, and the candles on the nightstand.

Jefferson's grandchildren clearly enjoyed Edward's story, and realized how fortunate they were to live in the comfort of their home. When it was time to go to bed, I retired to my usual room, and Patsy led Edward upstairs to the family's quarters. Before retiring that night, Edward came down to say goodnight once more.

"I want to thank you for introducing me to Jefferson and his family as your son," he said.

I knew he didn't like to be introduced as my nephew or secretary, despite my vow of celibacy. With genuine affection, we hugged each other good night.

When we finished talking about Edward, Jefferson suggested we take a stroll on the south lawn. My anger had abated as it always happened when Edward was in my mind. As we walked outside the greenhouse, the children were gone but the mockingbirds were still singing. I enjoyed hearing them. Jefferson now wanted news from Washington and our common friends.

Philadelphia, America's cultural capital, had always been exciting to me, just like Paris, but Jefferson's presidency was centered in the recently established political capital. He had ruled benignly over the small town, and had many friends there. To me, Washington was a nuisance. Its obsequious officials and I didn't get along well. My only solace in such an environment was the diplomatic circuit—cocktail and dinner parties that made time there pass quicker. My duties as Portuguese ambassador had been tumultuous and unsatisfying, and my private life hadn't flourished either. I had to deal with two major issues that never ended. Some diplomats felt suspicious dealing with a priest. It made my work more difficult. The other issue was my lack of a permanent home. As Edward was boarding at St. Mary's, I had only to worry about my own lodgings.

Jefferson asked me about Robert Walsh Jr, the editor of the *American Review*; I had once introduced them to each other. I replied that Mr. and Mrs. Walsh were doing fine, but that of late I hadn't seen them. The truth was Walsh and I had had a rupture, and, from his question, I gathered no one had told him about it. In fact, that was another reason for my misery those recent years in America. Walsh had suggested that his family and I rent a house together. I had found this an excellent solution to my lack of a home base. We agreed on how to divide expenses and ended up moving into a nice place on Brent Street. The arrangement lasted for less than six months—and its failure was my fault.

I didn't feel entirely comfortable in the new set up, but could manage it. The Walshes and I moved in the same social circles. Sharing a home with them was far better than remaining in the boarding houses and hotels where I had been staying before. Mrs. Walsh was a fine lady and a distinguished hostess, and the Walsh children delightful. Robert Walsh was a well-known author, editor, and critic; he had published an article of mine, "General Considerations upon the Past and Future State of Europe," in his magazine. Since I met frequently with members of the American government, the arrangement suited Walsh's appetite for news. My contacts gave him direct access to information he might otherwise not have obtained. When guests visited, we discussed politics, trade, religion, the law, and many other topics.

Walsh had a self-righteous character, and this increasingly annoyed me as time passed. He was a practicing Catholic and the whole family attended Sunday Mass. It surprised him that I always had something more important to do than accompany them to the weekly service. I was the man of the cloth, after all. On Sundays, I liked to rest the aches and pains of old age; I read scientific journals on botany; and I put my correspondence in order. More than once Walsh criticized me for being the priest in our household but not an observant Catholic as he was.

Walsh knew I didn't want to discuss the topic, so he always took the opportunity to "educate" me on my faith when we had company. Once, while we were having dinner with several friends from the diplomatic corps, Walsh asked my views on *The Garden of the Soul,* a book by the English Catholic bishop Richard Challoner.

When I said the book was a masterpiece, Walsh shook his head in disagreement. He proceeded to lecture me on how the spiritual exercises we planted in the soil of our soul made it possible for religious growth to take place. Sunday Mass was another moment of the same practice, he added. When I replied that Northern Europeans, such as Bishop Challoner, were stricter about the rules of our faith than we Southern Europeans—adding that I confessed my sins only to God—he took further umbrage.

Since I didn't want to speak about this detail with Jefferson, I mentioned only that the dinner parties at the Brent house had always been very engaging. I then mentioned a dinner with Mr. and Mrs. Jack Smith one evening, not long ago. Smith worked on foreign policy under Secretary of State John Quincy Adams, and I stressed to him the fact that we had demanded an indemnity for the merchandise stolen from our ships and sold in Baltimore. I wanted Smith to know that I had insisted with the Secretary of State that a joint commission be appointed to study the issue in order to reach a conclusion. Our king was waiting for deliberation on this matter.

Jefferson didn't want to commit himself one way or the other.

Nor did I want to discuss John Quincy Adams with Jefferson. He was a powerful Secretary of State, and his views on Brazil's independence were always veiled, though quite clear. He considered Brazil corrupted by Catholicism, Iberian traditions, and the tropical climate. He saw the king of Portugal as degenerate, decadent, and depraved. I wouldn't ever tell Jefferson that I reciprocated Adam's low opinion of us: I considered him—a typical New Englander—cold, austere, and insensitive to the needs of the Luso-Brazilian Empire.

Adams had also discredited Jefferson and me on the idea of establishing an 'American System.' In Adams' view, his government was better off without a maritime alliance with the United Kingdom of Portugal and Brazil. In fact, he said, the two nations shared no common interests.

We came back to the greenhouse and Jefferson got to the workbench to re-arrange his tools. "Now that you've resigned your ambassadorship, what are your plans for the future?" he asked.

"I'm still unsure about the exact day of my departure for Brazil.

I plan to travel via London—Edward is coming with me—and we'll revisit the city for a short while. This will be my first time in Brazil. I want to serve my crown with whatever energy my advanced age still allows. The United Kingdom of Portugal and Brazil turned me into a South American."

"I suspect the king has a good position waiting for you."

"Yes, I've already been named to the Council of State."

"I remember thinking when you were appointed ambassador, how sweet life would be, at last, for you. How you would finally have sufficient funds to live on."

"Unfortunately, I've failed in my mission here. How I wish I had been able to strengthen the relations between our two countries; the countries I've loved most in my life. Just think how I loved the American Republic as much as I loved the Portuguese monarchy,"

"We consider you a father of our Republic. Your contribution to the American Philosophical Society has been substantial. And you have linked the Old and the New World in the field of botany. You are at home in every science."

"You honor me," I said.

"By the way, I gave the society the Lewis diaries that you recovered from Dr. Barton's widow and sent to me," Jefferson continued.

"I'm pleased I could help you to recover a few of them. I see you, my dear Sir, as the embodiment of the republican virtues I've always admired. You have imprinted this country with your beautiful and noble character. I'm only afraid that they might disappear without you one day," I said.

My host stood silent as if waiting to hear more, so I continued, "You recall, no doubt, how cheerful I was when I first arrived in this land. I believed in the American dream. I feel American now—perhaps as much as you do. That is why I deem it appropriate to have the Portuguese monarchy based in South America. An enlightened king is as virtuous as a republican president."

Jefferson kept his thoughts to himself, and so I finished quickly, "We'll see what happens." And then I asked, "Do you recall Andrada e Silva—the scholar the Lisbon academy paid to make a scientific tour of Europe? Do you know where he is now? Back in Brazil, a rebel working for its independence."

Jefferson nodded, "Is that so?" But he wasn't inclined to proceed with the discussion. He knew that I knew he had met many Brazilian insurgents when he was politically active.

"Why don't we take a walk and see the magnolias in the grove? We planted them together." As I agreed, Jefferson said, "The shrubs were doing well the last time I saw them. They will remain the symbol of our everlasting friendship."

I told Jefferson that if I had been born in North America, I would have wanted to be a Virginian like him. He replied to my words with a broad smile.

Chapter 12

Eleonora: Crossroads

At the Vicaria Prison, Castel Capuano, outskirts of Naples, August 13, 1799

My contribution to the Neapolitan Republic was to be the editor-in-chief of the newspaper *Il Monitore Napoletano*, from February to June 1799, a short five months. Ours was probably the first republic of *philosophes* the world had ever seen. We were called the Parthenopean Republic, after the Greek colony that once existed where Naples now stands. Our newspaper had a political intent: to report news about the activity of the newly established provisional government. The predominant theme of my writing was the cause of liberty. It was consuming work all day long. Once a week, I continued holding my salon. As I started my new work, I decided, on a whim, to cut my hair short, ending at the nape of my neck. I loved it! The style was called "à la guillotine," following the new French style. Many French women were now cutting their hair to show solidarity for those who had been beheaded.

Was I naive? Was I courageous? I didn't give such thoughts much consideration, I simply believed in what I was doing.

If I perish, I hope the thirty-five issues of *Il Monitore* will survive me; each issue had about four hundred copies. We sent copies to France regularly, I trust they will not disappear. I'd like to think my political persona will outshine the ages. Like the Neapolitan sunshine: it will remain here, even if I succumb. Like Mount Vesuvius: it will stay here even if I depart. I always had a pedagogical intent; I never incited people to violence.

I hoped all along the French would protect us—us, the citizens of Naples, living in their Neapolitan sister republic. But in June of 1799, the French Army received orders from the Directory in Paris to withdraw from the city. The excuse was that they were needed somewhere else. In reality, the Directory was divided as to how prioritize the French revolutionary expansion under way. Moreover, the French Army needed financing to sustain the troops on the ground. Naples had no money to give them, the crown had left for Palermo with all that the royal banks had. Without French military protection it was practically impossible for our Republic to survive. During the following five months—with chaos spreading throughout the city—the French presence in Naples became, gradually, untenable.

As it turned out, Cardinal Fabrizio Ruffo, on Ferdinando's orders, assembled an army of volunteers called the *Santafede*, the Defenders of the Holy Faith. These were a bunch of brigands recruited in the southern regions of the Italian peninsula. Armed with a banner of throne and altar, and with the white Bourbon cockade set in a crucifix, they invaded Naples by land. The Republic was unable to resist their might after the French departure, which had taken place only a few days earlier. Admiral Nelson—the new self-appointed commander of the Mediterranean Sea—completed Cardinal Ruffo's work with the help of the British fleet at the head of his warship, the *Foudroyant*. This detail is important: Nelson returned to Naples from Palermo with Lord and Lady Hamilton aboard his vessel. They were overseeing conditions in the city for the safe return of the king and queen.

I was with the republican government in Sant'Elmo's fort—the same place where we had greeted the French—when we surrendered. With Ruffo's approval, both sides signed an armistice, or capitulation, with various foreign powers witnessing the event. But the terms of the agreement, regrettably, failed to be enforced. Otherwise I would not be here in this filthy cell, possibly facing death. The signed treaty stipulated that we were allowed to do as we pleased: either remain in Naples and renounce political life forever, or depart for exile in France, never to return.

As the negotiations were under way, something unforeseen—and unimaginable!—took place. The *lazzaroni* of Naples are sanguine, and they roamed the city not only seeking revenge but shouting, "Death to the Jacobins!" Bloodshed ensued. We republicans tried to go into hiding but many of us were caught. Jacobins were forced from their houses, killed, and their heads paraded on spikes throughout the city. The carnage was similar to when the French had entered Naples—only worse. Since the national banks were empty, life had been difficult for all. Prices for food shot up and the *lazzaroni* had been, of course, suffering the most. Barbarically, they resorted to cannibalism and the practice spread in Naples. And who did they eat? The Jacobins.

I left Sant'Elmo fort with the provisional government and we all marched out with guarantee of safe conduct and military honors. The few remaining French troops still in the city escorted us out. Other republicans—sheltered in the city's remaining forts—left their strongholds under the same terms. We were led to the bay, where transport ships for those who chose exile in France were waiting. We would be departing for Toulon.

The French had left by land but, even with the armistice signed, we still hoped they would return by sea to safeguard our lives. A blockade by Admiral Nelson was under way, however, organized to prevent that possibility. Our bay was filled with foreign warships that, surrounding the British fleet, were ready to support the Bourbons' return to Naples. Far in the distance, I saw some vessels bearing the name of the language I had always spoken at home: *Principe Perfeito, Rainha de Portugal, Afonso de Albuquerque,* and *San Sebastian.* It was clear now: the Portuguese fleet, earlier stationed in the Mediterranean Sea under the Marquis de Nisa, had arrived in Naples to support Admiral Nelson's plan against the French.

Under royal military watch, lines had been set up in Castel dell'Ovo, a fortress by the bay, for us republicans to sign various documents. I had chosen exile, fearing for my life. Before I was ushered to the *San Sebastian* with various companions—we were all in chains—I put my signature on a couple of lists that bore my name agreeing that, if exiled, I would never return to Naples. I had surrendered—the monarchy had my agreement to never engage in subversive activities in Naples again.

I intended to keep my promise. Under the circumstances, what future lay ahead for me there?

Poor Admiral Francesco Caracciolo, the distinguished naval officer who joined the republicans and commanded our fleet! Admiral Nelson—his orders promulgated from the *Foudroyant*—had him hanged from the yard-arm of the *Minerva*, the ship he once proudly commanded.

There was a hot, strong wind at sea the day I boarded the *San Sebastian*, and we were told we could only sail away when it abated. We were terrified to hear what had happened to Caracciolo. It showed not only Admiral Nelson's lack of mercy, but also his thirst for revenge. Was he, more than Cardinal Ruffo, in control of events now? The only sign we had of that possibility was that, in one of those evenings, a few vessels belonging to the British fleet came closer to the *San Sebastian*. They seemed in control of events.

My dear friend, the medical doctor Domenico Cirillo, had been thrown next to me in the lower deck. In the past, I'd always enjoyed the cheerful stories of his friendship with Benjamin Franklin. Deeply worried now, he couldn't figure out the reason for the delay in our departure. It seemed to Cirillo that upon Nelson's return to the bay aboard the *Foudroyant*, he had replaced Cardinal Ruffo in deciding the city's future. Distraught, he confessed he had pleaded for his life through Lady Hamilton. He had taken care of her, and her mother, for so many years that he hoped his case would be heard.

A couple of days later, while we were still waiting for departure, the inexplicable happened. A group of soldiers came inside the brig and called out a few names. I was one of them. It seemed clear what was happening: the previous orders had been reversed. Those who had played major roles in the Republic, like myself, were ordered back to land. It didn't matter anymore we had signed documents agreeing never to set foot in Naples again. Now, only those who had played minor roles in the Republic were allowed to remain in the vessel. I refused to walk out of the *San Sebastian*, so I had to be carried out with feet up in the air. Behind me, Dr. Cirillo, with a panic-stricken face, was kicking the soldiers who had grabbed him.

I was brought back to the Vicaria prison. This time Suor Amadea della Valle was at the entrance's loggia, she seemed to be waiting for my arrival. The soldiers removed my chains and she escorted me to the cell I'm in, in the jail's basement. This cell is not much different from the one I earlier described in the *panaro*. Her eyes expressed a grief hard to put into words. Did she already know my fate, even if I didn't?

When we entered the empty cell, she had two nuns bring in an old straw mattress, a table and a chair. Then she told them they could leave. Immediately after, she took from one of her pockets parchment paper, a quill, and a glazed ceramic flask of ink. She also handed me a black leather case, which included a small pocket in the back. It surprised me that a nun's large skirt could contain so many provisions.

Slowly, she sat down in the chair and told me that, if I wanted, I could write. Leaning down, she opened the table's only drawer and directed me to look inside. There was a hidden compartment in the back, and she easily opened it with a knock against the dark wood. She told me to write only at night—and to leave my writings and implements in the secret compartment at all times.

I only nodded my head in gratitude.

Perhaps this was her way of giving back, for as soon as *Il Monitore* came out, I always sent her a copy hoping she passed on the newspapers to her prisoners.

With a caring expression, eyes cast down, Suor Amadea said that the Giunta di Stato, the High Court of State, had been appointed by King Ferdinando who was still in Palermo. My case would be brought to trial soon. She didn't know yet where, but probably I would be escorted downtown, back and forth, for the hearings. She voiced surprise at the speed with which the appointed judges had already started to work in the case of other rebels.

Then, she quickly kissed me on the cheek and left. I only saw her once again.

Left alone in my dingy cell, I felt dejected at the fall of our hard-earned Republic. I longed for the times I was addressed as Citizen, not Marquise Pimentel. I was proud of my revolutionary work; I wanted liberty and equality for all. I just hope the judges have read *Il Monitore* as I intended it to be: the plea of a Neapolitan *literata* for the people of Naples to embrace the Republic as the supreme form of government.

To keep my mind active, I recite words from my articles in *Il Monitore*, for they still fill my heart: "Finally we are free and for us the day has come when we too can pronounce the sacred words liberty, and equality, and announce ourselves to the Mother Republic as their worthy offspring, and to the free peoples of Italy and Europe, as its worthy brothers and sisters."

The "free people of Italy" were the Jacobin Republics established by the French in the northern territories—in places like Venice, Milan, Genoa, and Bologna during the *Triennio* (1796–1799), the three years of revolutionary control of Italy by revolutionary France—the Jacobin period of Italy.

I addressed the people directly in my work. I said: "I hope that the plebe (the lowest of the low, the *lazzaroni*) might, with the help of the people (popolo), get to the cultural and instructional level of the latter."

I knew that the *lazzaroni* were vulgar and brutish. I knew that they didn't trust us, the republican *literati*. I despaired at their wretchedness; ignorant, knowing no better, they worshipped the monarchy and wanted it back. Nevertheless, I remained at their side to the very end. I admired their strength, their vitality, even if misguided. I wrote: "Justice demands that the *lazzaroni* be educated, more than condemned, and it is never too late to instruct them."

I exercised the most balanced position in page after page. In the last few issues, I addressed the people as *Majestas Populi,* the people as sovereign. I called for unity: "I have appealed to the courage of all. Because liberty cannot be loved in half…and cannot produce its effects until everyone is free."

Yes, I repeat to this day, liberty is not only for the entitled. The *lazzaroni* of Naples needed education to understand this. In France, the literacy rate is almost half of the male population and one-third of the female; but here, in Naples, only the *literati* are able to read and write.

I called for rooms for public instruction, places where the republican ideals could be taught along with the singing of patriotic songs. I wanted puppet shows with new story lines in the streets, to show there were other characters besides Pulcinella. I wanted "gazettes," sheets of paper to be read aloud in piazzas for those who couldn't read or write. I wanted to edit revolutionary catechisms, texts that went beyond the Bible and explained the beauty of classic literature. Yes, the alphabet would be printed in the back, as Suor Amadea had once wanted in the catechisms she had chosen at Palazzo Reale.

In order to fulfill this idea, I studied the dictionary of Neapolitan dialect that Ferdinando Galiani once wrote. I covered again all its grammar, syntax, and spelling. I knew it from before, I had written verses in dialect. But now I wanted to communicate with the *lazzaroni* in their native tongue, understand the way they talked to each other. If we talked the same language, we could create a strong bond. Galiani had already died, but I recalled with pride the time I had accompanied him to the San Carlo Royal Theater. I recalled also Joseph, how he followed his footsteps enthusiastically and wanted to become, like him, a diplomat.

I had to word carefully my criticism of the French stationed in the city. There were things they did that I didn't approve of. Above and foremost, they always wanted to see the *Il Monitore*'s issues before they went to print. I saw this is a form of censorship. But there were many other issues, equally bothersome. The French insisted we use the republican calendar to number the issues. André Thouin, from the Jardin des Plantes, had turned the season's drawings into works of art. I admired his idea of honoring the natural world, and of using the seasons as the new reference point. But the new dates were confusing to the *lazzaroni;* in addition they saw them as a foreign imposition. I had abandoned Catholicism—but they hadn't. They enjoyed our traditional calendar with the depiction of the days the Catholic saints where born and died. In their superstition, saints, more than nature, had divine powers.

I half-won this fight because I succeded in my request. *Il Monitore* was printed with the dates of both calendars.

A major problem concerned the conduct of the French troops stationed in our city. The tension never abated while they stayed with us. Unfortunately, they behaved far from honorably. Entering Naples had been an expensive military operation. The French demanded that we pay heavy sums for their help in sustaining our Republic. We had no way to satisfy their greed. After crossing the upper part of the Italian Peninsula, the troops were starved. They demanded food, but we were short of supplies, even for ourselves. I hinted at these problems in several of my issues, mindful not to antagonize them. To accumulate the amounts they demanded, the troops entered our churches and palaces and stole many of our national treasures. Those riches, I asserted, must be returned to Naples as soon as possible.

I also reported on the hostility of the *lazzaroni* toward the French troops. This problem was political and never abated, as much as I tried; and it was worse in the provinces than in Naples. There were constant armed insurrections with fierce street fighting. Many lives were lost. I tried to increase acceptance of the Republic, regardless of how fragile and unstable it appeared to all. For me, self-reliance and independence was, with each passing day, more and more imperative. This is why, perhaps naively, I said "We are free, at last," when the French troops left. I truly didn't realize what was about to descend upon our city.

I had lost my Catholic faith, but I still hoped the clergy would be active in educating the masses in the new republican principles. This is why I joyfully reported on our patron saint San Gennaro, and his miracle. When the saint's blood, kept in phials, liquefied in our cathedral—as it had happened each year from time immemorial—I wanted everybody to view the event as an omen of divine protection for our republic.

One of our readers was Queen Carolina in Palermo, I heard she grabbed the issues as soon as they came out. It seems she considered this the best way to be informed about the work of the provisional government. But she called *Il Monitore* "*a documento d'orrore,*" a horror document. Well, since I entered the Vicaria for the first time, I consider her to be, herself, horror personified. I also addressed Cardinal Ruffo as the "Monster Cardinal" in my last issues. And that is who he was, the way he invaded our city with his army of ruffians.

Suor Amadea visited me for a few minutes yesterday. She was very pale, as white as the starched white wimple that covers most of her face. She held my hands as she spoke. She said she wanted to inform me that King Ferdinando had triumphantly returned to the city. She had heard that Carolina was still in Palermo, too frightened to bring the children back. The monarch was saluted by horns, sirens, and cheers from all the foreign warships anchored in the bay. Many *lazzaroni* had welcomed the king in large hordes, rowing out their small dinghies near the royal flotilla. Others saluted him with white handkerchiefs from the bay's many quays. Afraid, the king had not disembarked, but he waved to his people from afar.

She excused herself for bringing such bad news and left as pale, or paler, than she had come in. As she was leaving she took a rosary out of her large pocket and asked me if I wanted it. I declined the kind offer but thanked her.

Today has been warm and humid, and its sticky moisture reached this basement. I had a strange vision after Suor Amadea left. I was washing myself, maybe a way to get rid of the alarming update about the king's return. I enjoyed such moments of luxury! Men and boys of the lower classes often jump into the bay for a scrub. I would gladly do that now, if I could, despite my decorum. Or I'd settle for my old steel tub, where I could lie back and relax in lukewarm water with a piece of glycerin soap. Or even better—I might wash with a bar of palm, honey, or coconut oil. How soothing those smells would be. After my bath, I might even write a good poem, like in the old days.

I miss the canary I once kept in Sant'Anna di Palazzo, he always sang along as I splashed in my bath water. I miss the sunshine, the darkness here is hard on me. Without it, I'm a flower deprived of water. I miss my walks to the fish market going along the *pedamentina*, the streets made of stone steps.

Now that the king is back in Naples, the likelihood I will be executed is strong.

My thoughts bring on a loneliness I've never experienced before. The unknown feels intolerable. I think of my dearest brothers, Miguel and José. I don't know where they are but I hope they went into hiding to be safe. They were never as outspoken as I, but they'll be suspects for being my relatives. If I am charged for treason, the charges are enough to imprison and condemn them for life. I couldn't care less that Michele has become a magistrate; I never had anything to say to him after our engagement ended.

I have too much time to think, to wonder—will Joseph ever answer my letter? There's still time, and I hope he will. I sent him a desperate missive to London, where he's living now, asking him to intercede on my behalf. The British papers reported often Admiral

Nelson's support of our monarchy in the Mediterranean Sea. He must know about my work in *Il Monitore* and the republican surrender.

The channel I used to reach Joseph was not the Portuguese legation in Naples. I no longer wanted to deal with them. I wouldn't go into minute detail about what I did to send that letter, for I don't wish to endanger the young Portuguese sailor who helped me and deserves my highest esteem. His eyes showed compassion for a woman in chains. I loved his wave of dark hair that fell over his forehead, and imagined my son Francesco might have looked like him if he had grown to adulthood. I don't think the young man realized the danger I placed him in by asking for help.

The two of us whispered at night during his shift watching the prisoners. Unable to sleep, I first enjoyed just looking at him. Soon, he noticed me, the only female prisoner. I couldn't get enough air, so I asked to be moved closer to the door where he stood. He obliged. Then I asked for a sip of water, and we started to converse. He confided about the voluminous correspondence between Lady Hamilton, lodged in Admiral Nelson's *Foudroyant*, and Queen Carolina, still quartered in Palermo. He knew Portuguese ships were carrying several letters a day, back and forth, between the two women. He said the sailors couldn't figure out why there was so much to share. I smiled at the comment, remembering the intimate scene I had witnessed between the two women when I was the queen's librarian. But why would the sailors know about this?

Returning to Joseph and my letter to him. He thought of me as a lofty idealist in my youth. I now see that as a compliment. I believed then, and still do now, in dreams of renewal and redemption. If he, too, believes in them, then he'll try to save me.

We had such an enjoyable time while studying Latin with Professore Grassi! When we read Dante's *La Divina Commedia*, I felt exalted reading his description of Beatrice in Canto 30: "Thus in the boson of a cloud of flowers..."

If I ever get out of these prison walls alive, I hope to see Joseph again. He is not, though, a romantic fantasy anymore. Louis-René is and, if I set my feet in France, I will find him. I adore pronouncing his name now. For strength, I roll it between my tongue and the ceiling of my mouth. I'm ready to start a new life at forty-seven, my longings are still intact. I marvel how I can feel such attraction to a man at my age. I never imagined my sensuality could ignite again after the passion I felt for Joseph in my youth.

The hot wind of the last few days seems to have abated. Are my republican friends still waiting to depart Naples for Toulon? Or have they sailed away already? How I wish I could go with them, be far away! Even if our Republic failed, the French one still stands—and I hope it will last forever.

I loved my parents, Uncle António, my brothers, and my late, darling Francesco. I loved my poetry, my books, and the revolutionary ideal of liberty. I loved the *lazzaroni* in this city, and the Jacobin republicans who fought at my side to improve their lot. And I loved the city of Naples, the city where, in the end, my dreams collapsed.

I believe in humanity. The question that first prompted me to write this memoir now has a simple answer: what turned me into a revolutionary? The sum of my life.

I have another question to answer, maybe an impossible one: how do I see myself in relation to other women? As an equal; with the advantage of an education. So, perhaps, a better question is: how do I see myself in relation to men? The answer is the same: as an equal; with the advantage of an education. And where do I stand, despite all that has happened to me, if I still believe in humanity? I stand proud of my femininity, of my work, and of my moral and political involvement in the controversies of my time and place. I crossed from the private into the public sphere as few women have done.

It's still the night, dawn has not appeared on the horizon yet. My cell is windowless, but I see through the cracks of the door that there is hardly any light coming through the corridor.

Oh my God, something is happening—something different. Why are there male voices in the distance singing "Il Canto Dei Sanfedisti," the royalist chant that celebrates the return of the monarchy?

Am I dreaming? Am I hallucinating? Today is the thirteenth of the month, thirteen is a number I never liked, it forebodes bad luck.

And why am I hearing steps in the distance? Soldiers' steps, stomping the cold stone pavement with soiled boots.

How many are there? Are they coming for me? I hope not. My memoir isn't finished, I have more to say. But I'd better hide it now and lie down on my mattress. Wait—I need to sign it first, for who knows how close my end really is.

Eleonora Fonseca Pimentel

Chapter 13

Joseph: Contemplation

I have a friend in Portugal, in whose welfare I feel great interest.... It is the Abbé Corrêa.... If [he is] at Lisbon, and it should ever fall your way to render him a service or kindness, I should consider it as more than if done to myself.
—Thomas Jefferson's letter to General Henry Dearborn,
    October 31, 1822

To enjoy the fresh air, my son and I have been sitting in the Royal Botanical Garden of Lisbon. September is my favorite month here, when nature is quiet and balmy. What a fine young man Edward is at eighteen! Needless to say, I'm wearing my cassock again. I had abandoned it while I lived in America, but here I must adhere to social conventions. I'm a priest, I'll die one. Edward and I arrived in Lisbon more than a year ago, more precisely on August 6, 1821; I had lived abroad for twenty-six years.

This is Lisbon's garden par excellence; it is small, cozy, and a delight to my soul. It is located on one of the city's seven hills, close to the Royal Palace in Ajuda. Edward and I enjoy sitting on the wooden bench placed under the famous botanical specimen, the *dragoeiro* or Dracaena Draco. Its shade gives me the spiritual nourishment I deserve—and need—at this stage in my life. Its trunk secretes a reddish resin, a substance called dragon's blood. When I examine the tree's outer bark, it reminds me how rich my life has been, despite its misfortunes. The sap of the *dragoeiro* is used to stain certain pieces of wood, one of them the Stradivarius violin. Jefferson would enjoy this detail, he loves music. I keep myself alive coming here as much as I can, hoping my blood reinvigorates my body, if only for a little while longer.

"Over a year has passed and I'm still shocked by the course of events. We should have been in Rio de Janeiro, instead we ended up in Lisbon," I say to Edward after taking a sip of water with lemon peel I had brought in a traveling jar. "I wish I'd been informed about the independence of Brazil—and the king's return to Portugal—while we were still in America. It continues to appall me how ships with news take so long to reach their destination."

Edward replies, "Brazilian independence changed the course of our lives forever, there's nothing you could have done about it."

"It's lucky our beloved King João swore a liberal constitution before being allowed to set foot back in Portugal." I look up at the tree's shade as if to ask for divine protection. "The new law of our land made me very happy. It appeased the people, and probably prevented an uprising."

"But the French executed Louis XVI even after he signed a similar document," Edward says.

"I'm confident all will go well here. Besides, I never imagined the king would bestow so many honors, financial and otherwise, upon me." I caress my son's hand. "Fortunately, you'll soon be in Paris to study medicine."

"I'm excited to return to France after all these years," Edward agrees. "I find life here disagreeable. The city's dirty and provincial. The illiteracy and the superstition bother me."

"You were brought up in Paris and enjoyed America, both more forward looking. You know, it's only now I feel vindicated for the sacrifices I've made all my life."

"You should. There's a reason you're called the Benjamin Franklin of Portugal."

"Maybe my originality of mind and simplicity of manners led to that designation," I continue. "If you were to remain in Lisbon, you'd always face the stigma of being the son of a priest."

"I never liked it when you hid in America that I'm your son." Edward returns my tender touch. "I'm not ashamed of whom I am."

"You're legitimized now and my legal heir."

"How did that happen? You've never explained this to me."

"I simply petitioned the *Desembargo do Paço*, our Supreme Court, and the petition was granted in the name of our king."

"I guess I never realized the importance my legitimacy has for you."

"Indeed. I feel I can die in peace now. This recognition will benefit you in the future."

"Thank you."

"Biographers might be surprised, one day, by my return to Portugal. But from the day you were born, I had this request to his majesty on my mind. Other events in my life contributed to my feeling that way. I didn't protect others who were dear to me—I'm not proud of that—so I took extra care to protect you, my son."

I don't want to talk to Edward about Eleonora. Since he doesn't ask for details, I continue to talk without hesitation. "To succeed, I needed to be as close to King João as possible, either here or in Brazil. It was necessary to ingratiate myself in royal circles; choose my alliances carefully. We, the Portuguese, have a saying, *longe da vista, longe do coração*, far from sight, far from the heart."

"The saying might apply to the Portuguese, but never to us," Edward says. "I feel very close to you."

"That's so comforting. To think that to legitimize you, I had to turn down a position in the American Temple of the Enlightenment, the University of Virginia! Sometimes I surprise myself."

"I feel responsible for your decision."

"No, you shouldn't. I left America for many reasons, not only because of your legitimization." I take a small packet of pistachios from my pocket and offer some to Edward. "I'll write soon to André Thouin at the Jardin des Plants, asking for his assistance, in case you need it."

"I appreciate it, though I know how to take care of myself— I learned that from you."

"Don't forget to visit the gardeners who helped your mother with the apothecary business."

"I plan to."

"Never forget you are a love child. Carry that with pride."

"I've always felt cherished."

"I'm glad. I'm going to miss you, but such is life. Your exuberance is so dear to my heart!"

"You must take care of yourself while I'm gone."

"I will, I promise. Coming back to why I left America. I expressed my irritation at the American government when I visited Mr. Jefferson for the last time."

"You've told me. Mr. Jefferson was a kind and learned man, I'm sure he was concerned with your complaints."

"I think he genuinely was; he cared for me. I enjoyed calling him the great, great Mr. Jefferson. In my view, America got its highest pedigree from him."

Edward remains silent, so I continue.

"We were both *philosophes,* we understood each other. I hope he kept my letters the way I kept his. I have his here in Lisbon in a leather box. The last one I received just before leaving New York is most affectionate."

"How so?"

"He said our two nations should remain in harmony. He wished me luck. But I feel so disheartened with the course of events! Had Brazilians not pushed for independence, our shared geopolitical ambitions could have been realized."

"Those dreams are over now."

"Indeed. Mr. Jefferson's soul is tender and genuine. Since our return, he wrote to General Dearborn, the American minister in Portugal, asking my whereabouts. Here is a man who never gives up his dreams."

"Have you replied to him?" Edward asks.

"No, not yet. When I last saw him, and I thought we were moving to Brazil, I told him that I would have liked to be a Virginian like him. I was leaving Virginia's plantation society to enter Brazil, another plantation society.

"Noteworthy to think of those territories in that light," Edward says.

"It is. I failed as a diplomat, and I'm disappointed to my core. The American government never listened to my views on privateering and Portugal never received an indemnity for its merchandise robbed at sea. It wasn't my poor health that prevented me from doing a good job as ambassador."

Edward gets up. "That doesn't matter anymore. I'm sorry, but I'm afraid we'll need to continue this discussion at home. I still have a few good-byes to make at the Department of Foreign Affairs."

"Your work there was brief but useful." Edward kisses me and then takes his leave. After a few steps he turns around and waves good-bye with a full smile.

With my son gone, I turn to my own thoughts. The shade of the *dragoeiro* is delightful, it covers my entire body. I sip some more water, and I really enjoy the lemon taste. I feel I've accomplished all I can at my age. I don't need to fight anymore. I can appreciate what I have, I just need to look around. Once again I think of the idea of happiness as expressed in the American Declaration of Independence. It is said in medical circles that even a small drop of happiness can contribute to long life. I think Jefferson—and the Founding Fathers—were aware of this truth. I've lived longer than most of my generation. As I look back, perhaps this happened because I enjoyed living abroad, traveling, and learning from other naturalists.

True, I've got some ailments: one of them is that I can't sit for long. So I'll get up now and stroll around to enjoy the pleasures of this garden. I've got my cane, I use it to strengthen my back as I walk. There are more than five thousand species here, a tribute to Portugal's vast colonial domains and imperial past. The marble balustrade that separates the garden's upper level, where I'm now, and the lower one is magnificent, made of carved white stone. The lower level has extravagant fountains with aquatic vegetation, ringed by French and Italian-styled flowerbeds. The views are so luxurious and thrilling that my mind wanders freely.

My thoughts turn to *Candide*, that masterpiece of the previous century. I wholeheartedly agree with Voltaire's maxim, *"Il faut cultivar son jardin."* I quoted those words in various letters to friends. But I disagree with Dr. Pangloss, *"Tout est pour le mieux,"* all is for the best. It's a maxim I don't share. I now recall how Voltaire enjoyed Eleonora's poetry; he called her *"beau rossignole de la belle Italie,"* beautiful nightingale from beautiful Italy. That Eleonora had such a tragic death is just an illustration of my thinking. I wonder what Voltaire would have thought of me, had we met. He hated all priests—he considered them a bunch of hypocrites—as well as the church, which he addressed as *l'infame,* infamous. Voltaire is an entertaining writer, and I must confess that, if it weren't for the Inquisition, his views would still amuse me.

I greatly admire the Turk in *Candide*, the farmer who has a small farm outside of Constantinople. Candide says his estate is small, but he nevertheless loves it because it prevents him and his family from three major pitfalls: *l'énnui, le vice, et le besoin,* boredom, vice and need. These ideas are a starting point to help me organize my reflections. They touch on my three vows to the Catholic Church—chastity, obedience, and poverty. I will begin with the last of these, *le besoin*—need.

The vital decision of my youth, to become a priest, sprung directly from it. I had to free my widowed father from taking care of me, his oldest child. It took a toll, but I don't regret my choice. I belonged to a community that gave me the opportunity to be part of a worldwide scientific network. Lafões's sound advice and patronage paid off nicely when I became Secretary of the Lisbon Royal Academy of Science. I contributed to the circulation of ideas on botany, my lifelong passion. I exchanged plants and seeds across the Atlantic Ocean, and I shared information on soil conditions for optimal vegetable growth and dissemination. Part of a circle of *savants,* all empiricists, we connected the old and the new world of science.

What an honor!

As to *le vice,* vice, I admit I was not immune. Like all vices, mine were far from noble and, if I could, I would erase them from my past. Alas, this is impossible. All along, I have felt human, all too human; I never felt holy or godly as some members of the Catholic Church do. I am now convinced that my mental ups and downs were a result of the humanity I experienced. Or better expressed, my vices were a result of the way I tried to suppress my hidden desires.

I recall now how, one late evening in Philadelphia, I saw two men embracing in a passionate manner as I walked along. It was dark outside and I was coming home on foot from a dinner with my colleagues. I always enjoyed such strolls after stimulating conversation; they helped me process all the information I had heard. I lived in the center of town—and even though the streets were dimly lit—those walks were safe as people were always around. When I turned a corner, sometime later, I saw that the two same men, both in handcuffs, were being led away by policemen.

This scene brings back sad memories of my own peccadillos.

The worse of my transgressions were sexual. *Fornicatio,* lust, is something my church condemns as a capital sins for its members, men or women. I tried to hide my sexual secrets even from myself. The church's remarkable duplicity, provided plenty of ways to do so.

The confession of my *delitos*, sexual sins, to the Inquisition is, notwithstanding, a sore in my past. I signed my admission, it's forever registered in *Cadernos do Nefando*, Abominable Sin Book. The church is known for its excellent recordkeeping throughout the ages, and I am a living proof of that practice. I will go into these matters now, the abundance of nature surrounding me prompts my entering the crevices of my soul.

In 1795, when I left Lisbon, I was struggling for my survival. The sins I confessed were common at the time. We should not forget this branch of the church operated in the Kingdom of Portugal from 1536 until very recently. This is a long time! I had been denounced for several acts of sodomy with women, men, and even *moços*, boys. In my naivety I thought the outdoors, the streets of Lisbon, provided safe encounters. When I disclosed these sins, I believed that if I gave the Inquisition a part of me—if I discarded a part of me—the judges would leave me alone.

I was totally wrong. I was still forced out of Lisbon after those admissions. The Inquisition's main goal has always been the same throughout history—to break a mans, or a womans, spirit. I contemplated suicide at the time, my life had lost all meaning.

During my interrogation, the sexual distinctions the Catholic judges made were obscene. The Edicts of the Faith, a sort of bylaws, specified sinful sexual activities for those under religious vows. And it treated participants or observers differently. I was asked about masturbation, fellatio, oral sex, penetration, and even anus ejaculation with spilling of seed. The judges wanted to know the number of occurrences in each of these practices. I knew beforehand that admitting sexual gratification of one's acts brought a sure conviction.

Those judges knew what they were asking. I wonder how they felt, if they ever admitted their own lust. The questioners looked so sordid! Like others, I swore to keep secret the aspects of the trial upon its conclusion.

I would have gone mad had I denied my sexual desire and

pleasure. I needed such encounters to quiet my tormented soul. If they were crimes, let God Almighty absolve me, if he is merciful and compassionate. I acknowledge I was weak and that my flesh ruled me. I was aware of the consequences of my acts. The lesser punishments for sodomy included public whipping, confiscation of property, and imprisonment. Some sinners faced far more severe treatment in autos-de-fé—religious ceremonies of penance set up in public squares filled with jeering audiences. Some were strangled before being set on fire; others burned alive in wood pyres.

I still feel lucky to have left Lisbon when I did. But these incidents might explain my melancholic madness, the ups and downs I've experienced all my life. Though I'm sure leaving Eleonora in Naples contributed to my ordeal.

Later on, my sexual habits cost me the respect of an American colleague, Mr. Robert Walsh, Jr. I have no idea what came over me to allow such a conversation to take place. I felt half-crazed. When I shared a house with the Walshes, I found Mr. Walsh increasingly vain and excitable as time went on. Maybe, ultimately, his devout, vocal Catholicism irked me. My irritation reached a peak, so I decided to shock him. One day, in a moment of acute exasperation, I told him about some of my sexual transgressions in America. He obviously judged my actions as evidence of moral turpitude, and we were never on speaking terms again.

He was the only American I know of who wished to see me leave the country. Maybe the judges in Baltimore who examined my cases on the privateers were equally happy!

I must drop the mask and confess my darkest side to Edward before I die. It's better he learns about my past from me rather than from somebody else. I regret what I did, but my sexual indiscretions are bound to be known one day. I need to decide the best way to approach this matter. We could talk again under the *dragoeiro;* or I could write him a letter, something he would read after my death. Either way, I hope he'll have it in his heart to forgive me. We have lived together for several years now, he knows I'm not perfect.

Edward is a broad-minded young man. When he finishes his medical degree, he would like to practice in the area of sexually transmitted diseases. This is a field of medicine attracting a lot of attention at the moment. He has read the *Confessions* by St. Augustine while at St. Mary's—an invaluable work I recommended. He knows about the imperfections of the flesh, how easily it gives in to wild gratification. He also knows how St. Augustine's prevarications did not prevent him from being canonized, later on, as a saint in the Catholic Church.

As I dwell on these issues—the gratifying of one's desires—Jefferson comes again to mind. He seemed virtuous and honorable at all times and I certainly respected him with all my heart. But I've always wondered what went on behind the closed doors of his life. Sally Hemings went about the house much the same way as his daughter Patsy did. Sally was in Paris with the family, while still a young girl; she must have been thirteen or fourteen. She certainly wasn't older than the boys I was with in the streets of Lisbon. When I stayed at Monticello, Sally came in and out of Jefferson's room throughout the day. Did she go there at night? Her constant presence in Jefferson's family life always made me wonder about the parentage of the mulatto children who played and sang with Jefferson's grandchildren. I'll never know. But the gossip that circulated in Philadelphia never answered satisfactorily this question of mine.

To finish this matter, my relationship with Esther gave me the greatest sexual satisfaction of my life. Eleonora was an ethereal dream, hardly real when I sometimes look back. Esther, on the other hand, was flesh and blood. When I met her, fathered Edward, and remained in the church, I kept my private life a secret. I knew I had sinned, but also knew I'd do it again, if given the chance. The intimacy Esther and I shared, along with the gift of Edward growing up—how his eyes smiled at me—were invaluable. Esther has since died but our son is the living proof of our relationship. The Protestants allow their clergy to marry, they're aware of the naturalness of human beings coming together in the flesh. Thus, their members avoid the condemnation of lustful sin.

Yes, I have desired both men and women all my life. Is the attraction to both so rare? I know for sure carnal craving is fulfilled inside the Catholic Church in more ways than I care to describe here.

One of my other vices had to do with money, my vow of poverty never sat well with me. I, of course, couldn't live on the meager stipends I got from the church or the crown. These resources couldn't sustain my basic needs, my travels, and my wish to acquire books or see colleagues in distant lands. I didn't covet money for its own sake. I have to admit, nevertheless, that I envied those who had enough for all the extra pursuits. I, too, wished to have those.

I must dwell now on boredom, the third vice Voltaire's charming farmer, the Turk, describes. I'm proud to say that I never suffered from this sin. I wish I had written or published more, but boredom was never the reason for my limited output. And I wasn't lazy, a trait of so many of my compatriots.

I cannot forget to mention, either, that I've always set my own rules. Thus, I couldn't comply with obedience, another vow of mine to the Catholic Church. I always had to do as I pleased.

I'm a man of the Enlightenment, my spiritual circle is broad and diversified—how could I have behaved differently from what I describe above? Like Candide, I've always been on the move, engaged, my pace even frantic at times. I traveled extensively, both in miles and through the network of friends I cultivated. My curiosity was boundless. Wherever I went—whatever room I entered—I agreed, I disagreed, and I argued. I've been considered, and rightly so, a great conversationalist. My life was directed to scientific inquiry, to empiricism as a path to knowledge, and to the pursuit of diplomacy on the larger world stage. I trusted experience over doctrine. I was against fanaticism, fear, and cruelty. I must add, without conceit, that I impressed the men and women I met: scientists, ambassadors, even presidents. Besides Jefferson, Mr. Madison and Mr. Monroe enjoyed my company. I loved America's Founding Fathers.

I've inhabited a world that has been the most satisfying of gardens, and I consider the flora that the earth and the rain sustain a rare elixir. Naturalists knew this, the reason I had species named after me. This was my ultimate privilege, and I'm proud of its many varieties: the Correa *virens*, the Correa *speciosa*, the Correa *pulchella*, among others.

I feel I am at the end; I am old, infirm, and utterly disenchanted. Despite the number of doctors I've seen, my legs are heavy and swollen, and my toes larger than my fingers. At seventy-two, my body is giving way. After Edward goes to Paris, I will go to Caldas da Rainha, north of Lisbon, to bathe in the spa's curative waters.

This evening I must not forget to tell Edward where the trunk is with the materials that I would like him to send to the American Philosophical Society once I am gone. There are pieces of clothing I used when I visited Jefferson in Monticello and while ambassador to America. I always dressed as a civilian while I was there. The clothing is neatly folded, with camphor in the creases. I hope these items will be on display, one day, at the society's museum. I also included several documents in the trunk; a few pertain to Edward's mother. I only told Jefferson, not anyone else, that Esther was Jewish. How could she be otherwise with a first name like that? Thus Edward prolongs the cycle of my Jewish ancestry. I placed the quill with which I wrote this work in a small leather case. A dried *Correa pulchella* lay next to it.

The trunk is locked and I must give Edward the key. The lock also has a code, besides the key, and I'll send that to him by letter. I could make the code a riddle for my son, and have it be the name Eleonora. That would start him thinking!

Edwards's certificate of legitimization isn't in the truck, it's in a separate leather case.

I wonder how I'll be remembered one day. As an exponent of *Les Lumières*, a natural *philosophe*, a botanist, and a man of reason? Or as a diplomat who, as ambassador, supported the ancient régime—the old order established in Portugal centuries ago? I hope the first, for it was the cornerstone of my life, my truest pleasure and fulfillment.

I'll walk now to the far end of the garden, to the aromatic corner. I always stop there before going home. This last stroll is a moment of satisfaction for me, a *promenade philosophique*, my philosophical walk. The herbs in this small space have such an intense piquancy that the mixing of the many aromas reminds me of a Mozart symphony. I pause to silently recite some revered names: bay leaf, dandelion, garlic, thymus, lavender, parsley, and cinnamon.

As I pace down the stone steps that lead to the lower level of the garden, I'll enjoy the view of the Tejo River. The water is usually serene at this time of day, virtually motionless. I can see already the cupola of the famous Church of Memory down the hill. The church was built to celebrate the failed attempt on the life of King José—the event that led to the killings of the high nobility by the Marquis de

Pombal, a significant detail Eleonora omitted in her work. It's the late afternoon, and the garden's iron gates will close soon. As I exit this oasis of quiet and rest, I look up at the sky. I see it's iridescent with the day's waning—like a rainbow.

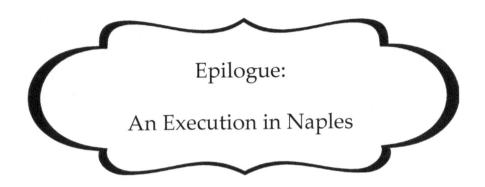

Epilogue:

An Execution in Naples

Kingdom of Naples, August 20, 1799

Isaw it with my own two eyes. Eleonora Fonseca Pimentel was escorted by royalist soldiers to the scaffold in the squalid Piazza del Mercato in the city center of Naples. Her life was tragically cut short at the age of forty-seven. She was the only woman—and the last republican revolutionary—to be executed that day. Seven men preceded her. They had all supported the short-lived republican government that ruled the city under the auspices of the French government, the Directory, for about five months. Eleonora was condemned along with other rebellious *literati*: enlightened nobles, distinguished men of letters, and radical members of the clergy. The group represented not only the oldest and most respected Neapolitan families, but also members of the bourgeoisie who had pushed for progressive reforms.

I hereby record the details of Eleonora's finale. After surrendering with other republican revolutionaries at Sant'Elmo fort, she was placed in a transport ship headed for Toulon, France. Clamped in irons like the other prisoners, she signed the required document stating that she would never return to Naples. The republicans' departure from Naples had been agreed upon with an armistice under the auspices of Cardinal Ruffo, whereas the insurgents acknowledged military defeat. Eleonora's order to go into exile was, however, reversed when Admiral Nelson arrived in Naples aboard the *Foudroyant* accompanied by Lord and Lady Hamilton. She was then removed from the ship and brought to the Vicaria Prison.

A session led by the *Guinta di Stato,* the High Court of State, took place in the complex of the Convento di Santa Maria di Monte Oliveto a few weeks later. Eleonora was condemned to death in this building, convicted of being a republican: a rebel, an insurgent, and a revolutionary. She had indeed supported the republican government as a sympathizer of the French army intervention in Naples.

Soon after the ruling, Eleonora was moved to the nearby Convento di Santa Maria del Carmine Maggiore, the convent located at one end of Piazza Mercato. The Bianchi Congregation, who ministered to those about to die, tended to Eleonora and the other convicts in their last hours.

In a chapel appropriately designated *Il Confortatorio,* Place of Comfort, Eleonora and her male companions had a chance to exchange final words. For brief moments, Eleonora enjoyed the consolation of being with her kindred friends. The intelligentsia surrounding her were the best the Neapolitan Enlightenment had to offer in the fields of poetry, music, art, philosophy, and the sciences. As time ran out, one member of the group said, "We're about to find out the answer to Socrates's question: Is there an eternal life?"

Before leaving the Convento del Carmine for the scaffold, Eleonora asked to drink a cup of coffee. I can well imagine how she swallowed the drink languidly, lovingly. She needed this last earthly satisfaction to face her last steps.

As soon as she finished the coffee, Eleonora pronounced the famous quote by Virgil, *"Forsan et hoec olim meminisse juvabit"* — perhaps one day it will be good to remember all this.

Eleonora suspected that she might be hung, and so asked for an undergarment to wear under her black dress to protect her private parts from public viewing. Sadistically her request was denied.

In the late afternoon, Eleonora left the Convento del Carmine and passed the Vicoletto dei Sospiri, Alley of Sighs, escorted by soldiers on both sides. Members of the Bianchi Congregation followed, dressed in white robes. She may have used a clamp to fasten her skirt between her legs, the skirt was tight near her feet.

As she walked, the crowd screamed and cursed. They spat and hurled insults at her: the Jacobin Marquise had dared to defy the Bourbon monarchy. Now her minutes alive could be counted.

I came to Piazza Mercato in the early morning that day, and found it already filled to capacity. For the public, the slaughter of a noble figure was an event worth witnessing. As this one involved a noblewoman, the lurid appeal was intensified. The scaffold had been placed high. With bloodthirsty gusto, the crowd anticipated the sight of Eleonora's sexual organs.

Eleonora's face remained composed and serene. For a split second, she attempted to sing the "Hymn to Freedom"—which she had composed while imprisoned—the Neapolitan version of "La Marseillaise." But Mastro Donato didn't allow her to do it. He rapidly secured the rope around her neck and pulled hard.

The *tirapiedi*, the man who clung to her feet for added weight, swung from side to side with gruesome relish.

To the executioner's shouts of "Long live the king!" followed a chant that seemed to reach the stars high in the sky: "Long live Carolina, death to the Jacobina."

Eleonora's corpse remained suspended from the scaffold for the next twenty-four hours. Then it disappeared. No plaque in Naples marks her grave.

During that night, the natural elements seized Naples as if by divine wrath. Neapolitans paused, slowly filled with dread. Mount Vesuvius, the tempestuous volcano, erupted with luminous red flames, its lava a river of liquid fire pouring down the mountain, its roars deafening all. It seemed the 1794 eruption was about to repeat itself. Copious thunder and rain descended upon the city's terrified dwellers, preventing sleep for all.

I stand as a witness of Eleonora da Fonseca Pimentel's death in Naples, the world must know about it. I believe Eleonora has been silenced but her voice will reverberate for all eternity.

I'm asking my niece Margarita to bring this memoir of Eleonora with her when she goes to France this week to begin life in exile with her husband, Alessandro. Also a republican, Alessandro was imprisoned on a transport ship in the Bay of Naples. The vessel already arrived in Toulon.

I placed the memoir in the black leather case I had given Eleonora recently. I found the pages with her writings scattered around the drawer's secret compartment. I'm sure she placed them there in a hurry, perhaps alarmed when the royalist soldiers came to fetch her. How I miss my Eleonora, dear friend and compatriot! I put this letter of mine in the case's back pocket and tied the case with a red ribbon.

Suor Amadea Della Valle
Madre Superiore
Vicaria Prison

Author's Note

During the summer of 2012, I visited the superb library of the American Philosophical Society to research materials on the life of Abbé Joseph Francisco Correia da Serra (1751–1823). He had become a member of the Society upon his arrival in America (1812–1820), or possibly even the year before. At this venerable institution, he enjoyed the privilege of lecturing to his peers, as well as attending various committees regularly. Considered a naturalist of the first order, it is his work as a botanist that stands out as his greatest achievement. Soon a close friend of the Society's president, Thomas Jefferson (1743–1826), the priest-*philosophe*-diplomat visited the latter's Virginia plantation, Monticello, seven times between 1813 and 1820.

The American Philosophical Society gave me generous access to its archives, in particular Correia da Serra's correspondence. After a few days of search, unable to find the materials I had hoped to uncover, I felt at a standstill. I wanted to establish a historical connection between Correia da Serra and Eleonora Fonseca Pimentel (1752–1799); she had been brought to the scaffold in Naples in 1799. As adolescents, they both had lived in the city with their families. It's unlikely that they didn't know of each other, given the small and closed knit Portuguese community that had moved from Rome to the Kingdom of Naples in 1760.

Correia da Serra was a familiar figure to me. The first time I encountered his name was when I visited Monticello, Thomas Jefferson's plantation, and came across a room in the mansion bearing his name. I was in my twenties, and became intrigued that a connection between Portugal and the United States was highlighted centuries after the death of both illustrious men. Much later, when I met with Ambassador João de Vallera at the Embassy of Portugal in 2007, the Abbé's oil portrait in a gold frame hung behind the ambassador's desk, a centerpiece in his office. I was filed with awe: Correia da Serra's veiled expression reminded me of a male version of Da Vinci's *La Giaconda*. What was behind that subtle smile of his, I wondered?

I came across Pimentel for the first time during a visit to Naples, more than a decade before my trip to the American Philosophical Society. Near the Spanish Quarter, I noticed a public school that bore Pimentel's name and the discovery puzzled me. Portuguese myself, this was a Portuguese name I had never heard before and yet it was honored in Italy.

Strolling through Rome later that year, bingo! Near Piazza del Popolo, I came across a plaque on an imposing *palazzo* at Via Ripetta that bore Pimentel's name. The plaque said she had been born in that building and had died in Naples in 1799. The inscription's last line said she was a *Martire della Libertà*, a Martyr of Liberty. By then, I had already found out she had been editor-in-chief of the republican newspaper *Il Monitore Napoletano*.

It took me years to investigate my findings. I searched libraries in Lisbon, in particular the Biblioteca Nacional of Portugal and the Academia das Ciências of Lisboa, with a variant of the original question: why hadn't Correia da Serra living in London at the time of Pimentel's death, tried to rescue her from her fate? I wanted information, or even lore, starting from the time they had both lived in Naples until Eleonora's horrifying death. There was neither evidence nor a plausible answer to my question. Most of Pimentel's works and letters are lost, so I couldn't rely on Portuguese and Italian historical records.

A third figure thus emerged in my research. Could the abundant and affable correspondence between Correia da Serra and Thomas Jefferson provide the information I needed? There was none, even if they discussed Napoleonic France. My novel's plan had been all along to interweave narrative, memoir, and biography. Consequently, I decided to use my imagination by following closely the lives of these three major figures of the Enlightenment. My main interest was exploring these characters' "truth of the heart," as they related to each other. I kept events, historical references, and dates as accurate as possible.

In the early nineteenth century, it took a while to reach Monticello in Virginia. Besides Jefferson's legendary generosity, this might explain why Correia da Serra stayed for weeks at a time. From Philadelphia, around 268 miles, it took more than a week to reach Virginia. From Washington D.C., around 118 miles, it took four days. I estimated Correia da Serra's first visit in 1813, a few months after his arrival in America. As for Pimentel, the precise day on which she was removed from the transport ship in the Bay of Naples and brought to the Vicaria Prison on shore is not known. But we do know she was condemned to death by hanging on August 17, 1799. She died on August 20, 1799, three days later. Thus, her dairy in the novel covers June 29 to August 11, 1799, the period she was most likely waiting to hear her fate.

The Republic of Letters was scattered throughout the Western world during the Enlightenment. The intellectuals driving this movement lived on both sides of the Atlantic, from America to distant Russia. Many of them lived in Europe, and particularly in Southern Europe. It is never too late to emphasize that the European Grand Tour ended in Naples, the capital of the Kingdom of Naples (also called, in different periods, the Kingdom of Sicily or the Kingdom of the Two Sicilies). The kingdom occupied a portion of the Southern Italian Peninsula in the center of the Mediterranean Sea: the boot, the lower part of the leg, and the foot of a region easily discernable in a map of the Mediterranean Sea. The educated elite lived in the city of Naples. From there to Palermo—the kingdom's second capital, to the south—stretched a vast agrarian territory ruled by the laws of feudalism characteristic of the ancien regime. Even if Jefferson didn't visit this region, his correspondence shows how he admired Italy, its food, landscape, art, and architecture. It is no coincidence that Monticello has an Italian name, a place that celebrated eighteenth-century notions of American republican virtue and European civilization.

Both Joseph Francisco Correia da Serra and Eleonora Fonseca Pimentel are known by two different names. In America, Correia da Serra is mostly known as Correa or Corrêa. I chose Joseph instead of José for his first name because this is how he usually signed his letters to Thomas Jefferson. Besides her famous noms-de-plume—Epolnifenora Olcesamante and Altidora Esperetusa—Pimentel is known in the Portuguese world as Leonor, the name she used when writing to Portuguese acquaintances. De or da between her first name and surnames—she uses both in the few letters known—indicates Portuguese nobility. To simplify her name for foreign readers, I decided not to use either of these particles. As she considered herself a citizen at the end of her life, Pimentel would have discarded them, anyway.

I used the title Abbé for Correia da Serra, as this is the designation equally used at the time for any male with an ecclesiastical affiliation.

It is a historical fact that Correia da Serra had a son with Esther Delavigne in 1803, and that he was called Edward Joseph, Eduardo José. Edward attended St. Mary's Seminary in Baltimore, travelled with his father back to Lisbon, was legitimized, and later became a medical doctor in France. It is also a historical fact that Correia da Serra confessed his peccadillos to the Inquisition. They are registered in the Inquisition records, *Cadernos do Nefando*, Abominable Sin Book. It is documented that Correia da Serra belonged to a New Christian family—Jews forced to convert to Catholicism—both on his father's and his mother's side. This might explain why the family fled to Rome in 1757. Little is known of Esther Delavigne, except that she was young and audacious; the name Esther indicates she might have been Jewish.

A contemporary footnote exists to this story. In 1999, to celebrate the 200th anniversary of the fall of the Neapolitan Republic, an opera was staged at the San Carlo Theater in Naples, starring Vanessa Redgrave in the role of Eleonora. Written by Roberto de Simone, the work is called *Eleonora, Oratorio Drammatico*, and it's available on YouTube.

Acknowledgments

E. B. White said it better than anyone else; New York gives you the gift of privacy, as well as the jewel of loneliness. The reason, I think, is the concentration of talent in such a small area. For this purpose, I am especially grateful to the members of the Historical Novel Society, New York City Chapter, for their interest in the Guest Speaker Program at the Jefferson Market Library. I have co-chaired the events from 2016 to the present, and I'm grateful for this opportunity. At the library, I would like to thank Frank Collerius for the use of the Willa Cather room for our monthly meetings. What an incredible space in the heart of the West Village!

I got very involved in the New York literary scene while working on this novel. It started with the privilege of being Visiting Scholar at the New School in the spring of 2014 and 2015. I thank Professor Gina Luria Walker for this incredible opportunity. Then, I got to know a group of talented writers, editors, and academics. I would like to thank Julie Mosow, Judith Sternlight, Lisa Petrini, Magdalen Livesey, and Mary Kole, as well as the late Professor Josephine Diamond, Christina Britney Conroy, Faith Justice, Ursula Renée, Susan Wands, Melodie Winawer, Andrea Chapin, and Elizabeth Gaffney. The 57th Street writing group was committed, well-informed, and fun: Gro Flatebo, Laura Schofer, Finola Austin, Barbara Lucas, and John Nuckel. Patricia Morrill, Loretta Goldberg and Lisa Yarde have been cherished friends and advisers all along. Mark Gottlieb provided a list of useful contacts. At the Columbia Fiction Foundry, I am especially grateful to Richard Hensley and Tania Moore.

I visited Monticello and, during my time in Virginia, I heard inspiring lectures by Professor Elizabeth Dowling Taylor and Jim Wootton. Both kindly commented on parts of my first manuscript. At the American Philosophical Society, I was kindly assisted by Earle Spamer and Estelle Markel-Joyet. Later, Michael P. Miller graciously forwarded to Portugal all of the correspondence I had read during my visit. Professor David Eltis of the Trans-Atlantic Slave Trade Database was most generous with information. Professor John A. Davis kindly clarified a few historical issues pertaining to the Neapolitan Revolution. Alison M. Foley, Reference Archivist at St. Mary's Seminary and University, sent me the registration page where the name Correia appears. This refers to Eduardo José Correia da Serra, the Abbé's son. At Columbia University and at the Catholic University of America, I was helped with my research by Meredith Levin and Joan Stahl.

There were others in Portugal, equally talented and big-hearted, who provided help and inspiration for this work. My gratitude goes especially to Emeritus Professor José Barreto, historian, of Instituto de Ciências Sociais, the University of Lisbon. His knowledge of the history of the Portuguese empire in the eighteenth century is unparalleled. He answered all of my requests for information, and I had many.

Professor José Luis Cardoso did something I will never forget: he gave me a private tour of the Lisbon Academy of Sciences. In the meeting I describe in the Author's Note, Embaixador João de Vallera encouraged me early on to proceed with this theme. He considered it original, innovative, and deserving of attention.

Several scholars helped me with the history of the eighteenth century: Professor Valentim Alexandre, Professor João Pedro Marques, Professor Daniel Pires, and Professor João Medina. Professor Onésimo Almeida at Brown University provided me, as in the past, with useful ideas and contacts. Professor Guilherme d'Oliveira Martins kindly read and commented on the manuscript. Professor Elsa Rita dos Santos knew about Eleonora Fonseca Pimentel much earlier than I did. Not only did she discuss Pimentel with me, but kindly forwarded materials originally written in Italian, books I would otherwise not have been able to read. Professor Daniela Galli contributed with advice on the Italian language. Professor Annabela Rita from the Center for Lusophone and European Literatures and Cultures, the University of Lisbon, is someone I continue to consult with regularly.

A few institutions provided support and information. I would like to mention Carlos Vences, from the National Library of Portugal, Leonor Pinto from Academia das Ciências de Lisboa, and Cristina Salles and Maria Leonor Roquette from the Luso-American Development Foundation.

I enjoyed a magical moment in Providence, Rhode Island, when I made a presentation about this book to the Historical Writers of America in 2018. I would like to thank a few of those present who provided invaluable advice: Linda Cardillo, Nancy Rubin Stuart, Paul Van Heest, and Charlie Heinemann.

Among my friends in Portugal, I would like to thank Celeste Maia and Robert Bentley, Dinah and João Nuno Azevedo Neves, Cláudia Mota Pinto and Alberto Musalem, Miranda Van Gelder and Xico Greenwald, Amélia and Rey Hutchinson, and the late Ana Vicente and António Pedro Vicente; Teresa Salles Caldeira, Mariana Abrantes, Lídia Barreiros, Manuel Liquito, Marta Tavares d'Almeida, Francisco Marques Bom, and Pedro Abecasis. In the United States, I would like to thank Martha Daza, Kady Dalrymple, Jean McCurry, and Ramona Payne.

Last but not least, I would like to thank the solid presence in my life of Mané Pedreira d'Almeida, Ana Mantero, Vera Mantero, Carmo Cunha Rego, Dra. Mafalda Garcia, and Dr. João Ribeiro da Silva.

My colleague Gail Spilsbury did the final editing of this book. She is an amazing editor who works wonders on a foreign writer's English prose.

I am solely responsible for the content of this novel.

March 2, 2020

About The Author

Julieta Almeida Rodrigues is a writer, professor, scholar, and interpreter. Born and raised in Portugal, she earned a Ph.D. at Columbia University, where the renowned Margaret Mead was her dissertation sponsor. She is the author of two collections of short fiction, The Rogue and Other Portuguese Stories and On the Way to Red Square. The latter is a fictionalized account of her life in the diplomatic circles of Moscow in the 1980s (New Academia Publishing, Washington DC). She published a narrative work about Sintra, Portugal, entitled Hora Crepuscular/Drawing Dusk/La Hora Crepuscular (Agir, Execução Gráfica). She is a member of the Pen Club of Portugal, the Fulbright Commission Team of Evaluators in Portugal (2014 Prize for International Cooperation, the Prince of Asturias Foundation), and of CLEPUL, Center for Lusophone and European Literatures and Cultures, Faculty of Humanities, the University of Lisbon. She has taught at the University of Lisbon and at Georgetown University, and has been a Visiting Scholar at the New School (twice). She has spoken at the Foreign Service Institute, U.S. Department of State, The Chawton House Library in the United Kingdom, The International Conference on the Short Story, The American Portuguese Studies Association, and the Historical Writers of America, among other locations. She is a member of the Steering Committee of the Historical Novel Society New York City Chapter and runs, with a colleague, its Guest Speaker Program at the Jefferson Market Library. She divides her time between Manhattan and Sintra, Portugal.

CPSIA information can be obtained
at www.ICGtesting.com
Printed in the USA
FSHW020403040620
70614FS

9 781734 865912